Autumn of the Witch

Seasons of the Lukoi Book 4

Iris Foxglove

Acknowledgments

Thank you so much to our editor, Alicia Z. Ramos, our cover artist, Garrett Leigh at Black Jazz Design, Justy for being an awesome first-reader, and our PA, Kim, for her enthusiasm and hard work. We appreciate you all so much!!

We'd also like to thank @Natendo_Art on Twitter for the beautiful commissioned artwork included in this book.

Foxglove would like to dedicate this book to their sisters. We conquered our own shadow, and came out the other side triumphant.

Author's Note

Author's Note

Please be advised that the natural power exchange/biological imperative kink element to this story is intended as fantasy, **and should not be considered a factual representation of BDSM as practiced between consenting adults in real life**. The dynamics portrayed in this and other Iris Foxglove titles are entirely fictional, and should not be considered a guideline for the safe practice of any activity described herein.

This book contains m/m, m/f, and m/m/f content.

Additional content advisories include: discussions of mental illness, cultural misunderstandings of said mental illness, anxiety, chronic pain/illness, difficult familial relationships, death of siblings/young children (not described), guilt and horror themes/imagery.

Thank you for reading!

Chapter One

"There's something wrong with him."

Micah Fire-Keeper hunched over the desk in his small, ramshackle cabin, delicately painting the eyes of a wooden puppet. The puppet had a red coat knitted with wavelike patterns, her shoes were black and glossy, and she was smiling coyly up at Micah as he traced her lashes over the wood. When he was done, she would be able to tap across the worktable, and he would wrap her up and give her to one of the families who lived closer to the shore. Maybe they would love her. Maybe they wouldn't. But for now, she was beautiful and new, already smiling.

"He's just shy, Fia."

"Shy doesn't look like this."

Micah's parents were long dead, lost to a sickness when Micah was fifteen, but that didn't stop them from commenting on his behavior. He always remembered them the most when he was finishing a project, their tense voices just a touch too loud.

They never understood why he preferred quiet, why he jumped at strange voices or froze up when he met someone new.

It wasn't that he didn't like people. It was that when he was in the middle of a crowd, the sound and the smells and the feeling of being stared at were too much. It was like being tossed into a lake and told to swim when he hadn't learned how to float yet. He was left to flounder, and all anyone did was ask, "Why is he so unhappy?"

Instead of thinking it over or even asking him, his parents had decided there was something wrong with him. Then everything else he did was just another sign that he didn't fit in with their idea of a proper Lukoi.

Micah finished painting the smiling puppet and pushed his chair back.

His cabin was a riot of color. There were lengths of dyed cloth hanging over his bed, clay jars of paint and glaze lining the walls, and scraps of fabric and wood shavings everywhere, along with half-finished projects. In the middle of it all, squat and fat like an enormous bullfrog in an overturned bowl, was the kiln. The fire inside glowed, baking a tray of clay figurines that would go on strings of dragonflies and sparrows on a web made to simulate flight.

He hadn't been allowed to tinker when he was a kid. His mother thought it made things worse—fed his need for quiet, exacerbated the choking anxiety that seized him every time he was pushed into the crowd during feast days. She thought if he focused on *fixing himself* instead of playing with toys, maybe a lever would flip in his brain and it would all settle properly. She was always grabbing things out of his hands, tearing the cloth braids he made, her eyes wet with fear. The only thing she didn't take from him was the book.

The book was his father's. Or, rather, it was his father's grandmother's: an old book full of recipes and diagrams and little inventions, some as simple as a new type of compass, some complex mixes of gears and strings and levers. Micah found it when he was ten, and every time he looked through it, he felt a deep tie to the woman who wrote it. His great-grandmother had loved these diagrams and had meant to pass them on to her descendants. To him.

"I met Iya Fire-Keeper once," Dragan had said, shortly before Micah's parents passed. The kuvar was surprisingly understanding, not trying to force Micah into anything that made him uncomfortable. Micah had gathered the courage to ask him about her, since Dragan seemed to know everything about the village, and Dragan had gazed at the distant mountains before answering.

"It's rare to be that old and still hale enough to survive a winter here," he said, still focused on the snow-capped peaks. "But she was always inventing something, even to the end. She had two houses. One near Red Mountain, with a kiln she used to bake clay, and another here. The one near the mountain should still be there."

Micah turned to look at the mountains, holding his arms tightly. "Can I take her name?"

"Her sobriquet?" Dragan's brows raised, and Micah shrank back, shame building in his chest. "It isn't unheard of. If you earn it, yes. She would have wanted someone to carry on her skills, I think. Why else would she have written that book?"

Micah clung to the book after that, reading the old instructions long into the night and imagining his great-grandmother's hands working on the wood carvings and the recipes, bringing them to life.

When his mother and father died only a week apart, Micah took them outside to burn on the pyre in spring, and then he went back in and spent all night carving a crow with wings that moved, straight from the pages of the book. No one took it from him. He gave it to a woman who was expecting a child that summer, and she smiled at him so warmly that Micah went home and finally let the grief come, the bitterness and loss washing over him like a winter storm.

For a while, every creation was a release. Even the ones that went wrong, when he moved beyond the instructions of the book and started making his own. But he found joy in the work, too, and he found himself smiling and humming while he spent too many hours on a doll with a secret compartment or a set of interlocking gears that made a picture instead of hunting and shoring up his house for the winter.

Micah earned his sobriquet, in the end. He'd gone alone to the mountain. He found his great-grandmother's house, which had fallen to ruin around the ancient kiln, and rebuilt it. He shivered through winters alone in the draughty shack, surrounded by toys and carvings and clay figurines, and he held her book to his chest and carried her name with him, his own private legacy.

He assembled the strings and made the puppet bow in the cluttered mess of his desk. She was perfect.

Outside, the mountains loomed over his shack, and the trees beyond his window shimmered in brilliant golds and reds like the flames in his kiln. He could do something with that, maybe —a miniature forest on a plate that spun, the leaves' colors changing. He'd have to think about it.

It would be another week or so before he could trade the doll for supplies. Zev, one of Micah's few friends on Lukos, was supposed to bring the kuvar to help fix a crack in Micah's wall. He was always doing that: trying to help out here and there, cleaning while Micah worked, talking to him in his quiet, gentle way. He didn't seem to mind Micah's aversion to crowds. More than that, he understood it. Even though the idea of heading toward the other houses in Lukos filled Micah with terror, like a claw dragging at his heart, he had to admit that he missed Zev when he was gone.

Lonely, he thought, setting the puppet aside. *I'm lonely*. But just as it had been with his parents, he didn't know how to solve the problem without fucking things up. Zev had a mate. A life. Micah couldn't ask him to stay the night just because he felt the emptiness of his house as keenly as he felt the oppression of a crowd. They were both fully grown—it wasn't done.

Micah took the pottery out of the kiln to cool and pushed scraps of wood carvings off his bed. The doll smiled at him, her coat a slash of red against the wooden tools behind her as Micah curled up under his blankets and closed his eyes.

As Micah slept, the wind rose until it whistled through the boards and rushed through the small shack. It stirred the cloths above Micah's head, ruffled the puppet's yarn hair, and rattled open the door of the kiln, sending sparks flying from the embers to land amid the wood shavings on the floor. The wind quieted, and for a long moment, everything was still. Then the air moved again, like the lungs of an ancient dragon, breathing in.

He smelled the smoke first.

Sasha was a lot of things, ridiculous and loud and prone to breaking stuff if he wasn't paying attention, but one thing he took no small amount of pride in was how good he was at hunting. He'd been doing it his whole life, and he was good at it. Viv always said it was one of the few times he could be quiet, could stop moving around so much and focus on the scents, the sounds, the air around him.

Everyone back at the Compound was used to him by now: the big, cheerful man with shaggy black hair and a loud laugh, a submissive who wanted nothing more than to have his tiny, feisty wife cut her name into his back and whip him with a flogger made of thorns after he spent a day hauling wood to the pile and whistling while he chopped it into logs for the fire. Viv was bossy as fuck, and half the Compound was terrified of her. Sasha had loved her from the moment he saw her—and fine, at first maybe it was puppy love, and then as they got older, more like "Climb on my cock and scratch me until I bleed and leave your teeth marks in my chest while I fuck you so good you come six times in a row" than "love," but love had to start somewhere, didn't it?

A few weeks earlier, he'd hiked to the wolf-people's village —hard not to think of it that way, still, even though only one of them was really any kind of wolf—to talk with Zev's friend Victor Owl-Eyed about Gerakia and whether maybe the warm summers there would be better for Viv. While Sasha didn't want to admit it, she needed more help than he could give on his own. Whatever strange sickness had taken her siblings was troubling her again, and he would do anything he could to keep it from getting worse. If it meant leaving Lukos, like Dragan Wolf-Breaker's daughter had, that's what they'd do.

He didn't like the idea of leaving. Sasha liked his cozy home with his gorgeous, vicious sadist wife, and the Compound was mostly running smoothly after the whole thing back in the spring with Evgen.

In any case, they wouldn't be going anywhere before winter, and he needed to put by enough meat and other supplies to see them through the cold months ahead. He could have gone home when the gathering clouds started threatening rain, but he'd opted to keep hunting and had a nice buck to show for his efforts ... and that's when he smelled the smoke. It wouldn't normally concern him, since the people of the village where Victor lived obviously had fires in their homes, just like the ones who lived in the Compound. But this smoke was coming from the wrong direction.

And maybe, if Sasha hadn't already met the toymaker in the woods ... maybe he would have relied on the coming storm to put out the fire and simply taken his buck and gone home to show off his prowess to his wife. She did like it when he carried a whole deer home for her, and thinking about the way she showed her appreciation made him shiver with something other than cold. But he *did* know about the toymaker—Micah, he was Zev's friend—and how he lived in a house deep in the woods. Though "house" was giving it a pretty loose definition; it was a shack. And if Micah was on his own, and the place was on fire ...

With a low curse, Sasha set off at a lope toward the scent of smoke. He knew Micah didn't like unexpected visitors, and he'd leave if he saw it was some kind of bonfire or something. But as he got closer, he knew that wasn't the case.

There were flames leaping too high in the air, catching trees and dead leaves, and the sound was like nothing Sasha had ever heard. It sounded like the fire was *eating* the landscape, like it was a living thing devouring whatever was foolish enough to get in its way. The wind grew hot enough that Sasha started coughing, and he dropped the buck as he broke into an all-out run. He didn't think he was going to find anything but ashes, but he had to check.

Zev was Sasha's friend, and while Micah had been as friendly as a porcupine the first time Sasha encountered him, Sasha knew that Zev counted *Micah* as a friend, and that meant something. Sasha wasn't the sharpest arrow in the quiver, but even *he* knew you didn't fuck off and live alone in the woods if everything in your past was sunshine and rainbows.

So he let the deer's carcass fall to be food for the—four-legged—wolves and raced to find out whether Micah was still alive. He was coughing nonstop now, and his eyes were stinging from the smoke, but he could just make out the shape of a man trying to ... go back *into* the heart of the fire, which used to be his shack. House. Whatever, it had been his home, and Sasha felt a rush of sympathy even as he shouted, "What the hell, man, get away from that. You're going the wrong way!"

Micah didn't respond, so Sasha shouted again. "Hey! You know me. I'm Zev's friend, Sasha. I'm all right! Coming to get you!"

"—off," was the reply, and Sasha ducked under a smoldering tree limb and tackled Micah to keep him from running back into the blaze.

"Get off me and let me *go*," Micah snarled, a tangle of soot and limbs and wildly unkempt hair.

"Sure thing, buddy." Sasha got to his feet—he was much more nimble than people thought, given his height and build—and hauled Micah up with a fist in his shirt. "As soon as we're away from the fucking *fire*. What the fuck is wrong with you?"

Micah was scrawny, tall but thin, and while he fought like a snow cat, he couldn't escape Sasha's grip. He was lighter than the buck had been—which, damn, he could use some meat on his bones. But first things first: no burning to cinders on Sasha's watch. Zev would be sad if that happened, and he'd been sad enough as a young pup. He didn't need to go back to it now that he was mated and happy and all.

Sasha liked it when people he liked were happy. He didn't much like Micah, but that was only 'cause he didn't know him very well. Didn't mean he wanted the guy to roast like a deer over a spit.

He dragged Micah toward the edge of the thick cloud of smoke—but then Micah kicked him right where it *fucking* counted. Which, honestly, wasn't the kind of pain he was usually into. "What— *Ow*, buddy, that's a hell of a way to say *thank you,*" Sasha growled, still holding on to him. "Also, you think people haven't tried that before?"

"I need— There's ... something in the house. I—I can't— I need it. Let me go; I don't care if I—"

"You must have smoke in your brain. You can't go back in there, or you ain't comin' back out." Sasha looked at Micah and sighed. "What is it you need? Like, really need? I'll go look for it. You'll catch on fire. You're like a scarecrow."

Micah pushed his hair out of his face and *stared* at him. "You— What? No."

His dominance fell hard in the smoke-clouded air, but Sasha was used to his wife, and he shrugged one shoulder. "Then I'm hauling you to Zev. Your choice."

Micah swore. "A book. It's ... probably gone, but it's— If it isn't, I need it."

Sasha hesitated only a moment before grabbing his own shirt and pulling it over his head. He wrapped it around his face and said through the fabric, "Stay here, or I will be *so* pissed."

Micah just watched him, like a soot-covered wraith, as Sasha turned and ran into the house. He did foolhardy stuff all the time, but this, this was bad even for him. But hey, Viv'd take it out of his hide, and that'd be okay.

"You," Micah called, dominance even heavier than before, enough that Sasha shivered and paused in his stride. If the guy didn't hurry, though, there'd be nothing for Sasha to rescue.

"Yeah?"

"The book. The cover, it's leather, and it's got a design with lines coming out of it. Like the ... the sun."

"Sure." Sasha drew in a deep breath, covered his face again, and ran into the fiery death trap of a house. Most of it was gone, but there was a small table near the back and next to the bedding—which was, fuck, on the floor?—and there he found the notebook, just as described. Sasha grabbed it, and right as he turned, a portion of the roof collapsed and blocked the way he'd entered. Cursing, he pressed the book against his chest, turned, and *kicked* the wall—mostly out of annoyance, but luckily the cabin was constructed of wood with the strength of a toothpick, and it gave easily beneath the weight of his boot.

Then, as fire singed the bare skin of his back, Sasha did a front roll and kept going, thankful for the tumbling he'd done as a lad. He came to a stop at Micah's feet, covered in dirt and sticks and ashes. With a grin, he tore his shirt from his face and sucked in air that wasn't free of smoke but was better than inside the house—or what was left of it.

"Sorry about your wall," he wheezed and handed over the book.

Micah took it, silent, his eyes wide in the moonlight.

"Prolly should get out of here," Sasha said, hopping to his feet. He grinned. "C'mon, let's go to Zev's. The rain should put the fire out before it goes too far, but best to, y'know. Move."

"Who *are* you?" Micah held the book tight, breathing too fast, and the glazed look in his eyes ...

Sasha frowned. "Sasha," he said. "And I know that look. You're panicking. Want me to carry you?"

"You—you ran into a burning house and ... you're just— Why?"

Sasha coughed and spat on the ground, trying to subtly urge Micah to move. "You're Zev's friend. Zev's *my* friend. Friend of my friend, yeah? So, c'mon, hop on my back and—"

"No." Micah shook his head wildly, hair going every which way. "You—you're mated. Yes?"

"Uh, married, yeah. Same thing. Why?" Sasha took a step toward him, and Micah retreated, like Sasha was ... well, a huge guy covered in soot and dirt and Micah was a twitchy, terrified dominant clutching an old leather book.

"Go home. To—to your person. I'll go to Zev. I know the way."

Sasha blinked. "You don't want me to help you?"

"No," Micah breathed, and then, before Sasha could say anything, he turned and *ran*.

Sasha took a step toward him, then stopped. He was still coughing, and maybe ... yeah, maybe he should just go home. It was quite a distance to the village, and if Micah knew the way ...

Viv would worry, since she had some preternatural sense for when he was putting himself in situations that could hurt him. And the fire was starting to die, thankfully, as sheets of rain rolled over the forest. So, if Micah had his book and was headed to the village, Sasha could go home.

It would be fine. Hell, maybe fortune would smile a little longer and he'd find that deer he dropped. Stranger things had happened—like when he ran into a burning house to save an old book and didn't die. Life sure was an adventure.

* * *

Vivian was waist-deep in a spell when her husband came home.

Literally waist-deep, because she was kneeling in a tub of lukewarm water with charcoal lines and arcs drawn over her arms and face, holding a squirming, deeply unhappy cat wrapped in a blanket.

It wasn't even her cat. One of the girls from the Compound, a rabbity creature named Ella, had staggered into Viv and Sasha's cave with the cat under one arm and a bag full of onions to trade with under the other, tears rolling down her cheeks.

"Sunshine's not eating," she'd said, and Viv had looked at the one-eyed, ornery, bulky monster of a cat. Sunshine seemed to sense a kindred spirit in Viv, because she started yowling piteously, and Viv knew that was it for her afternoon.

People called Viv a healer ... if they liked her. If they didn't like her, they called her what she was: a witch, the only one in Lukos with enough inborn magic to cure a cough or heal a grumpy, pissed-off cat. There used to be more of them, but the ones who joined the Compound not-so-mysteriously dwindled in number pretty early on. Most of what Viv knew came from guesswork. Magic ran in her family's line, but the ability skipped generations, so everything she knew was patched up at best.

But part of that knowledge was that magic tended to work better when it was amplified by something. Like water.

"Why the fuck did you feed your cat bird bones?" She held Sunshine up, drawing on the magic that ran through her blood. Using it was like spinning thread from wool, twisting the warm fibers of her magic into something she could grasp, and the sensation strengthened as Sunshine's abdomen began to glow. "You know bones get lodged inside, right?"

"I didn't," Ella sobbed, wringing her hands together. "I swear. I thought cats loved eating birds. I even cooked it first."

Viv looked into Sunshine's only eye. Sunshine blinked at her, slowly, settling down as the healing force of Viv's magic took root.

"You spoiled little princess," Viv said, smiling at the beast. She didn't smile often—only around Sasha or animals—and Ella looked taken aback when Viv glanced her way.

"Is that it?" Ella asked. "I thought maybe ... people said you sacrificed things."

Viv rolled her eyes. Of course they did. "Do you want me to? It won't go well. Death causes death. A sacrifice just leads to trouble."

"Oh." Ella looked almost disappointed. "Okay."

Viv didn't bother hiding her frustrated sigh. Rumor was an insidious thing. It was why, when Sasha proposed to her, Viv went to the headman to demand they be allowed to live outside the tunnels and caves that made up the central portion of the Compound. In her own cave, with full control over who came and went, she didn't have to worry about things like rumor. She could actually get work done.

She was still holding the cat when the wooden door blocking the mouth of the cave swung open and Sasha strode in. Viv wrinkled her nose at the scent of smoke and frowned at the smudges of soot on Sasha's cheeks and arms. He stopped at the base of the stairs and looked at her, hands on his hips.

"Aw, baby, are you doing magic? That's so fucking hot."

Viv tossed her long blond hair out of her face and glared at him. "Why are you on *fire?*"

"Not on fire. That's the thing. I'm definitely the opposite of on fire. Unless you mean I'm sexy, because I am very much that. Oh, hey, Ella, how's your dad?"

Of course Sasha knew her. Sasha knew everyone.

Ella blushed and fiddled with the neck of her gown. "Fine. Thanks."

"Is there a reason you have to specify that you aren't on fire?" Viv asked. She held Sunshine out to the girl. "Go on. Take her. She'll sleep for the rest of the day, but she'll be fine."

"Thank you, madam witch," Ella said, grabbing Sunshine with both hands. Sunshine was already asleep, paws limp, and Ella bobbed a curtsy before scrambling up the steps.

Viv waited for her to close the door after her before she gave in to the tremor in her legs. She gripped the side of the bathtub, unsure whether she had the strength to get out again but unwilling to ask for help.

Not that she needed to. Sasha was already there, lifting her out of the water. He kissed her, and Viv ran her nails along the back of his neck, just enough to make him shiver and smile.

"Love you," he said, but there was concern in his gaze, enough that Viv had to look away.

She knew Sasha had noticed how tired she'd been of late. How she had to lean on the wall to steady herself when she walked the low-roofed tunnels of the Compound. She knew he remembered her siblings' deaths, how everyone assumed she would die every time her own sickness sent her into a relapse. Viv was the only one of her mother's children to reach adulthood, and no one expected her to last much longer. No one but Sasha, who married her anyway, who *courted* her, bartering for new dresses and kissing her fingertips like he had all the time in the world to love her.

"You have charcoal on your face," he said, sitting her down on the edge of their enormous bed so he could help her out of her wet gown.

"And you have soot on yours, but you aren't a witch, so you have no excuse."

"Nope. Just lucky." Sasha went to his knees and unlaced the front of her gown. Viv longed to grab his broad shoulders, then flog them until he wept, pleased and lost in that quiet place he went to when she was just cruel enough to fulfill his desires. "Ran into that friend of Zev's. The one who makes toys, right? His house was on fire."

"What?" Vivian lurched out of a daydream of putting Sasha in clamps. "Was he hurt? Where is he?"

"Just shocked, I think. He's fine. Gods, look at your sexy legs. Can I touch you, babe?"

"Down, boy." Viv pushed the rest of her gown off and grabbed a blanket, wrapping it around herself. She was always so cold, lately. Another sign of an oncoming relapse. "What do you mean, he's fine? Did Zev come and get him?"

Zev had spoken to her of Micah. She'd met the man once, when he was injured trying to rescue Zev, but things had moved too quickly afterward for them to get better acquainted. Zev insisted on visiting in the spring and summer, though, making the long journey down to check on her and give her honey and other treats from the wolf-people, who kept bees. He knew Viv had a sweet tooth, and it was nice to see him now, tall and proud, his voice sure.

He'd said that Micah was reclusive. Not fond of too many people—Viv could relate to that; she was notoriously prickly, herself—and clever, even if he didn't have a wealth of common sense where his own safety was concerned.

"I'm trying to fix his house for him," Zev had said the last time he visited, maple candies spread out on the table between them. "But I don't know if he'll make it through the next winter, Viv. That place ... it isn't safe. But he'd rather eat knives than come back to the valleys."

Now, Viv ran her fingers through Sasha's hair, scratching at his scalp, and pulled just enough to make his eyes flutter closed and his lips curve in a lazy smile. "Did you leave him with Zev?"

"Mm. No. He took off. Viv, if you keep doing that, I'm gonna ..."

"You're not going to do anything without my permission," Viv said, a sharp spike of dominance in her voice, and yanked hard. Sasha moaned, always a slut for pain, and put his hands on the edge of the bed, on either side of her. "You can hold me."

"Oh, Viv, I'll hold you however you want me to." Sasha climbed over her, hauling her up the bed. She hadn't thought herself a cuddler before meeting Sasha, but he was so good at it that she couldn't help but melt into his heat, wrapping her arms around his neck. "Viv. Viv, beautiful woman, can't wait for you to fuck me up. Can I get my collar, Viv, please?"

"Go on." Viv smiled as Sasha reached for the collar at the end of the bed, the one she liked best. It had an O ring at the front and was etched with markings that would, if she had the power for it, send a sharp current of magic through whatever was tied to it. She liked to link the clamps to it and watch Sasha beg for the pain while he drove into her, his hands tight on the headboard.

But not tonight. Tonight he just looked lovely in it, his smile going wide when Viv played with the ring and caressed the leather.

There was still soot on his jaw, a dark smudge like a handprint dragged over his cheek.

"You're sure he went to Zev?" she asked.

"What?" Sasha blinked. "Oh. Micah. Yeah, he had to. Where else would he go?" He watched her for a moment, braced comfortably over her. "Viv? Babe?"

"I don't know if he would," she said. "Zev talked about him before. I think we might ... want to go see Zev. Tell him."

"Yeah. Maybe. Micah did seem a bit, uh. He was gonna go back in that shack, actually. While it was on fire. All for some book, believe it or not."

Viv, who *loved* books, very much could believe it. "A shame it burned."

"Oh, no, I got it ... Oh." Sasha wilted under her glare. "Look, he was gonna go in himself. I had to!"

"Oh my gods. You risked your life for his book."

"I mean, yeah. I figured I was in better shape to do it and come out again. Didn't even have a name or anything. Just a weird symbol on the cover."

Viv raised her brows. "What kind of symbol?"

"Like a circle, with a bunch of lines going out around the edge, kind of like a sun."

Viv went still. "You're sure."

Sasha smiled and kissed her cheek. "Yeah, pretty sure. I saved it from a fire. I'd remember that."

A circle like a sun. Lines radiating outward. She knew that

symbol, knew it intimately, innately. She'd sketched it herself hundreds of times, making the shape with her finger as she cast her spells.

The sign of a witch.

"Sasha," she said, and there must have been something in her voice, because Sasha sat up, his bright eyes grave. "Sasha, you need to find him. You need to find him now."

Chapter Two

Micah was in trouble.

He'd been trying to make a shelter against the rain for hours. He couldn't bring himself to go to the village, where people would stare at him, whisper about madness, try to *fix* him. Dragan and Zev would be kind for a while, but then Micah's strangeness would be too much, and if even *they* tried to force Micah to join the crowd at the fire at night ... it would shatter him. It was better to remain lost.

His new shelter wasn't much. Micah was good with his hands, but he was shit at making the things a dominant was supposed to, like lumber, nails, or a foundation. His parents never bothered teaching him, because his father thought he would always be too "immature" for a mate. Then they'd died before he could get the courage to ask. So he was sleeping under a net of tree branches propped up by a slightly bigger branch that kept falling over, surrounded by what little he'd been able to scrounge from the wreckage of his home.

The doll he'd been working on was lost. So was his set of clay disks that told stories depending on which way they were turned, and the stringless puppets he was crafting that would move through a combination of wooden gears and a screw on their backs. What Micah had now was his book, which he kept under his jacket, a few figurines, and pieces of a clay wolf he'd been trying to turn into a music box for Zev.

When he'd come back to his house after the fire was drowned by rain and wind, Micah had wept. He wept harder than he did when his parents died, and then harder still when he realized why: because his creations were so much more a part of him than his family had been. He'd poured a piece of himself into everything he made, while his parents had always kept themselves at a distance, untouchable. The three of them had lived together for fifteen years and turned out to be strangers, and Micah hated that he cried more for the loss of his kiln and his tools than he had for his own parents.

It had been five years since they died. Five years, and he had nothing to show for it but ash and bits of burned ceramic. Five years, and he was still a child, weeping into his dirty hands because his toys had been ripped out of his grasp once again.

Then he'd heard something rustling in the bushes, and fear had clutched at his chest. He couldn't risk Zev or the others seeing him kneeling in the soot and mud. So he'd grabbed his book to his chest and run until he couldn't run anymore.

If it had been people from the village, he could only hope that man wasn't with them. Sasha, Zev's friend, the loud one with the broad shoulders who radiated the need to submit like a small sun. He'd charged into Micah's burning house after a *book,* and the look he'd given Micah hadn't been pity or revulsion or even fear—and the experience had left Micah breathless and light-headed in a far different way than before.

He wasn't sure he could handle seeing Sasha again. Not like this, dirty and cold and entirely unimpressive. He needed to ... get his bearings, first. Figure out what to do.

He coughed, pain lancing through his chest. It was getting

colder. Autumn was a brief thing in Lukos, a splash of color that flickered over the mountains before the snow came, and Micah curled his fingers around the book and thought of his great-grandmother, who'd written her notes so carefully in its pages. He opened the book to a recipe for "A Starving Man's Soup," which had the ingredients listed in neat rows.

Watch the fire, his great-grandmother had written. *Give it a circle, and it will push at the edges. Build your stones high.*

Her notes were always like that. He had to interpret them: building the stones high meant making a well for the oven, for instance, and circles were good for retaining heat. He wondered what his great-grandmother had been like. Whether she would have liked him. What she would have called him on cold nights, curled up together by the fire while they worked on soups and trinkets and little toys that moved at a touch.

Just as he was starting to really feel sorry for himself, there was a lurch in his stomach, and one of the damp leaves at his feet burst into flame. It burned brightly, spitting as it touched the wet leaves around it, and Micah cried out and stamped on it, heart pounding. Where had the fire come from? There was nothing around but the wet branches of his shelter. He hadn't even managed to make a campfire.

But a fire had come for him. Micah clutched the book to his chest, fingers tracing over the circle on the cover. Maybe his parents had been right, and he was mad. Maybe it wasn't only fear and the overwhelming sensation of too many eyes, too many faces, that kept him from a crowd.

No. No, Zev said it happened to him, too, sometimes. He didn't like crowds, either. He, too, went breathless and had to go somewhere quiet for a while. It wasn't madness.

But Zev didn't see fire where there wasn't supposed to be one. Micah leaned down and picked up the wet ash that had once been a leaf, smudging his fingers with it.

It was real. He tried to focus on his breathing, the way Dragan had taught him when he was younger, but that just set off another coughing fit. Even if the fire had been real, that didn't mean Micah knew what to do about it. So he crouched there, huddled under the branches with the scent of smoke from the burned leaf permeating the air around him, more alone than he'd ever been in his life.

* * *

As much as Sasha wanted to start combing the woods for Micah immediately, he knew he'd get nowhere fast if he didn't ask for help. And the best hunter he could think of—aside from himself, of course—was Zev. So he took off through the damp grass toward the village of the wolf-people.

Calling it a village was overstating it a bit. It was a few dozen houses spread over a fairly large area. The kuvar's house, one of the few made of both wood and stone, had a fire pit outside it, with a ring of stone benches for gatherings. There were similar places at the Compound, of course, and people were slowly finding their way back to each other after everything went to shit when they found out Zev was being forced to serve their former leader, Evgen, with some weird magic Sasha still didn't really understand.

The door to the kuvar's house was propped open with a stone, so Sasha assumed that was a sign he didn't have to knock. He called out a hello and walked in, checking the corners of the room just in case Micah had come here after all. But the only person he saw was the kuvar. Dragan Wolf-Breaker was ridiculously good-looking and bled so much dominance in a single *glance* that, if Sasha weren't hopelessly in love with his spitfire of a wife, he would probably swoon at the man's feet. Dragan was seated at the table before the hearth, writing carefully on parchment—and he wrote the way Sasha always did, with his tongue caught between his teeth.

At Dragan's feet, dozing with his head on his paws, was a snow-white wolf. The wolf lifted his head and gave a soft *woof* before trotting over and head-butting Sasha. His tongue lolled out, and he sat on his haunches.

"Feeling wolfy today, buddy?"

Aksa barked.

"Yeah, yeah, same, same." Sasha scritched him behind the ears, and Aksa snuffled happily. "Writing your memoirs, Wolf-Breaker?"

"Writing to my daughter," Dragan said. "In Arktos."

Sasha had heard that the kuvar's daughter, Elena, had left Lukos for the desert country across the sea and was now married—or mated; maybe that's how she'd say it—to the ruler there. "Is Aksa gonna swim the ocean and carry the letter?"

"No," Dragan said, and then, with a perfectly straight expression, "the letter would get wet."

Sasha snorted, then laughed out loud. "Like I know how to send a letter across the world?"

"A ship, boy," Dragan said, his dominance filtering through a heavy air of amusement. "Before the snows come, Owl-Eyed will meet a woman who visits here from the scholar's country. He gives her his books to publish, and she will bring my letter to Elena." Dragan smiled. "She is ruling in another country, my daughter. Did my mate tell you this, Black?"

Sasha nodded, reaching down to pet Aksa—as Zev was called when he was in his wolf form—and flashed a grin at Dragan. "He did, Wolf-Breaker." They had a different system for names in the Compound, based on whatever sect your family came from, going back to the original group of exiles. Or something like that. It could get confusing. He would have taken Viv's family name, since she was awesome and he adored her, but she seemed to like his, so *Black* it was.

"She did well, she and her Aleks." Dragan looked proud, but there was wistfulness in his expression, too. He probably missed his daughter, considering he'd raised her all by himself after his first wife died. Or mate—Sasha always forgot that was the word they used. Something about wolves and how into them they were. Figuratively. Or, in Dragan's case, literally. Except not— They didn't— *Could* they, when Zev was a ...

The wolf barked, and Sasha looked between him and Dragan.

"Whatever you are thinking, stop," Dragan said, putting down the quill.

Yeah, they probably weren't into that. Whatever, he'd ask Zev later. "So, hey, I came by 'cause my little lady's worried about Micah."

Dragan gave him a curious look. "Why?"

"You didn't see the fire in the woods? Micah's house burned down. That's why I'm here, to make sure he's all right."

In the blink of an eye, Zev stood where the wolf had been. He was naked, holding his pelt, his snow-white hair loose but for a single braid—the one he'd taken after he defeated Evgen in the fight that had broken his curse. "What do you mean, his house burned down?"

"Uh, the ... honestly, Zev, I don't know how that isn't clear from the words. Fire? Wooden house? Whoosh?" He made a gesture with his hands to approximate flames devouring a cabin. It looked mostly like waving, but that's what he meant. "What'd he tell you, he fell into a pile of ashes and rolled around in it?"

"Tell us? When?" Dragan asked, exchanging a look with Zev. "It has been some time since we've seen Micah. He brought a toy to send to my daughter, for the child she will soon have." His voice rang with pride. "He did not look to be covered in ashes."

Sasha groaned and stared up at the ceiling. Viv was going to *murder* him, and not in the fun way. "You're saying he didn't come here? After his house burned down?"

"That's what we're saying." Dragan gave him a sharp look. "We did smell a fire a few nights ago, but we thought it was his kiln."

"You didn't go check?"

"No ... he likes his privacy." Zev looked anxiously at his mate. "I want to go look for him."

"I'll go with you," Sasha said, clapping his hands. "Viv's worried. I should have brought him back with me to begin with. If he's sick or injured, she can help. She's done it before, remember?"

Zev looked down—and Sasha swore silently as he realized Zev maybe still felt guilty about people getting hurt on his behalf. "Hey, don't worry about it. We're all glad you showed us what a creep Evgen was. And we miss ya, but you're happy here with your man, yeah?"

"Yes," Zev said. His chin went up. "But I'm going to help you find Micah."

Sasha gave an easy shrug. "We all three going, then?"

Dragan squinted. "No. My mate knows Micah and his scent, and Micah trusts him. I make him nervous."

Sasha grinned at him. "You make me nervous, too. I like it."

"You would." Dragan caught Zev by the scruff and pulled him in for a kiss. "I'll send word to Snow-Walker and his mate, maybe Star-Finder. It will help if we have more people looking for him."

Sasha headed outside with Zev, pulling his coat tighter. The chill in the air said snow would be there soon enough. "I'll miss you this winter," he told Zev as they headed toward the woods. "I mean, I figure you can't come visit the caves."

"Right." Zev smiled at him. "I think my mate plans to keep me busy."

"I think he does," Sasha agreed, waggling his eyebrows. "Good for you. Seriously. If anyone deserves being bent over and fucked for a few months straight, it's you, buddy."

"Thanks," Zev murmured, and the tips of his ears were red, though that might have been from the cold. He had his fur bundled loosely around himself, but he was barefoot, and though he wasn't as skinny as he used to be, he didn't have the same kind of padding most Lukoi did. "I'm going to shift now. Can you keep up?"

"Can I— C'mere, fur-face," Sasha shouted good-naturedly as Zev shifted to his wolf form. While he couldn't run quite as easily through the forest as Aksa could, he did fairly well.

Zev might have shifted to avoid Sasha's teasing, but Sasha knew it was also so he could use Aksa's better senses to find Micah. When they reached the burned-out husk of Micah's shack, Sasha looked at Aksa with concern as the wolf whined and pawed at the ground.

"I got him out," Sasha said, putting a light hand on Aksa's head. The wolf whined again and trotted around, pawing at the piles of sticks, sniffing the air and moving back and forth as he attempted to follow Micah's scent. After a moment, he woofed and took off at a lope, so Sasha cursed softly and followed.

It wasn't long before he heard a cough a few paces away and saw Micah's sad, limp form huddled under a lean-to. It had started to rain again, and if Sasha was cold ... hell, that poor kid must be freezing. By the time Sasha leaned down to place a hand on Micah's shoulder and shake him gently, Aksa was whining again and nosing at Micah's neck.

Aksa turned and blinked at Sasha, who slipped his hand under Micah's lank hair and pressed his fingers to his pulse.

"He's alive," Sasha said to Aksa, who was circling anxiously. "I'll take him back to Viv, okay, buddy? Go back and tell your man, yeah? Don't want him to worry."

Aksa barked, then nudged Sasha before turning and doing the same to Micah. Micah barely moved, and he was so cold his skin was turning blue. Sasha wouldn't be in any danger sleeping outside in this weather, but then again, he had a good deal more meat on his bones than Micah. If they hadn't arrived ...

Well, no point thinking about that. Sasha lifted Micah's limp body, sighed, and turned to make the long trek home.

"Guess I should tell you a story, huh," he said as he moved, at a pace he could keep up for hours, toward the mountains. "It'll make the time go faster. How's about a tale of epic romance, yeah? Everyone likes those. I'll tell you all about how I wooed and married the best little sadist in all the land ..."

* * *

Micah barely remembered being carried out of his shelter. There were patches of overcast sky, a familiar voice rising and falling through the fog in Micah's mind, leaves trembling in the wind—and then warmth, the sound of a door closing. He opened his eyes, and it took him a moment to realize where he was.

It was a house. Not a house like his own or his parents', made of wood with furs to insulate the walls, but one made of stone, like the kuvar's. Except the ceilings were sloped and roughly hewn, with stone dripping down like a petrified waterfall in places, pebbled and wavelike in others. The stairs were carved out of the rock, but the walls were reinforced with wood planks and long rolls of cloth. Lukos didn't support enough goats or sheep to give that much wool, but he was surrounded by beautiful decorative rugs someone had hung between wooden beams. There were an alcove with cushioned benches, a kitchen and a chimney built into the stone, and a room farther in with a massive bed that was only just visible.

"I don't smell any goats," Micah said. Sasha, who was still holding him up, gave him a bemused look. "For your walls."

"The wall cloths? Oh, nah, we make those with cave poppy. You know, plants? All fuzzy on the inside? They're everywhere down below, in the main portion of the Compound. That's where we are, buddy. Sort of."

Micah wasn't sure it mattered. At least Sasha hadn't dragged him to the kuvar's to be stared at. Sasha set him down on the cushions in the alcove, and Micah looked up at the rug on the wall. It was woven to create the image of a woman walking down a hill, her long red hair twisting into different shapes: a bear, a cat, a porcupine. It was masterfully made, and Micah wondered, as he shivered in a cold he should no longer feel, if it would be the last thing he saw.

"Let me look at him. Oh no, he's more of a baby than I remembered." Viv's voice was sharp with dominance, the words snapped out like a fire popping in the hearth.

"I'm full-grown," Micah said dreamily.

"Mm-hmm. Can you turn your head, or will you let me do it?"

"People don't usually ask." Micah's parents had just moved him around whenever they needed to, like an inconvenient piece of furniture. Micah let his head flop to the side and looked up. Despite her forceful tone and fierce, calculating expression, Viv was tiny, slim and almost as young as he was. She was wearing a gown that was just as ornate as the rugs on the walls and made out of the same material.

"Well, I'm asking." She frowned at him. "I'll have to touch you if you're going to get better. Will you fight me?"

"No." Micah wondered why he wasn't afraid. He usually was, around new people. Maybe it was because Viv had healed him before, when he first met her at the kuvar's fire. Or maybe because she spoke like him: bluntly, without trying to obfuscate her meaning.

"Good. All right, we need to regulate your temperature first. You're going to breathe on my count, and you aren't going to argue."

"She's gonna make you feel better, buddy," Sasha said, his tone much warmer than Viv's. Micah nodded—or he thought he did. He felt hazy, not quite aware. Maybe he was dreaming this and was going to wake up in his flimsy shelter, alone again.

Viv lay her hand on the book Micah held to his chest, and his eyes widened. Her expression softened a touch. "It's all right. I won't take it from you. But I need to put my hands on your chest for this to work. There's too much smoke in your lungs."

Micah's heart beat unpleasantly as Viv set the book aside, but she gave him a sidelong look and adjusted the book on the table behind her so he could see it. Then she leaned in and placed her delicate hands on his chest.

"Breathe in," she said. "And think of summer."

Now it was Micah's turn to frown. Think of summer? What did that mean? Summer was just a season, another stretch of time. It didn't have anything to do with why he was lying in some stranger's cave house with a bossy little dom holding his chest.

Viv flexed her fingers. "Think of summer. Breathe in." Micah tried to breathe, and her hands rose with his chest. "The trees are green. The flowers in the mountains are blooming. Breathe out."

Her hands sank. Micah thought of the little yellow flowers that sprouted along the base of the mountain where he gathered clay. They were poisonous but beautiful, and they spread over the grass in the summer like the tide.

"Breathe in," Viv said. Her hands rose. "With no clouds, you can see the stars at night. The mountains look like a bowl filled with them. Breathe out."

Micah hadn't thought of that before, but it was true that the stars were always visible in summer. Sometimes he would go outside to watch them, and he'd work feverishly in his workshop the next morning, giving shape to the unnameable feeling stirring in his chest.

"Breathe in." Viv's voice was soft now. Gentle. "The grass is high. There's sun on your face, on your skin. Breathe out. Open your eyes."

Micah looked up. Viv was looking down at him, her long, pale hair falling over one side of her face. There was a light in her, a glow just under the skin, but it faded as Micah tried to catch it, leaving her the same wan woman who'd wriggled the book out of his grasp. But even without it, she was beautiful, and Micah wasn't cold anymore.

"Now we just need to feed you," she said, staggering as she stepped back. Sasha caught her, heavy brows knit in concern, and Micah sat up, one hand outstretched. Sasha pulled a chair out for Viv, who collapsed into it.

"You know, you were dying," she said, ignoring the worried look Sasha gave her. "Was that what you intended? To hide in the woods, waiting to die?"

"What? No." Micah looked down at his hands and grimaced. They were filthy. So was the rest of him, caked with dirt and soot, and he moved to the edge of the cushions. "I just ... didn't want people to see me."

"Sometimes you have to let them," Viv said.

"I should go."

"No, you shouldn't. You can't. What I did wasn't enough to stop you from dying if you go out there a second time." Micah wanted to ask her what, exactly, she thought she'd done, but she was giving him a searching look, and Sasha was already heading toward the kitchen. "You'll have to stay until you're well enough to go ... wherever you want to go."

The familiar anxiety bloomed in Micah's chest. He didn't mean to be a burden. He hadn't asked these people to take him in. He didn't even know them. They were just friends of Zev's, essentially strangers.

"It's not a problem," Viv said, as though she could hear his thoughts. "If it was, you wouldn't be here."

She didn't seem like a person inclined to lie. "I'm not good company."

"So? Neither am I."

"Aw, babe, that's not true." Sasha turned from the oven, which was already radiating heat. Micah thought of the fire tearing through his house and clasped his hands together. "You're just ... prickly, yeah? Like a really hot porcupine, or those little ones, the ones that roll up and ..." He gestured broadly.

"Hedgehogs," Micah said. "I've seen those."

"I'm a hedgehog." Viv shrugged and propped her feet on a cushion. "Of course I am."

"Yeah, but you're a fucking gorgeous hedgehog, babe. Hope you like my whatever-the-fuck-I-grab-first recipe, Micah."

There was the sound of sizzling fat, and Sasha started humming, throwing things into a pot seemingly at random. Viv was smiling at Sasha like she'd forgotten Micah was there, so much affection in her gaze that Micah felt even more like an imposition than before. Then she glanced his way, and her cheeks flushed pink.

"There's a bathtub in the other room, if you want to use it," she said. "It's connected to pipes, so you don't need to pump water to fill it. If you want the water to be hot, trace the circle on the board next to the tub, but don't overdo it. And if you start coughing, come back out here."

Sasha glanced over his shoulder at her, but he didn't say anything, and Micah nodded, slowly getting to his feet. He didn't feel as weak or cold anymore, but now that Sasha was cooking, he realized he was ravenous.

"You can use one of my robes," Viv called, as Micah made his way into the other room. "You might be a little tall for them, but that's fine."

Micah could already see them: a rack of robes within reach of the tub, all of them made of the same cloth as Viv's dresses and just as colorful. Pipes led from the tub to a barrel, which had a stone column sticking out of it that reached up through the roof. The column didn't look like a natural part of the rock, and Micah wondered, as he stripped out of his filthy clothes, who had carved this cave. It looked like it should have taken decades to make a natural cave so comfortable.

He looked down at the bath. He saw the slate with a white circle drawn in the center, but it wasn't connected to anything but the edge of the bathtub. Micah peered around it, trying to figure out how it worked, until Viv called from the other room, "It's magic—I made it myself. Fill the tub first, then draw the circle."

"Magic?" Micah's voice sounded rough.

"Didn't Zev tell you I'm a witch? Just trace the circle and think about heat."

Micah groped around the pipes until he found the lever that let the water out of the barrel, and once the tub was filled, he turned to the slate. He traced the circle slowly, thinking of the hot spring out near the Lukoi village, and yelped when steam started to rise from the water.

"Did it work?" That was Sasha's voice, eager and booming.

"Yes?" Wasn't it supposed to? Micah stepped into the bath, which was warm enough to make him want to weep in relief, and sank down until he was entirely submerged.

He bathed quickly, scrubbing himself with a bar of soap that hung on a string by the tub, then fumbled for the drain. After he dried off, he put on one of the robes. It was magnificent and fit him well, even if he really was too tall for it, and when he stepped out of the bathing room, he braced himself for the stares and inevitable comments.

No one said a thing. Sasha gave him a quick once-over, and Viv nodded as if she was satisfied with something, but Micah was left alone to make his way back to the alcove, where he tucked himself into a corner and pulled the book off the table and into his lap.

"Here we go," Sasha said, dropping plates of seared meat, peppers, and onion on the table in front of them. There was a great deal of onion. He leaned down to kiss Viv, who tugged at his collar until he gasped and sank to the floor at her side. He was beautiful on his knees, big and muscular and worshipful, and Micah suppressed a spike of envy. No submissive would ever look at him that way.

Viv pushed a plate toward Micah. "Go on. Eat. Magic only does so much. Food goes farther."

Micah shook his head, still unsure why these strangers would care enough to do more than clean him up and send him on his way, and gingerly reached out to take his plate.

* * *

"So, he's a witch," Sasha said.

Viv looked up from where she was weaving warp threads through her loom. It was well-made, having been built by Sasha's older cousins as a wedding gift, and took up most of what Sasha liked to call Viv's *lair*. Weaving room was more accurate, but Sasha did like his dramatics.

"He heated the bath," she said. "And you know you've never been able to. I'd like to get a look at that book of his."

"Good luck with that."

Viv smiled wryly. They'd left Micah sleeping off dinner, wrapped up in blankets with the book hugged to his chest. "I don't like him going out there alone with wild magic. It isn't safe. But he might not respond well to learning he has it if he doesn't know already."

"If he stays much longer, it's gonna be too cold for him to leave."

Viv grimaced. "I know. I don't want to burden you with extra hunting this close to winter, but we might need to prepare for an extended visit."

Sasha stared at her long enough that Viv stopped fiddling with the thread and looked up. He sat next to her, balanced precariously on the end of her weaving bench. "You hate visitors."

"I don't hate them. I just like my privacy." Viv sighed. "Is it so strange, Sasha? This is the first time I've met another witch. I can't help but be a little protective."

"And he's underfed and alone," Sasha added. Viv narrowed her eyes. "Admit it, baby. You have a weak spot for people like that. It's why we went camping for a week to look for Zev."

"It'd be easier if you didn't know me so well," Viv said, and Sasha kissed her, cradling her cheek in one hand.

"I'm gonna barter for more thread in the Compound," he said, winking at her. "Maybe get something for the witch, though I suspect you're planning on making him something yourself."

"Clothes take days to make," Viv said, feeling her cheeks heat. Sasha smiled and walked off, and Viv turned to look at her loom. The threads were all cool colors, with a line of gold running through. They would bring out the pink in Micah's skin and complement his hair. "Depressingly predictable," she muttered, and got to work.

It was easy to get lost in the repetitive work of weaving. There was a rhythm to it, and it gave Viv time to think while her hands took up the patterns she'd learned as a child in Sasha's grandmother's lap. Her own parents had hand looms and shuttle looms, but Sasha's family were the true weavers, and they'd taken Viv under their wing like a flock of birds adopting a misplaced cat.

It was hard to deny the excitement Viv had felt when Micah heated the water in the bath. Witch blood ran in her family, but most of the spellcraft Viv knew, she'd figured out on her own. There was no manual to follow, no training, and Viv couldn't help but wonder if that had doomed her.

Because something was wrong, she knew that much. All three of her siblings had died before their sixth birthday. By the time Viv came around, her parents barely noticed her. Her father soon left her mother for a new, healthy family, and her mother treated her like Viv was already dead.

But maybe her mother was right. Viv couldn't help but feel like she was living on borrowed time. She'd been told as much ever since she was a child, and every time she had a relapse, the fever was harder to break. It wouldn't be long, now. Maybe she'd make it through the coming winter. Maybe not.

"That's beautiful."

Viv twisted in her seat. Micah was standing at the doorway to the weaving room, gazing at the loom. The pattern she'd chosen was simple, meant for a coat for a man who was skinnier than he ought to be, but he looked at it as though it were woven from sunlight itself.

"It's how we make our cloth, here," she said. "You don't have looms?"

"Sort of," he said. "My dad had sticks, and a kind of harness ..."

"I have those, too. This is different. Sit down, and I'll show you."

Micah still had his book under his arm as he sat next to Viv on the bench. "Is it magic?"

"I don't weave all my spells," Viv said. "It's nice to have another way, sometimes, to make something. Here, watch."

Micah hunched over his lap, watching her move the shuttle and pull the threads through the pattern. "I know what you mean. I make things, too. At home. Toys and ... I don't know what to call them. Creations, I guess. They don't do anything. They're just there to be ..."

"Appreciated?" Viv glanced at him sidelong, and Micah blushed. "There's nothing wrong with making something that gives people joy."

"But if it doesn't have a purpose ... maybe the fire was retribution. Maybe it means something."

"Maybe it was an accident, and bad things happen without a reason." Viv didn't mean to snap, but the words came out harsh anyway, her dominance heavy in the air.

Micah raised his brows. "I know that. There wasn't a reason for my parents to die when they did, either. I know things can just happen."

Viv stopped weaving and turned to him. "I'm trying to *encourage* you."

"Oh." Micah smiled, and his wan, surly expression shifted, making him look even younger. "You're not very good at it."

"No. Apparently."

"Neither am I."

Viv got back to work. "Then why don't we just tell each other what we think instead of tiptoeing around it?"

"I can do that."

"Good. I think you're too skinny and you need to take better care of yourself."

"And I think you're trying to be rude to hide how nice you are."

They looked at each other for a moment, and Micah's face creased in another brilliant smile.

"Give me a few years, and I might like you, Micah," Viv said.

"Yeah," Micah said, blushing red as the sun. "Me, too."

Chapter Three

There was a sound in the walls.

Sasha blinked, staring into the dark of his bedroom. Viv was asleep on top of him, as usual, using him for his body heat—which was just fine with him. She made a noise and pressed her face into his neck, much as Aksa had done to Micah.

The noise came again. It sounded like ... something was scratching.

Frowning, he rubbed his hands up and down Viv's back. She was wrapped up in the quilt and sleeping in one of his shirts, so he couldn't touch her soft skin, but he loved how she felt on top of him even if she wasn't naked. Smiling, he smoothed a hand over her hair and felt her warm breath as she shifted closer.

She always was cuddliest when she was sleeping, his Viv.

Sasha closed his eyes again, but he heard the noise almost immediately: scratch-scratch, a shuffle, like there were creatures trying to creep around very quietly.

Or.

Like a slight, twitchy dom was trying to *leave*.

Sasha gently moved Viv off him—she grumbled but rolled into the blanket Sasha had kicked off and eventually settled again—and got to his feet. He wasn't quiet, or all that fast, but he had the advantage of knowing his house well enough to move around in the dark. He ducked against the wall to stay in the shadows, passed the bathing room and Viv's lair, and saw a figure moving toward the door.

"You could go," Sasha said. "But it'd be sorta silly. Viv'd get worried, then she'd get mad at me, then she'd send me to bring you back. So maybe, you know, don't? Wait, were you looking for the bathroom?"

Micah was still as death, standing by the door. Sasha couldn't make out his expression, but he could hear him breathing, too fast, like he was afraid.

"Hey," Sasha said carefully. "It's okay. I'm not mad. What are you doing?"

It was quiet for so long, Sasha wasn't sure whether Micah was going to answer.

"Leaving," Micah said at last. His voice was so quiet, Sasha had to lean forward to hear him. It still seemed like moving was a bad idea, like he might spook Micah out the door.

"Why? Your house burned down." Sasha realized how that sounded and winced. "Sorry, man. I'm less tactful than usual when it's, y'know, the middle of the night. Why are you leaving?"

"I don't have to tell you," Micah said, and the dominance in his voice made Sasha smile.

"No, you don't," he agreed. "But I'd appreciate it if you did. I'd like to have something to tell Viv when she wakes up."

"You'll let me go?" Micah sounded suspicious. "You just said you'd come after me."

"Look." Sasha held his hands up. "I don't have on my boots. It's cold outside, and it's not even dawn, and it's probably gonna rain, 'cause my ankle hurts, this old sprain I got when I was a kid and tripped over a— It doesn't matter. My point is, I can't run after you right *now*, but in the morning, my little firebrand's gonna send me after you."

Micah sighed, and since Sasha's eyes had adjusted, he could see the way Micah's shoulders hunched. "I don't want to stay here and be a bother."

"Hmm. Right, sure. You're not, though. Viv doesn't like that many people, and if she wanted you out, you'd be out."

"You do, though," Micah said. "You like people."

"Yeah." Sasha shrugged. "I do. But she rules the roost, friend. She doesn't want you gone, though, so ..."

"Why?"

Sasha ran a hand through his hair, which was in need of a cut, and grinned. He knew why Viv wanted Micah to stay. Micah was a witch, and Viv was going to take care of him. "Guess she likes you. She told me to go hunting again, get some meat on your bones. She knows what your book's about, too."

Micah was clutching the book to his chest, Sasha saw. "I'm sorry." Fuck, he sounded miserable.

Sasha moved closer. Then, when Micah didn't bolt, closer still. "Hey. It's not— I'm not trying to make you feel bad. I just want to explain something. Viv's a witch. I think she wants to see if she can help you."

"I'm not— I'm not a— I'm just strange." Micah's eyes were wide in the dark, shadowed. "That doesn't make me special. Not like her."

"Plenty of people say the same about her." Sasha carefully laid a hand on Micah's shoulder. "I won't make you stay if you don't want to, but ... if you think you gotta go, could you talk to Viv first? In the morning. A good night's sleep, maybe some more food, and you need some clothes and—"

Micah jerked away. "This is what I mean. I'm too much

trouble."

"It's not," Sasha said. "You're not." He didn't try to touch Micah again, but he found himself wishing he could. Rub his back, work the knots out of his shoulders. Micah looked so *tense*. Sasha's submission was firmly weighted toward masochism, but he had a caretaking streak, too. He doubted Micah wanted to scratch him up, but if he did ...

Micah moved cautiously back from the door. "It's going to be winter soon."

"And your house burned down," Sasha repeated. "You think, what, you're so much of a bother you should just go and freeze to death?"

Silence.

"Oh. You do think that. Huh. Well, no, sorry. Viv'd be mad at me, Zev'd be sad, his mate would be sad. And you're a nice guy. You helped my friend when he needed it, so I'm gonna help you. Would you just ... consider not leaving right now?"

"I don't understand you," Micah said, which wasn't an answer. "And I don't think— Anyway. I'll stay. At least until morning."

"Thanks." Sasha nodded. "Want something to drink? Something to eat? You could use more food, probably."

"No." Micah went to the couch, where he sat and pulled blankets around him. "I'm fine."

Sasha wasn't sure he believed that, but one thing at a time. He went and stoked the fire, making the light flare up in the room. "I don't know how Dragan's community does things, but we wouldn't send you out with nowhere to stay in the winter. I can imagine what you must think of us, after Zev and Evgen—"

"I don't," Micah said, and his dominance made Sasha shiver. He wondered, though he'd never ask, what Micah liked when it came to subs. Hell, did he even know? Probably not.

"I just meant, I get it if you don't think well of us. I wish

I'd ... been able to help Zev more."

"You're good people. You and your mate." Micah looked lovely in the firelight with his hair loose around his angular face, his wide eyes somber and intent as he watched Sasha. "Which is why I don't think you should let me stay here. I think I ... do something. To people, places. I think I'm better off alone."

"Nah. Viv used to think that, too, see? And then she got me, and I was annoying until she loved me—and now, well, I'm still annoying." Sasha stood up, grinned, and went to the kitchen. "How about some stew?"

"I don't— All right." Micah must have realized that it was impossible to argue with Sasha when he was determined to do something. Being submissive meant he was used to channeling his natural alignment to help people, even when they didn't think they needed it.

"I made this, you know," Sasha said, shoving an earthenware bowl at Micah. He put his bare feet up on the table, wriggling his toes, enjoying the warmth of the fire and the comfort of the sofa, and even the slightly suspicious expression of the cute dom next to him. "I'm good at cooking. I have lots of skills, even if I ain't the best at smart stuff."

Micah took a bite, then another and another. "It's good," he said after a moment.

Sasha beamed. "Thanks. You can have more. I make a lot. And don't worry, it's fine that I'll have to get more food and stuff. Viv needs to eat, too. You'll both be fat and happy by the end of the winter."

"I can't stay here that long." Micah ate another bite. "I can't ... This isn't my home."

"It isn't, but it could be. We'll figure it out. Just ... eat, and rest, and see what happens, all right?"

Micah took yet another bite, then put his bowl carefully on his knees. "Are you ever in a bad mood?"

Sasha thought about it. "Sure. I get frustrated when stuff doesn't work right, or when I'm hunting and scare off a deer, that kind of thing. Or when people are mean to my friends or to Viv. But mostly, I'm pretty easygoing. How about you?"

"I." Micah paused. "I don't know."

"That's all right," Sasha said, putting his hands behind his head. "You've got time to figure it out."

* * *

Micah dreaded mealtimes when he was a boy.

It was easy to keep out of his parents' way when they were off hunting, fixing the house, or doing the other myriad tasks it took to make it through a winter in Lukos. Making himself scarce was one of Micah's earliest skills. But at breakfast or dinner, when his parents pulled up a seat by the fire, Micah had to drag himself away from his book and join them. His mother would inevitably try to make him talk, and Micah would sit there with shame twisting in his belly and a knot in his throat, unable to say a word.

Breakfast at Viv and Sasha's was nothing like that. Sasha burst out of the bedroom at an unholy hour, startling Micah from his sleep, and disappeared into a small alcove next to the kitchen. He came back with a bag from which he pulled a fruit with papery, pale yellow skin, which he peeled away to reveal soft white flesh. He bit into it and tossed another at Micah, who almost didn't catch it.

"Food on the run," Sasha said, as Micah peeled back the skin of his own fruit. It smelled strange but not unpleasant. "Those are maiden tears. No idea why we call them that. My sister grows them in her house, ends up with buckets of them."

Micah took a tentative bite and sat there with the fruit held to his mouth, staring at Sasha. The flavor was tart and sweet at the same time, wholly unlike anything he'd tasted before. He wouldn't have thought an island as harsh as Lukos was capable of making something so delicate.

"Good," Sasha said, while Micah had a quiet, revelatory experience over a piece of fruit. "I'll tell her to bring more. She'll be thrilled. I'm off to hunt; be back in ... when I'm back."

Micah forced himself to look away. "You're not waiting for Viv?"

"Nah, it's not her thing. Sometimes she'll forage in the morning, if she's feeling up to it, but I'm the hunter in the family. Stay here, and I'll come back with something you can really sink your teeth into, yeah?"

Micah wanted to tell him that the fruit was enough, but Sasha was already heading for the entrance, whistling softly.

He looked down at the fruit. Maiden tears. That probably had some horrible origin, if Lukoi folklore had any say in the matter. His father's stories were always grim warnings disguised as fairy tales: Don't go swimming in spring. Don't eat unknown berries. Don't be too quiet, or too loud, or too ... Micah.

Viv was still in the bedroom. If Micah was careful, he could use Sasha's hunting trip to take his leave. He could slip away, maybe find another shelter. His parents' old house had been torn down for salvage ages ago, but there was always something. Even the cave where the Lukoi first lived.

But while Micah didn't know Viv and Sasha as well as he knew Zev, he was more than aware that they'd traveled across Lukos as soon as they heard Zev was in danger. They'd been willing to fight Dragan for him, if it came down to it. Micah doubted he could convince either of them to just let him go.

Micah set the fruit down on the table and pulled out his book, thumbing through the pages. There was a whole section devoted to recipes, and he stopped at the one he needed, looking around at Viv and Sasha's kitchen.

Viv didn't come out for a while. When she did, her hair was carefully brushed and pulled back in a braid, and she was wearing a thick blue dress with deep red, puffy sleeves that narrowed at the wrist and black stripes along the hem that twisted like a snake when she moved.

Micah blushed. "Sorry."

"For what?" Viv narrowed her eyes. "For existing?"

"Oh. No, I ... I made a thing."

Viv propped a hand on her hip. Micah shuffled awkwardly, unsure what to say. He'd tried to use as little of Viv's supplies as he could, but it was still a risk to cook with someone else's food. He gestured at the tart he'd made, filled with ground nuts and topped with fruit he'd sliced in thin, overlapping layers. It made the tart look like a blooming flower, and Micah drew back, wary.

Viv gazed at the tart. "You made that."

"Was it wrong?" Micah held his breath as Viv approached. "I know I used your stores."

"So you made us a tart." Viv examined him with the same critical air she used on the pastry. "Can I cut into it, or is it supposed to be art? Because that's almost too pretty to eat."

Micah blushed. He'd overdone it. "I'll make it simpler next time."

"Don't you dare." Viv opened a drawer full of knives and started cutting a slice. "Sit down. You're eating this with me so I don't feel like a pampered empress or something."

Micah almost smiled. "We did away with emperors and empresses ages ago."

"Yeah, good thing. Useless people. Probably never baked a tart in their lives." Viv handed him a plate and cut another slice.

Micah sat on the couch where he'd slept, waiting for Viv to come over, but she ate standing up at the counter, leaning against it with her cloak bunched up behind her. She closed her eyes as she took a bite, then cursed and took another.

"This is ... How did you do this?"

"There was a recipe." Micah took a bite of his own slice. He didn't often bother to cook anything that took more than a few minutes to prepare, but when he did, he always used the book. He had to admit the fruit was a nice touch.

"Keep that recipe forever," Viv said, and when Viv raised her brows, he realized he was smiling.

They ate in silence after that. Each of them in their own space, Viv leaning on the counter, Micah flipping through his book, the quiet unburdened with forced conversation.

When she'd finished eating, Viv straightened and rolled her shoulders. "There was something in that, wasn't there?"

"Nuts and eggs. Fruit."

"Not that. I mean—" Viv cut herself off with a sigh and headed toward him. Micah tensed, but she sat a few cushions away, not even acknowledging that she'd changed direction as soon as Micah began drawing in on himself. "Can I see the recipe?"

Micah hesitated. He lay a hand on his book. All he had to do was pass it over. But he couldn't. He could feel the knot forming in his throat again, the panic and the fear, and he pulled the book into his lap.

Viv propped her chin on her hand. "Okay. The book is off-limits. I get that. Why don't I show you my book first?"

"You can't have one like this. My great-grandmother wrote it herself."

Viv stood, smoothing the wrinkles from her dress. "And Sasha's grandmother made this one. Come on. It'll distract you."

"People tried that, before." Micah got to his feet, holding the book to his chest. "Distracting me. They thought the fear would go away if I looked at something else."

"Bet they were real patient about it, too," Viv said. Her voice was thick with sarcasm as she led Micah to the weaving room.

"Didn't rush you or make you think you were inconveniencing them at all."

Micah narrowed his eyes. "Is this a witch thing? Did you look into my mind?" Because she was right: his parents, the other villagers—even Dragan, once—all of them acted like if Micah didn't stop panicking immediately, Lukos was going to fall into the sea. It always made the panic worse, because now there was shame and guilt mixed in with the rest.

"My mother had several children before me," Viv said, stopping at the doorway. "I lived in the same bedroom where they all slept before they died. Sometimes I'd wake up thinking they were pulling me down, trying to take me with them, and my parents ... didn't like that I was making a fuss. It upset them."

"Making a fuss is different from a night terror, though."

"I know that. They didn't." Viv shrugged. "I'm just saying it isn't a witch thing. What I'm about to show you is, though."

Micah followed her into the weaving room, where she opened the drawer of a long dresser and lifted out a rolled tapestry. It was a good size and masterfully made, with interlocking panels that told a story as she unrolled it on the rug.

"That's the history of witchcraft in the Compound," she said, running a hand over the fine threads. "Sasha's grandmother made it as a wedding gift. See, there? At the top? Those are what witches used to be in the empire we left behind."

Micah leaned over the tapestry. The top panel featured a group of people in white robes, collars, and iron crowns dancing in a field. A vast green country spread out beyond them, with a sun that shone over a distant city. The next panel was only a ship at sea, and the next, a wolf standing over a woman in the snow.

"The uglier side of our history," Viv said, tapping the wolf. "This was Zev's ancestor, the one who killed a witch as an offering to the gods and brought the curse down on his descendants. But there's more. This is the witch coven that remained—see the one with blond hair? That's my ancestor. They helped build the Compound. They shaped the tunnels that connect everyone's cave houses and spelled the earth to make crops grow without sunlight."

Micah stared at the panel depicting a woman kneeling in a field of vegetables. "Is this something you do now, blessing the crops?"

"No. They must have cast a powerful magic, because the soil's still good," Viv said. "But there were always witches in the Compound. Their spells weren't passed down all the time, though, because magic skips a generation now and then. Witch magic is tied to our bodies, you see. It grows in us, like a plant. If you use too much, you dig at the roots and put your own life at risk. You have to cultivate it, tend it."

The panel at the bottom of the tapestry was clearly Vivian, dancing between lines of people. Her hair was flowing in a breeze, and Sasha was holding her hand on one side, a woman Micah didn't recognize on the other. She looked happy.

"The person who made this must have loved you," Micah said, looking at the dancing figures.

"Sasha's people love everyone." Viv was smiling to herself.

"Why don't you have this hanging up?"

"Because it's mine, and it's personal." Viv touched one of the white-clad witches at the top of the tapestry. "It's my legacy. Our legacy."

Micah looked up at her. "I don't understand."

"You need magic to heat the water in the bath," Viv said. "And this morning I was so tired I could barely walk, but eating the food you made was like waking up new. You're a witch, Micah."

Micah drew back. "What?"

"You have magic." Viv held his gaze. "Maybe it takes a

different form with you than it does with me. I heal, but it's diffi-cult. I could never make a spell like the one you made this morning."

"That wasn't a spell. It was a *tart*."

"Balderdash."

Micah held his hands together to keep them from trembling. "I ... I thought I started a fire, before. When I was alone. It sparked in a bed of wet leaves."

Viv leaned forward. "Because you're a witch."

"Oh gods." Micah looked down at his shaking hands. "There really was something wrong with me."

Viv's voice went hard. "What?"

"All that time." Micah ran a hand through his ragged hair. "My mother was right. Everyone was right. There was some-thing wrong with me."

"Magic isn't a disease."

"How do you know?" Micah asked wildly. "Look at the witches on the tapestry. Exiled, dead ... there aren't any witches in my part of Lukos anymore. Maybe magic isn't a plant that grows in you—maybe it's a weed that chokes you."

"It's not." Viv stood, chin raised. "I'm a witch, and I'm not broken."

"But if it's magic, I can *fix* it!"

Micah hadn't realized his voice was raised until he heard it echoing off the stone walls, a strained, desperate chorus. *Fix it. Fix it.*

His mother had been desperate to fix him most of his life, even though other kids weren't forced to be social if they didn't want to be. And because she was always pushing him, and he was always jittery and scared, people noticed.

Then there was Niki, a submissive who had given Micah cider when his parents' pyres were lit and had taken his hand shyly behind the woodshed. Micah could still remember the disgusted look on Niki's face when he shoved a glass flower Micah had given him back into Micah's hands. They were sixteen, and Micah had thought he was in love, lying awake all night thinking of Niki's smile and callused fingers. But he knew then, as he stood at the edge of the fire pit where other members of the village were starting to fall silent, that he'd been very, very wrong.

Niki had told him to stop sending him flowers and notes, raising his voice so everyone at the fire could hear, and Micah realized that Niki was embarrassed to be seen with him. Micah wasn't someone a submissive like Niki would want to present to their family.

Dragan tried to intervene, but it was too late. Everyone had seen it. So Micah ran. He fled into the mountains, where no one was going to call him broken, and stayed there with his book and his kiln. But he'd brought them all with him: every negative voice, every pitying look, every frustrated sigh when he said something wrong or couldn't bring himself to say anything at all.

"Micah."

He blinked his gaze back into focus to find Viv kneeling on the floor in front of the tapestry, covering a portion of the last panel. Smoke drifted between her fingers, and when she moved her hand aside, Micah saw a hole burned into the cloth, obscuring one of the dancers' faces.

"Micah, intense emotion can sometimes trigger magic." Viv's voice was level, but her fingers shook as she brushed at the tapestry. "Take a deep breath."

"I did that." Micah stared at the hole. "I ... started a fire."

"I don't see you breathing."

He'd burned part of Viv's wedding tapestry—the thing she loved so much she kept it rolled up in a drawer, a precious symbol of her legacy. And he'd ruined it.

"I'm sorry." He backed up a step. "I didn't mean to."

"Micah, *breathe.*"

"I'm so sorry," Micah said again, and he turned on his heel, racing for the door to the cave.

* * *

"Oh, I'm a man, and I have a—uh—cone, a pine cone, and a pine cone is my trueeeeeest loooove," Sasha sang, swinging the basket of foraged goods while making sure none of the mushrooms he'd found escaped, a brace of rabbits slung over his shoulder. There were also berries, late-ripening ones that Viv used for a million different things—crafts, tea, pie—and some stones that she'd asked him to gather for ... something witchy. Sasha didn't always know, but he trusted his wife. She wanted stones? She'd get stones.

"I love my pine cone, and it loves *meeee,*" Sasha sang, smiling as he saw the smoke from the fires near the Compound. Their community might not be perfect, and they had a lot of work to do to address the fucked-up shit that happened for years under Evgen, but they'd get there. Dragan had offered them land to build a house and sobriquets to become part of the wolf-people's village, and he and Viv had considered it, but they'd decided to stay put. Their home was comfortable, and while Sasha didn't mind the idea of building a house, someone else would have to design it, since that was a lot of math and shit he didn't know. Working with his hands, maybe with Zev and his hot mate shirtless, sure, that would be fine. He was married, not dead, and it wasn't like Viv didn't think Zev was *pretty.* And every now and then when she wasn't feeling too great, she'd find a nice, hot dom to fuck Sasha senseless. Dragan and Zev didn't seem like the sharing type, though. Bummer. But while they hadn't made the move to the village, they'd spent some time there over the summer, and Sasha had wrestled happily with

Sava, Tomas, and even Dragan—though it had been difficult, given how much Sasha liked dominants pinning him down. He'd been in a lusty mood after, and he and Viv had fucked with abandon, him on his back on the soft grass and her riding him with her nails digging into his chest. It'd been a good day. Summer was good to them. Viv seemed stronger when the sun was shining.

It made him wonder whether they should take a chance and hop on one of those boats, like Dragan's daughter had. She was married to the ruler of the Arkoudai now. Maybe she'd find them a house where Viv could get enough warm sun but not so much that her perfect, beautiful skin would burn—

"Oops," Sasha groaned as he nearly tripped over a tree root, swinging basket dropping a few mushrooms and some of the rose hips on the ground. "Oh no you don't! You're gonna be tea for my gorgeous lady—there's no escape." He scooped up the fallen items and then glanced up ... and saw a person standing a ways off in the woods.

Sasha frowned, the hair on the back of his neck raising in alarm. It was late afternoon, but since the year was heading toward winter, the sun was already dipping below the horizon. But that didn't make people look like shadows. And this person —or this *thing*—that's what it looked like. It was human-shaped but indistinct, like the shadow on the wall of a cave in candlelight.

And it was ... not right. Sasha wasn't the brightest log in the fire, but he knew something *wrong* when he saw it. He straightened slowly, a hunter again—his songs gone quiet, his clever rhymes forgotten. Sasha moved toward the thing, eyes wide and unblinking, as silent now as he'd been loud earlier.

The ... person-shadow ... saw him. It didn't move, and Sasha didn't know *how* he knew it was looking at him, but he did.

They regarded each other, there, in the fading light. And then the thing turned and began to move deeper into the forest.

"Oh no you fucking don't," Sasha whispered. "You do not just ... stand there and be all—all weird and not-human at *me*, buddy." He followed, moving far more nimbly than anyone might expect given his large frame and heavy tread. But Sasha Black knew how to hunt, and whatever this thing was, it needed to be hunted. Because it was moving toward the Compound, and fuck that. They had enough shit to deal with without adding ghost-shadow creatures to the mix.

The thing didn't move right, either. It would sort of ... *glide*, then fade out and blink back, and Sasha was glad he had to focus his attention on tracking it, because otherwise, the thoughts of *What is this, and how can it do that* would probably terrify him. It faded and appeared a few feet away, still turned toward Sasha, and it took Sasha a minute to realize that it was *leading* him. And he was foolish enough to let it. Wow, yeah, he wasn't even the ... third-brightest log in the fire, was he, that he just ran after it?

"Nah. I'm brave. I got this." Sasha marched toward the thing, ducking under a branch and hearing leaves crunch under his feet. He didn't need to be stealthy. The thing wanted him to follow. "You just ... go on, now. Back to, uh, wherever you're ... Huh?"

It was gone.

Sasha blinked, but no shadow person appeared in front of him, not close by or even far off in the distance. A sudden horrible sensation crept up the back of his neck, and Sasha whirled around ... but it wasn't behind him, either. He chuckled, sheepish, and ran the hand that wasn't gripping the basket's handle through his shaggy hair. "Guess I imagined all that," he said, ignoring the slightly unsteady sound of his own voice. Of course he had. Shadow people didn't exist.

Feeling ridiculous, he turned ... and saw his wife.

Viv stood there in her favorite winter cloak, the hood pulled up to frame her lovely face. Strands of her white-blond hair contrasted with the thick black fabric, and her dark eyes were fixed on Sasha.

She smiled.

And he knew it wasn't her.

"What the fuck," Sasha hissed, and moved. He dropped the basket, reaching for her, but she blinked away and reappeared deeper in the woods, laughing, the sound wild and unnatural and nothing like Viv's actual laugh. "You do *not* take her face! Fuck you, no."

There was nothing quiet about Sasha's pursuit of the thing wearing his wife's face. Branches swung at him. Sasha hit them out of the way. His heart raced, his fury carrying him as easily as it had the night they'd gone to find Zev in Dragan's village. More so, even, because this was his wife. His Vivian. And Sasha might be ignoring the signs because thinking about them woke him up in a cold sweat, but Viv was going into one of the downturns she took when the weather grew cool, and they both knew it. That was always when he worried the most, both about her condition in general and that in her weakened state some common illness that should be easy to fight off would take her away from him. But if something was going to take her, it wasn't this phantom in the darkening forest, wearing her features and laughing someone else's laugh.

Sasha roared like a bear and sprang forward, arms outstretched, going in for the kill. Or at least the tackle. He wasn't about to wait for this creepy thing to drag him to some equally creepy village or wherever it came from. For a moment, it felt like he was grabbing on to ... something made of smoke and sulfur and slick oil, ugh—and then there were brambles scratching his hands, and he kissed the dirt as he fell flat on his face.

Spitting, he pushed up on his stinging palms and looked down at what he'd "captured." It was nothing but a mess of branches, wood, and moss. The taste of the moss was in his mouth, fetid and gritty. Sasha spat it out, heart racing, and looked around wildly. His basket was gone, as was the thing that had been Viv. He turned, on high alert, expecting it to be there again, laughing, staring out of hungry eyes that weren't Viv's at all.

He saw no one.

As Sasha stood rooted like a tree, the wrongness and strangeness of the encounter slowly replaced the chaos of the chase. He frowned, looking for the basket, but wherever he'd dropped it wasn't immediately visible.

And then he heard a voice call, "Sasha?"

It was Viv.

Whirling, he squinted as he saw her in the distance—but even so, he knew it was really her. "Viv!" He ran to her, stumbling a bit on the rough terrain, and caught her up in a hug. "Oh, baby, it's you."

"Yes, Sasha, put me—put me *down*. I just saw you this morning." She swatted at him, and when he set her down, he delighted in taking in all the intangible details that told him, yeah, this was his girl.

Which, wait. "What are you doing here?"

"I'd have told you, if you weren't busy tackling me. Where's your basket?"

"I'd have told you, if you weren't trying to stall," Sasha retorted.

She smiled, and she looked nothing like the creature in the woods that had worn her face. It was a brief smile, but it was enough to make him lift her off her feet again and hug her tight.

"It's Micah," she said when he'd once again put her down. "He ran off."

"Huh?" Sasha scowled. "No, he said he wouldn't when I caught him trying this morning!"

Viv opened her mouth, sighed, and shook her head. "I showed him my wedding tapestry and ... something happened. He caught it on fire."

"Like, on purpose? What the hell is up with today?"

"No. Definitely not on purpose. He's a witch, Sasha. And something spooked him, and I ... We need to find him." She glanced at him. "What spooked *you*?"

He shook his head. "Let's find Micah first, and then I'll tell you. Just ... if you see someone that looks like him, make sure it *is* him, first. Before you, ah. Try to tackle him."

"Before I try— Sasha!" She looked at him, her warm brown eyes so different from the cold, empty things that had been in her false face. "How exactly would I know if it's not him?"

He turned and crouched down so she could climb up, settling on his back with her hands curved around his upper arms. "Ask him to laugh. It worked with you." He heard something in the distance, a snap of a branch, and gave a whoop, good mood returning. "Hang on, gorgeous! We gotta go catch a spooked deer."

* * *

They found Micah sitting by a spring, holding the book open on his lap. The spring was one Viv hadn't seen before—she didn't wander too far from her house if she didn't have to—but it reminded her of the clear, cold pools in the depths of the Compound, where children would swim and feel bubbles rising from a fissure down below. Viv had tried to swim out to the bubbles herself many times ... and had nearly drowned twice, when her limbs grew too heavy and her breathing went short. This spring was small enough that Viv could have reached the middle easily, and it was shaped in a perfect circle, ringed by stone and moss.

Micah looked like he belonged there. Perhaps it was the way his hair was disheveled, or his lanky limbs that were too long for his clothes, but he could have been a bedraggled forest god seeking a moment of quiet in the middle of the woods.

He looked up, and Viv wondered how he'd gone this long without realizing he had magic. She could feel it on him now, so strong that it charged the air.

"You know, bears live here," Viv said, slithering off Sasha's back.

"So do witches, I guess." Micah traced a drawing in the book with his finger. "Sorry."

"Thought you said you weren't gonna run off." Sasha leaned down to look at the book, and Micah didn't close it—he just splayed his hand over the page. It was as though all the fear had drained out of him, leaving him quiet and withdrawn.

"I know. But I'm a danger." Micah stared at the water. "I started a fire in your house."

"A tiny one. And if you run off every time you make a mistake, you'll end up living outside forever." Viv plopped down next to him, even though the moss was going to ruin her gown. "With the bears. And the dirt. And the snow."

Micah sighed. "If I come back, I'll be staying the winter. And I'm not ... easy. I don't say the right things, and I'm ... I'm sorry for what I said about magic."

Viv eyed him sidelong. There was something deeper going on with Micah; she knew that much. Something to do with shame, which Viv never had time for. She had a feeling that people had tried to press Micah into a shape that didn't fit, and now he thought that meant he was broken.

"Fuck them," she said.

Micah turned to face her. "What?"

"Fuck them." Viv stood again, dusting off her dress. "The people who made you feel like you're better off gone. What do they know? Most people who think they have it all figured out are a tangle of fucked-up shit under the surface, so who cares what they think?"

"She has a soft way with words, my girl," Sasha said, and Viv made a face at him. He grinned, and she turned back to Micah.

"Come back and stay the winter. You can hide in a closet and eat cave fruit for five months if you want to. You can learn magic if you want to. You can shave your face and eat enough to sustain yourself, even. And maybe you'll leave in the spring and build a new house for yourself where the old one was, but you won't run off again—or, so help me, I will tie you to a post."

"I'm not a submissive, you know," Micah said. "You didn't have to be so ... forceful with your dominance."

"Nah, go ahead and be forceful all you want, baby." Sasha winked at her. "But maybe do it back home, yeah?"

"I think my great-grandmother was like me," Micah said. He blurted the words out like it was urgent, something that had to be said or it would burn through him. "I think she had magic. I think this book was part of it."

"So you come by it honestly."

Micah made a pained sound, and Viv drew back in alarm. She never knew how to respond to tears. She looked at Sasha, who winked and got to a knee at Micah's other side.

"I wish I'd known her." Micah's voice was tight.

"Yeah, I know." Sasha held out an arm, and Micah looked from him to Viv, clearly confused. "It's a hug, buddy. I can do it all day."

Micah turned into Sasha's arms, and when Sasha held him,

he clutched Sasha back, pressing his head to Sasha's chest. Viv remembered clinging to Sasha in much the same way when he'd first hugged her, and something unfamiliar and warm stirred in her chest. They looked nice together, Micah and Sasha. Maybe they would be a comfort to each other, if a fever did take her. Sasha needed people to look after the way Viv needed her magic—it was a part of him.

She looked down into the spring and went still as she saw her own face there.

It wasn't her reflection. The water was too clear for that. No, her face was looking up at her from a stone embedded in the bottom of the spring. The crags and bumps in the rock that made up the image seemed to shift in the sunlight, and silt stirred at the bottom of the spring, a perfect expression of terror molded in the stone. Viv swayed, her limbs going heavy, and her heart sped up, blood rushing in her ears. She turned to Sasha, like she always did when she felt a dizzy spell coming on, but she was already tipping sideways into the water, which closed over her like a fist dragging her down.

She woke to the smell of something roasting. The air was warm, and she tried to sit up, only to collapse when her limbs shook and her head throbbed. She was in bed, dressed in a nightgown with her hair still damp but feeling clean and brushed, and Sasha was radiating heat at her side.

"Hey, lovely," he said, and Viv made a face at him. "Yeah, that's the girl I married."

"I didn't mean to worry you." Viv covered her face with both hands the moment she heard her own voice breaking. She *hated* sounding weak.

Sasha took her wrists and tugged gently. He kissed her palms, and Viv stared at him.

"I still don't know how you're real," she said.

"My mom fucked a guy because he could throw a barrel

across an entire cave." Sasha's voice held a note of pride. "Ulfren. Muscles the size of your head."

"You didn't tell me that was Ulfren!" Viv laughed. "That explains why he tried to give me chickens when you and I got married."

"Yeah, he's a softie that way."

"Why would someone give you chickens?"

Viv looked over to find Micah at the door, holding a mug in both hands. "Wedding gifts."

"Oh, like a mating? We don't give people things for that. Just if you have a baby." Micah brought the mug over and set it on the table next to the bed. "I made you tea. It's from the book. Um. It's supposed to fortify you."

"Hypothetically, or by magic?" Viv let Sasha help her into a seated position, and Micah shrugged.

"Magic, maybe. This is ... still new, for me."

Viv reached for the mug, glared at her own shaking hands, and sighed. Sasha took the mug without her asking, but they glanced at each other when Micah turned his back on them.

"Micah?"

"You probably don't like people to see you looking sick." The tips of Micah's ears were pink. "So. Um. I won't look."

Viv felt the warmth she'd noticed when Sasha held him by the spring and looked at Sasha to see him smiling at her. "What."

"You like him."

Micah's ears turned red.

"Don't let it go to your head," Viv said to Micah's back, then let Sasha hold the mug to her lips. The tea was ordinary, just some rose hips and maiden's tears peel with medicinal bark, but the throbbing in her head went away almost immediately, and her hands were barely shaking when she took a second draught. "You'll have to show me how to make this."

"Sure." Micah still hadn't turned around. "Is it working? It helps me if I forget to eat."

"You do that a lot?" Sasha looked him up and down.

"It's not important when you're working."

"Pretty sure it is, but all right."

"Sit down on the bed and stop acting like a virgin on his wedding night," Viv snapped, and Micah turned, his face blotchy with an uneven blush. He walked woodenly to the bed and sat down, glancing back and forth between Viv and the mug. "I'm fine. I've been sick since I was a child—it comes and goes."

"Oh." Micah twisted the hem of his tunic. He was always doing something with his hands, it seemed. "I'm sorry."

"Not your fault. But I need to say something before I forget. Micah. You were looking into the spring for a while, right? Did you see anything in it? Anything strange?"

"Strange how?"

"Like a face. My face, made out of stone. I could have sworn it was there before I fell—damn!" Viv threw her hands up as Sasha fumbled the tea, spilling it over the blankets. He twitched the bedding away and set the mug down before getting up to grab a fur from the couch. "Sasha?"

"About that." Sasha looked troubled, which only ever happened when his grandmother was sick or Viv had a dizzy spell. Viv frowned at him, and he spread the fur over her legs before he continued. "There was something in the woods today. It was wearing your face."

"What?" Viv clutched the soft fur. Sasha wasn't prone to flights of fancy. "Something like a spirit, or magic, or ..."

"I don't know. It looked like you, but it wasn't you. Walked strange, smiled strange. I almost had it, but when I got there it was just ... sticks and shit. Nothing like you at all."

"And the face in the spring was made of stone." Viv looked

down at her hands. Why was something wandering around looking like her? What did it mean? "I've never heard of anything like this, but then ... we know a man who can turn into a wolf. Maybe there are other things out there."

"If it's after you, it can fuck right off," Sasha said, and Viv smiled at the heat in his voice.

"There's the fox-maiden." Micah's face was paler than usual. "But she only comes in winter. Could there be another witch? Someone who knows you, who's ... making things?"

"You're the only other witch I know." Viv immediately regretted her words as Micah's face fell. "No, I don't think it's you. Calm down."

"But if magic can come out of me when I'm emotional—"

"A working like that would have drained you, and you'd notice. Trust me." Viv patted his knee, and when Micah closed his eyes at the touch, she left her hand there. For a man who hid himself away, he seemed desperate for contact. "I'll see if I can search for this, if I have time. Maybe I can try to cast a fortune for it."

She doubted that would help. The fortune-telling spells she attempted for her own life usually ended poorly.

"And we can ask my nan about any spirits she knows that fuck around with other people's faces." Sasha picked up the mug again, and Viv was just able to take it from him on her own. "My nan knows everything about the Compound. She's the oldest of the Black family."

"It's how we're organized in the Compound," Viv explained to Micah. "I'm from the Red family. When the Compound was made, everyone was split into different sections and given names based on what they were in the empire. Guards were Black, witches were Red, criminals were Gray, and political prisoners were White. Then we all married each other, and it didn't matter so much anymore. Some people changed their names a little, calling themselves Crimson or Silver, but it's all the same."

"I would've been a Red when I married Viv, but she wanted my name."

"That all sounds ... complicated." Micah looked genuinely confused. "Sobriquets are simpler."

Viv shrugged and set the mug down. "Maybe. Micah, if Sasha talks to his grandmother, she'll insist on coming over. Will you be okay?"

Micah blushed again. "It's your house."

"Will you. Be. Okay."

Micah narrowed his eyes, and when he spoke, his dominance was almost as strong as Viv's. "It's. Your. House."

"Look, do you two want me on my knees or what?" Sasha laughed when they both glared at him. "Just asking."

"I'll be fine." Micah looked away. "I just ... might be quiet. New people are hard."

"Not my nan. She's great." Sasha got up. "She knows more history than anyone else in the Compound. Smartest lady here, other than my wife."

He was right. Sasha's grandmother might have been a champion in the fighting pits in her youth, but she was also smart as a whip and had told the best stories when Viv was young. Half of them probably weren't true, but it was still worth listening to her.

"She's like a mother to me," Viv told Micah, squeezing his knee. That seemed to comfort him somewhat, as he took a long, nervous breath. "She won't push you to talk."

"I ... I'll check on the carrots," Micah said, getting up to leave.

"He's cute," Sasha whispered, and Viv smiled as she realized they were both watching Micah go.

"Yeah. I suppose he is."

Chapter Four

Sasha sent a message off to his nan, who promised to come by in the morning. That was good. She'd know how to help, and by then Sasha would hopefully be over the sheer terror of remembering how Viv looked, pitching into the water. He didn't think he was ever going to forget that sight. It was even more frightening than the shadow creature that wore her face one minute and was a pile of sticks and moss the next. That mystical shit made him uneasy, but it was nothing compared to Viv being in physical danger.

She'd been so light in his arms, shivering and pale, unconscious from her impromptu swim. He'd rather face a horde of shadow-moss people wearing whatever faces they wanted than see that again.

At dinner, Viv ate more than she normally did, and Sasha wondered if it was because she was trying to put Micah at ease or if she was actually that hungry. If she was doing the first, she might really *be* one of the shadow people. The second, now, that would be a good sign. She did have a nice flush to her skin, and while he worried for a moment that the color might be from a fever, her eyes were sparkling and she was far more engaged in the conversation than she would have been if she were unwell. No, it was probably due to the witch shit she was talking about with Micah, since that did tend to get her all riled up. Sasha, who had nary a magical bone in his large body, let them talk uninterrupted. But Viv sat on his lap after she finished her meal, and the way she pulled her fingers through his hair while continuing to chat magic with Micah told him she was feeling fine.

That was proven to be true when they went to bed and she climbed on top of him, kissing him with her hair falling soft over her shoulders and tickling his face. "Thank you," she said, small hands on his shoulders. "For getting me out of the water."

"Uh. Babe." Sasha put his hands behind his head and grinned up at her. "I don't think you gotta thank me for, like, not letting you drown. That's base-level married stuff, right there."

She laughed, low and husky, and the sound made him shiver. He loved her laugh. He loved *her*. He didn't want to think too long about what it meant that her smiling and laughing over dinner was abnormal compared to her usual energy levels. Now wasn't the time.

"You're in a good mood," Sasha said, shivering again as she sat up, wriggling on top of him, her cunt a warm, wet press against his bare stomach. The fire in their bedroom was stoked high enough that Sasha slept naked, and Viv had pulled her nightgown off, too.

"Mm-hmm." She kissed him sweetly, but only for a moment. Then she bit his lip, hard, and harder *still*, enough to make him moan and grab at her hips. "Oh no, what's this? Eager, are we?"

"For you? Hell, yeah." Sasha grinned, canting his hips up, pushing his rapidly hardening cock against her ass.

"What do you want more?" She wriggled down, making his

eyes cross as she slid her wet slit up and down the ridge of his cock. "For me to ride you or hurt you?"

He grabbed at the bedding, twisting it in his fingers as she teased him. "What kind of question is that? You know I want both."

"Both?" She tilted her head, playful in a way it seemed like she hadn't been in forever, and her fingers scratched lightly through his dark chest hair. "You'll have to earn it."

"Oh *no*, what terrible, awful thing will I have to do for —mmph."

Viv silenced him by sliding up his body and sitting directly on his face. "You can pleasure me. Twice, I think, and then I'll think about scratching you bloody while I ride you."

Sasha would go for three times. What was he, a quitter? He buried his face in Viv's sweet cunt and grabbed her hips, pulling her down, inhaling her scent while she gasped and wriggled on top of him. He loved when she did this. When she used him for her pleasure, nearly smothering him with her gorgeous snatch— even if she hated that word. He couldn't help that it was such a beautiful cunt, it snatched his breath and his will to do anything but make her come all over his face, could he?

"Sasha, are you *giggling?*"

He shook his head, but he was, kind of. Having her like this, warm and eager, riding his face ... it made him so happy, so turned on, so *everything*. He'd loved her from the moment he'd asked her to be his luck and kiss his knuckles before a fight in the ring. He'd lost, as she'd told him he would, but he was masochistic enough that being thrown on the ground and beaten up a little wasn't a problem. He'd swaggered over after, bloody and bruised, with the taste of dirt in his mouth and sweat stinging his eyes, and she'd sighed and said, "I told you so. I'm no one's good anything."

"Yeah, but it was a hell of a fight. And maybe I lost, but I got a kiss from the prettiest girl in Lukos, so there's that."

She'd stared at him like he was a fool, then rolled her dark eyes, but he'd made her smile. He'd liked that, seeing her small face light up, the way it seemed she couldn't help but like him. Sasha had plenty of people who were into him for a fuck or whatever, but one had told him, "I'd keep you gagged—you talk too much," and while the idea was sorta hot, it wasn't all that appealing to be with someone who only wanted him for his muscles or his big dick. Both of which Sasha had, but nah. He liked to think that, while he wasn't the cleverest guy around, he was funny or charming or at least fucking endearing. Viv was one of the few who seemed to like his brain as much as his muscles or aforementioned dick. She liked his mouth and the stuff he said with it, which was pretty great. And she liked the things he could *do* with his mouth, as evidenced by how fast she went tense and liquid-hot and came.

Sasha turned his head a moment to breathe, then dove back in, worshipping her with his tongue while she ground on his face, bucking against him, mindlessly seeking her pleasure again. Sasha could do this for hours, and had—getting her worked up and wet, buzzing enough to take his cock without too much oil. She tasted delicious, spicy-sweet, and he loved to look up at her while she gasped and made those soft, tense sounds of pleasure as she neared her peak.

As she convulsed a second time with his tongue inside her, he wondered, idly, what she'd look like riding Micah's face. They'd shared before, a few times, other dominants who could hurt Sasha when he needed a little more and her energy was low. She liked to watch him deep-throat cock, but he couldn't remember watching her ride someone else like this. His brain was fuzzy with lust and his desire for submission and pain, so maybe he was forgetting, but hell, it would be hot to watch her and Micah. Having ... hot dom sex. Yeah. Fuck—

Viv gasped out a curse and ground down on him, and he went dizzy from lack of air while he felt her cunt ripple like a wave. She rose up enough to let him catch his breath, gasped out, "I changed my mind—let's do three," and his laugh was cut off abruptly when she sank back down on top of him.

The third one seemed to be the strongest, and he wondered, as she cried out and rubbed herself frantically on his mouth, if Micah could hear them. Viv might have put up one of her silence spells, but he had the thought that she might *want* Micah to hear ... and that idea got his own cock even harder.

When she shifted down to take him, she didn't even need the oil. Sasha groaned as he entered her, so fucking slow and wet, and started playing with her perfect tits while she settled on him.

"Fuck, babe, you're so good. I'd go into exile for that wet cunt of yours."

"Sasha," she said, but smiled and smacked him, hard, her nails on his cheek a delicious sting. "You're ridiculous."

"You wouldn't, for my cock? You like it." He thrust up, just a little, and she laughed and tossed her hair back, shaking her head.

He loved making her come, making her laugh ... all of this. He loved her so fucking much he would literally fight Death for her. Punch that fucker in the face and kick him while he was down—or her, or them. Whatever gender Death was, Sasha didn't care. They'd be beaten to a pulp if need be, to keep his wife safe.

Viv scratched him, leaving red trails down his chest and abdomen, and she came again with one of his hands between her legs to rub her clit while she bounced on him.

"C'mon, baby, pull my hair. Make me feel it," Sasha begged,

then gasped in pleasure when she complied. "Yeah, fuck, you feel so good. You like that? Like my cock? It likes you."

She was too far gone to make fun of him, so she just nodded, sweaty, her hair sticking to her face and her breasts bouncing as she rode him. "You're—good—at this. Always—have been."

"Practiced just for you," Sasha agreed, smiling as she went tight around him, coming as hard on his cock as she had on his mouth. "That's, what, four? Wanna go for six?"

She laughed weakly, shaking her head. "I want to hurt you until you come."

"Fuck, baby, you're the fucking *best*," Sasha crowed, and she slapped him, pulled his hair, scratched him up while he fucked into her. "Yeah, yeah, make me bleed, ain't I been a good boy?"

"You have." She put her hands on him, and the air went tense around them. A spark of violet flashed, and Sasha's breathing went all fucked up and fast when he realized what she was going to do. This took a lot of energy, using her magic this way, and he could hardly wait for the *zing* that would send him over the edge.

"Gonna make Micah make that tea—and dinner—for you all the time, if I get this," Sasha panted, on edge, his cock swelling. "Mmm, that cunt of yours is heaven, baby. I— What?"

She leaned down, smiled, and the magic zipped through her, shocking him into a moan as she bit at his ear. "I wonder how he'd hurt you. Micah."

So he wasn't the only one thinking it, then.

"Ain't sure he's a sadist up to your levels, baby," Sasha managed, because even on the edge of orgasm he could still talk. "But I wouldn't mind if he wanted to try. You feel like sharing?"

"You'd be nice, together," she said, settling back on his lap, letting him fuck up into her while she kept tracing fingers imbued with magic over his chest. When she flicked at his nipples, it felt like a current going down to his balls. She smiled. "Don't come until you ask."

"Aw," Sasha whined, but it wasn't really a problem. "Think he'd like taking my dick as much as you do?"

"Who wouldn't?" Viv kissed him. "I love you."

"Love you, too," Sasha managed, then cried out when Viv did something with her magic, making her eyes brighten, and he felt it *inside*, like some kind of lightning directly on his cock. "Please, baby, have mercy."

"You don't want that," she teased, smacking him again and again, over and over while she scratched him bloody with her other hand and the magic pulsed.

It felt like fucking a storm. Sasha managed one more "Please, please," and then she nodded and he barely heard her "Go on, come," before he came like a wildfire and drove his cock in as deep as he could get. Viv pinched his nose and covered his mouth while he came, to give him that last little edge of submission, and he nearly blacked out with how good it was before she let him breathe again.

After, he gathered her into his arms and kissed her face, her neck, her cute little tits, her soft stomach, her thighs. She played with his hair, not pulling, drowsy as he rested his face on her stomach.

"Did you mean that?" He looked up at her, her face serene in the firelight. "About, uh ... Wait, is the door silenced?"

She opened her mouth, then gave him a wide-eyed look. "Oh, I—think I forgot."

He snorted. "Sure. I'm not buying that, but we can pretend, if you want." He yawned. "You did a number on me. Been awhile."

He saw a slight flash of something like guilt, which made him feel bad, because he knew that if she had the energy, she'd put him in his place like this every night.

"Always feels so good when you make me wait for it," he continued quickly. Having her alive and well was more important than ever being scratched again. "But you need a drink. I'll go get you some water." He kissed her stomach and climbed off the rumpled bed. "Want anything else?"

She pushed her hair out of her face. "Maybe a piece of that tart. If there's any left." She held up a hand. "No jokes about tarts, Sash."

He grinned and kissed her, then glanced around for his pants, which seemed to have vanished. Well, Micah was probably asleep, and if not, he'd seen a naked man before, right? And hey, if she was serious ... a little advertising couldn't hurt, right?

"Be right back," he said, whistling, and headed out of the room.

* * *

Micah lay on the couch with the blankets in a tangled mess over his lap, eyes fixed on the ceiling.

He knew how sex worked. His father had awkwardly explained the process during possibly the most embarrassing ten minutes of both of their lives. Moreover, a small section of his great-grandmother's book was dedicated to things that weren't toys, recipes, or routines to do around the house. Her careful notes on self-pleasure were almost as mortifying as his father's talk. And Zev would sometimes show up at his place still dreamy-eyed, talking about how *strong* his mate was.

But none of that had prepared him for the sounds coming from Viv and Sasha's room.

It certainly didn't prepare him for what he saw when the sounds stopped and Sasha emerged with red lines crisscrossing his bare chest and his gaze gone hazy and soft. It took Micah a moment to realize that he was under—in subspace, as his father had called it. Micah sat up, holding the blankets over his lap to obscure his erection, and Sasha turned to look his way.

"Oh. Hey. Getting water. You want some?"

Micah stared at the scratch marks on Sasha's skin. Viv had done that. He wondered if that had been when Sasha started begging, his voice desperate and low, like he was going to die if he couldn't come. Sasha followed Micah's gaze and pressed at one of the marks, smearing a faint trail of blood over his shoulder, and Micah's dominance flared like a flame in his belly, roaring to its full height.

"Does it hurt?" His voice was hoarse. He wanted Sasha to say yes. Please, gods, let him say yes.

"Yeah. Not as much now." Sasha winked. "You should see what she can do with her magic."

"You can use magic for that?" Micah had to control his breathing. He couldn't look away from the blood. Did he like it? Was that what he liked? Blood? What kind of dominant liked *blood*?

"Or her nails. You can touch if you want. Go on."

Micah tensed as Sasha swaggered over, naked and glistening with sweat. When Sasha got to his knees so Micah could have a closer look, Micah inhaled sharply. He raised his hand tentatively and touched a line of scratches running down Sasha's chest. They weren't deep—they'd likely be gone in an hour—but Micah could feel the welts as his fingers brushed over them, and he let his nails catch on one. Sasha gasped, just loud enough for Micah to notice, and Micah snatched his hand away. "Didn't mean to."

"You can go deeper, you know." Sasha winked. "She won't mind."

Micah looked to the open door to Viv and Sasha's room, then back to the marks on Sasha's chest. He raised his hand again and slowly lined up his fingers with the scratches Viv had made. He dug his nails in, and Sasha closed his eyes, his smile blissful.

Micah dragged his fingers down, and Sasha let out a sharp moan that went right to Micah's dick. Micah pulled away again, breathing hard, and clutched his own wrist to his chest. He wasn't sure if he was afraid of himself, the temptation Sasha offered, or the strange tension rising between them.

Sasha opened his eyes and got to his feet. "Thanks, boss."

"I'm not ..." Micah could feel his face going hot. "Go get your wife her drink. She's been waiting."

"Sure thing." If Sasha felt the dominance in Micah's voice, he didn't seem to mind it. He leaned down and winked at Micah again. "Boss."

Micah clenched his fist. When Sasha's back was turned, Micah looked at his fingers. There was blood smeared over his fingertips. He'd made Sasha bleed, and Sasha had liked it. And Micah ...

Micah licked his fingers. They tasted metallic, like sweat and blood, and he looked at Sasha's back and thought of the way he'd cried out for Viv. He wondered if Viv felt the same way when she made those marks over Sasha's chest and shoulders. Whether he liked a flogger, or if it wasn't enough.

Sasha returned with a mug of water that he set down on the table by the couch, and Micah stared up at him, Sasha's taste lingering on his tongue.

"Thank you. That was ..." What did a dominant say, here? "Good. You're ... a good person."

"Aw, thanks." Sasha retreated into the bedroom with the other cup and a piece of tart wrapped up in a cloth, and Micah raised the mug to his lips.

He'd never been so thirsty in his life.

He didn't touch himself that night. He lay back on the couch with his hand to his mouth until he finally let exhaustion take him, and he dreamt of nails dragging over flesh, blood on his lips, smeared over Sasha's mouth. When he woke, it was so early that the clever skylights someone had carved into the ceiling were still dark, and the fire in the living room fireplace was out. Micah groaned and hobbled over to it, lighting the tinder with a flint before he remembered that he had magic now.

Or he'd always had it. How strange. It was easier to think of it as something new, rather than something that was as natural to him as his dominance. But it seemed he was learning about both.

He used one of the recipes from the book for breakfast, cooking by the light of the fire. He cut holes out of a sliced squash to form rings and cracked quail eggs inside, and thankfully he recognized the spices hanging up over the stove. His great-grandmother had written, "Be careful not to break the circle. Circles have power." Circles were everywhere in her diagrams and recipes. This one was supposed to "wake you in the morning." Micah had always thought it was just folk wisdom, but now he wondered how many of the recipes and diagrams were actually useful spells.

Spells she'd passed on to him.

Sasha was the first to get up. He was wearing nothing but a pair of trousers, and his hair was a mess. The marks on his body were already gone. He looked at the eggs. "Huh. Never thought of doing it like that."

"They're not ready yet," Micah said when Sasha reached for one, and he took the pan and put it back over the fire. "Are you going to ... fix your hair, or ..."

"We're both wild men," Sasha said, touching Micah's hair, and Micah blushed. He knew he didn't take care of himself at the best of times, so he probably shouldn't be bossing Sasha around, but it was easier to focus on someone else. He shrugged and backed up a step.

"And if you both come here," Viv called from the bedroom, "I can fix that."

"The eggs, though."

"Eggs first, then your hair." Viv sounded amused.

Sasha brought the plates to the bedroom, and Micah sat gingerly on the edge of the enormous bed while Viv ate with a plate propped up on her knees. She was in a thin nightgown that clung to her frame, and Micah wasn't sure where to look, so he kept gazing off toward the wall.

"All right," Viv said, when she'd polished off two rings and was reaching for a third. "I love Sasha's cooking, too, but if this is something you enjoy, Micah, you're in charge of meals from now on."

Micah pinched his lips together and took a few breaths before he could find the courage to say anything. "Sure. I like doing it."

He liked watching people eat more, though. Sasha was ridiculous, exclaiming over everything and eating with obvious relish, but it made Micah feel warm to see both of them enjoying something he'd made. And maybe it was a spell after all, because Viv went from a sleepy drawl to quick-witted chatter in minutes and was on her feet as soon as her plate was empty.

"Stay put," she told Micah, her dominance snapping out. "I'm going to brush your hair."

"I could shave you," Sasha said, and Micah opened his mouth, unsure how to respond. It was a great deal of attention, but it felt like an extension of breakfast, with Sasha and Viv chatting away while Micah was allowed to be silent and listen. He nodded, and Sasha grinned.

Viv settled behind Micah on the bed while Sasha got

shaving supplies and crouched on a stool. His knees kept knocking into Micah's, and Micah closed his eyes when he felt Viv touch his hair.

"You're tangled," she said. "It'll hurt."

"Lucky you," Sasha said, and Micah smiled. Viv touched the back of his neck to steady him while she eased a comb through his hair, and Micah leaned into the contact. He would have pulled away when he realized what he was doing, but Viv moved her hand so she was making slow, small circles on his back, and Micah couldn't bring himself to stop her.

Sasha touched his cheek, and Micah opened his eyes. "Doin' okay?"

"Yeah," Micah said. "Yeah, I'm okay."

When Viv was done brushing his hair, she kept running her hands through it while Sasha shaved him, and Micah wished Sasha would take his time so he could feel their warmth that much longer.

He left them to get dressed and was surprised to discover that Sasha had found another robe that fit him better than Viv's. It was dark green with yellow trim, and Micah wrapped a belt around it, wondering whether he could knit one for his next doll. If he could make dolls anymore, that was. He'd need a kiln, and he wasn't sure he could build one in someone else's house.

Someone knocked on the front door, and Micah jumped as Sasha loped across the living room. The knocking continued, insistent and sharp, and when the door opened to reveal not one but two figures standing in the morning light, Micah withdrew to one of the far couches near the bedroom, bringing his book with him.

"Nan! Inessa!" Sasha's shout echoed—which made sense, as the house was originally a cave, but Micah shrank back all the same. "Where are the kids?"

"My man has them. Look at you!" The younger of the two

women, who looked to be around Sasha's age, wrenched Sasha down into a hug. She was attractive, with the round face and large frame that Lukoi looked for in a mate, and she was wearing a gown just as fine as one of Viv's, with little birds flying across the hem. She kept kissing Sasha's cheek, and Sasha was pushing at her and laughing. "My little brother, all grown up. Little baby Sasha!"

"Nan, stop her."

"That sounds like your problem," said the other woman, who had stark white hair done up in numerous braids and wore a thick red gown. She held her arms out to Viv, who embraced her. "Sweet girl, how are you?"

"I'm doing well, Nan."

Micah wondered if he should slip into the bedroom, but then Inessa spotted him and charged his way. Micah couldn't help it—he cringed, and Inessa stopped, brows furrowed.

"That's Micah," Sasha said. "Don't stomp over to him like a fucking bear, Ness."

"Don't fucking swear, Sasha," Nan shouted.

"Hey, Micah!" Inessa waved, but Micah couldn't even wave back. He could feel the fear returning, the lump forming in his throat, his heart beating too fast. Viv gave him a look, and he slumped down. She'd been patient until now, but if he couldn't even behave normally around two people, what would she think?

"Sit down, and I'll show you the unicorn," Viv said, and Nan and Inessa sat on the other couch with Sasha. Inessa kept looking at Micah, but Viv paused as she headed for the weaving room and placed a hand on the table in front of Micah, like she knew he couldn't bear to be touched just then. "Do you want to come with me?"

She was asking if Micah wanted to hide in the weaving room. He shook his head, and she tapped the table with her fingers before moving away. She came back out with a tapestry in her arms, and she unfurled it to reveal a beautiful scene of a unicorn in a field of flowers, its pearly horn cleverly fashioned to give it the look of gleaming bone.

"Damn!" Inessa whistled, but Viv was looking at Nan, a small line between her brows.

Nan squinted at the fabric. "You listened when I told you about the weave for the flowers. That's good. If you have time, I can show you how to give the fur texture."

Viv sighed, which was strange. Micah would have wilted with his work under that kind of scrutiny, but it seemed like Viv wanted it. "Yes. Next time."

"You said in your message your new friend's a toymaker?" Inessa turned her focus back to Micah, and Micah held his breath. "You know, I have a boy with a birthday coming up. Timon. He's eight this year, obsessed with the ocean. I'll trade you more robes for a boat."

Oh, gods, she was talking to him. Micah tried to open his mouth to reply and looked to Sasha for help.

"Don't boss people around, Ness."

"I'm not bossing, I'm just talking to him."

Micah clutched his book, and Nan gave him a quick glance before turning to her granddaughter. "Inessa, my bones ache. Can you fetch me a warm drink, please?"

"Sasha, fetch Nan a drink. It's your house."

Sasha and Inessa broke into another comfortable argument, and Nan gave Micah a tiny nod. Micah only just managed to nod back.

"So," Nan said, patting Viv on the knee, "what's this about a spirit with another person's face?"

Viv explained in a soft voice while Inessa and Sasha got drinks and distributed them, and Nan's frown deepened, her mouth pressed into a thin line.

"I see," she said after a brief silence. "There are many stories about mirror people. That's what they're called. But they're meant to be just that: stories. Tales to explain why some live unexamined lives, or why people have sudden changes of mood or think they see something in the distance that isn't there."

"Are there any tales that … aren't just stories?"

Nan shrugged. "I can look into it. Winter isn't so close that I can't make the trek here again. But in all the stories, the mirror people are most dangerous to the one they imitate. And … it's strange, but I think they all need to be invited in. You need to welcome them into the house, thinking they're your lover or friend. So, if this is real, if it isn't just your mind playing tricks on you, you'll need to make certain you have a way to know who is the real Vivian and who is not."

"I can always recognize my Viv," Sasha said, and Nan leaned over to pat his leg.

"I know. As I said, they're stories. But I'll look into this, see if there are any old tapestries or paintings that can help. And if I see you, Vivian, what should I ask to know you are my girl?"

Viv's cheeks went pink. "My favorite story. Out of the ones you used to tell."

"'The Witch-Girl's Gown.'" Nan smiled. "Yes, that'll do."

"I think it's probably nothing," Inessa said. "I mean, sticks? Moss? A stone in a spring? You probably ate something bad, Sasha, that's all."

"You wouldn't say that if you saw it."

Micah slowly opened his book. He'd read something about mirrors once. How to make one, in any case, out of glass and metal. It wasn't a story like Sasha's grandmother's, but it was something to focus on, and when he found it, he looked at the writing on the page and narrowed his eyes.

Mirrors work when ink is scarce. Micah read the line over and over, but he couldn't parse it. What did mirrors have to do with ink? What made ink better? What was the mirror in the book for? The diagram was simple, and he could probably recreate it. There was a drawing of someone looking into the mirror, and another of a bowl of ink. But he didn't know if it would do anything. Maybe it wasn't the right spell for the situation.

"Remember to ask Micah about the boat, Sasha," Inessa said, and Micah glanced up. Inessa and Nan were already getting to their feet, and Micah hadn't said a word to them the entire time. He stood uneasily, then froze when Nan looked his way. She nodded again, and he raised his hand, unable to do more. Then she left a bundle on the table and gave Viv a pat on the shoulder before heading to the door.

Micah didn't breathe again until Nan and Inessa were gone. Then it all came out in a rush, and Sasha gave him a concerned look while Viv shrugged and started going through the bundle.

"Sorry," Micah blurted, standing stock-still by the couch. "I couldn't help it."

"It's fine. My family's a lot." Sasha grinned at him. "My sister has four kids now, all boys. When we're together, it's like a pack of wolves got set loose."

"He isn't kidding." Viv picked up the bundle and approached Micah, looking him up and down. "You know we don't think less of you just because you're nervous."

"There's nervous, and then there's me."

"Okay." Viv rolled her eyes. "We don't think less of you for being you, how's that?"

Micah looked from Viv to Sasha. "I don't understand either of you. None of this makes sense."

"Look, I just had to deal with stories about mirror people who apparently hate me personally," Viv said. "We all make more sense than that. Come with me to the weaving room, and we can use this cloth Nan brought to make you some more clothes. I need a distraction."

"I could make the boat for your nephew," Micah said, "if I had some wood, and cloth, and something to seal it so it doesn't rot in the water."

"I can get you all those things." Sasha beamed. "You want clay, too? I can get you clay. I remember Zev saying half the shit you made was clay, and we have caves full of it."

A tiny spark of hope lit in Micah's chest. "Do you have a kiln? Or a glass oven?"

"I mean, there's gotta be one somewhere in the Compound. There's a glassmaker in the White family. Bet I can make your own oven if you tell me how, though."

"It'd take up too much space," Micah protested, but Sasha was already on his way out the door, grabbing a bag from a hook on the wall. Viv sighed and turned to Micah.

"Come on. Let him be useful. It'll give me time to dress you."

Micah sighed, still too jittery to say all the words that were rattling around in his head, and followed Viv into the weaving room.

* * *

It was best not to dwell on it.

Viv jabbed a pin through the blue-and-green coat Micah was awkwardly modeling. He looked nice in robes, so she let the coat extend a little past what was fashionable for men in the Compound. It wasn't like he minded, based on how he kept running his hands over the fabric when he was supposed to stay still, and why *shouldn't* men dress the way Viv liked, for once?

They weren't being chased by mirror people.

Not that she was dwelling on it. She wasn't. It didn't matter if there was some fairy-tale villain scuttling around wearing her face. It would be winter soon, and that thing could freeze in the snow for all she cared.

"You're afraid of it, aren't you?"

Viv shot Micah a withering look, but Micah stared back at her, blinking slowly. She brandished a pin at him. "Don't antagonize the tailor."

"I wouldn't. I just want you to know it's all right to be scared. You have a reason for it."

"And you don't?" Viv gestured for him to unbutton the coat, and Micah took it off gingerly, as though it were made of spiderweb. Viv sat down with the fabric over her lap. "Fetch me a needle and the spool of blue thread."

"You're bossing again." Micah found the thread regardless, and he sat down on the floor in front of her, letting the rest of the material drape over his knees. "I can take the other side. I sew clothes for the dolls, so I know how."

Viv handed him the spool, then hunched over her own set of seams. "I don't know how to feel, to be honest. If this thing is real—and Sasha isn't given to flights of fancy, not about something like this—why would it go after me? Because I'm a witch? But you are, too, and nothing's happened to you. And why now? I don't like questions I can't answer. I don't like worrying about what will happen if I leave the house ... even if I don't, much, these days."

Micah was sewing quickly, capably, frowning at the seam as he stitched it closed. "You've been sick."

"Since I was a child, yes. I fell sick one day, and I never fully recovered. It was awful—they said my siblings died of the same thing. When it comes back, which it does, it's the fever that's dangerous."

"And you're scared of that, too."

Viv glanced at him, but he was still looking down at the

coat. "It's been worse, lately. I don't know how I broke the fever last time. Any attempt at healing myself falls flat."

Micah must have guessed what it took for Viv to say that. Her failing health was always an unspoken subject between herself and Sasha, a looming wave ready to crash over their lives at any moment. But now that there was a tangible threat, something external she could shout down instead of her own body, she realized she didn't want to go quietly that winter. She didn't want to leave Sasha alone. She didn't want any of it.

"Wait."

Viv glared at Micah, her vision blurry, as he got to his feet. He pulled at his sleeve and leaned over to wipe her eyes, and Viv let out something that was more of a sob than a laugh. He kept brushing at her cheeks, softly, like he wasn't sure he was doing it right, and then the coat was on the floor and he was holding her, rocking back and forth.

"I can help you," he said. "I think. My book, it has recipes for the lungs, for the stomach. For the heart. For the blood."

"They might not work on me," Viv whispered, wrapping her arms around his waist as he pressed his cheek to her hair. "This isn't something that can be cured. It comes back."

"But maybe it'll be easier to beat the fever when it does. You're the nicest person I've ever met. You're kind, and you're thoughtful—"

"I'm selfish and brash, and I use my dominance too much."

Micah cradled the back of her head, his breath warm in her ear. "You're clever and good, and I see why Sasha loves you."

"You've only known me a few days."

"And I haven't hugged anyone since I was eleven." Micah pulled back, and Viv saw his eyes were wet, too. He was still shifting from foot to foot, and Viv's mouth twitched in a half smile.

"We're almost dancing."

"Do you like to dance?" Micah's eyes lit up. "I used to watch them dance at the fire on festival days. I made a doll that spun on a track to copy the movements."

"Really?" How on earth did people let someone like Micah disappear into the woods? Viv smiled as Micah took her hands, holding them out between their bodies like they would in a line dance. "I usually have to stop after one song."

"I can make you something to help, maybe, for when you're tired." Micah stepped forward, guiding her around in a half circle with their palms pressed together. "Wheels for your shoes, so Sasha can spin you around." He spun her, and Viv couldn't help it—she laughed as she twirled, and Micah smiled at her, earnest and hopeful.

"I don't know about wheels on my shoes," she said, and Micah spun her again so her back was to his chest. He touched her elbow with one hand, her shoulder with the other, and Viv could feel the calluses on his fingers. "I don't know this dance."

"They do it in the spring." Micah hummed the bars of a song Viv didn't recognize, and he moved his hand to her stomach, holding her close.

"Hey! Who wanted bricks?"

Viv sighed as a door slammed and Micah jumped away from her as though burned. Sasha strode in, a bulging bag on his back, and waggled his eyebrows at Micah.

"I didn't ask for bricks," Micah said warily.

"Yeah, but I know a guy, and he said they work to make kilns. We've got a spare room we can build it in and everything."

"But it'll heat up the whole house."

"Oh no," Viv said, deadpan. "Heat. On Lukos."

"Yeah, we're fucked." Sasha joggled the bag. "Oh well. Show me how to put it together, boss."

Micah blushed. "I was helping Viv ..."

"We were dancing," Viv said, so Micah wouldn't think it

was something they had to hide. "But I'll bring my sewing with me if you let Micah boss you around."

"Yeah, I'm good with that."

They didn't finish the kiln that night, since there weren't enough bricks, but Viv enjoyed sitting back and watching while Micah and Sasha took their shirts off and got sweaty working with the bricks and mortar. The spare room was just another small chamber in the cave that was their house, with a few shelves and alcoves carved into the walls. Micah spent all afternoon talking about how to shape a kiln and how much firewood they'd need, and for a while, Viv almost forgot the shadow that lurked outside, gliding about in her form.

She made Micah bathe before he tried on the finished coat, and Sasha whistled while Micah walked about the house in it before taking it off to cook a dinner that was supposed to "strengthen the bones." Viv didn't know if her bones were strengthened by it, but it didn't hurt.

The only damper on the evening was when Sasha went to the door and placed a wooden beam across it, "Just in case."

"I'm coming with you when you pick up the rest of the bricks for the kiln," she told him the next morning, while Micah handed out a breakfast of tea and fried disks that turned out to be sliced fruit. "I haven't been out in a while. I know you won't be able to carry me back along with the bricks. It's fine."

"I can join you." Micah was wearing the coat again, tracing the patterned cloth on his sleeve.

"There might be people around."

Micah shrugged. "I might need to be close to one of you. Or behind you. I do that with Zev, sometimes. It helps."

Viv knew he was only offering because he didn't want Viv or Sasha making such an effort on his behalf without him. She didn't like the idea of him going somewhere he'd be uncomfortable, but it might be good for him to test his limits. And they'd be there to help if he needed it.

Micah took a long breath when they stepped outside of the cave. The main part of the Compound was nearby—a series of family caves all connected to each other by winding tunnels and stairs. Viv had insisted on living apart, in a cave home someone from the Black family had abandoned almost a century before, but she still knew every step of the Compound. She used to walk the tunnels with Zev when they were young, whispering to each other until their parents found them. Except Zev turned out not to have a parent at all, but a captor.

She hadn't heard of Evgen, the former headman who'd used Zev as a tool and a servant, since he was exiled into the wilderness. Some in the community tried to pretend none of it had ever happened, but a few were talking seriously about elections and reform, while others had moved to the village by the hills, leaving their cave homes empty.

"We have a communal stock of supplies," Viv explained to Micah as they walked. He flinched every time someone passed by, so Viv kept on one side of him while he stayed close to the wall, running his hand along the smooth stone. "You have to give some to take some, and there's usually someone there to mark everything down so no one takes too much."

"Which means we'll be talking to at least one person, but they'll be bored as fuck," Sasha said. "Easy as pie."

"Pie isn't easy, though."

"It's a saying," Viv said, patting Micah on the arm. "And maybe your pies are complicated because they're magic."

"No, it's because of the butter. I hate churning it, so it always ends up soggy."

"Hey, I'll churn all the butter you like," Sasha said in his most suggestive tone. Viv made a sound of disgust, and he laughed.

Then he stepped into the trading room, and his cheerful expression faded like a candle blowing out.

"Oh." Viv's mother, Daria, stared at the three of them, her arms wrapped around a heavy bag of wool. "Sasha, Vivian."

"Morning, ma'am," Sasha said. Micah looked from Daria to Viv—clearly, he must have seen the similarity in their faces—and Viv tightened her grip on his arm.

"Vivian, it's good to see you." Daria stepped forward, pushing a lock of blond hair behind her ear. "You're ... you're well?"

"Doing better."

"Oh. Oh, that's good. I'm so glad." She adjusted her hold on the bag. "And who's this? A friend?"

Viv opened her mouth to say that her mother had no right to ease into her life after spending so long avoiding having any part of it, but she stopped as Micah cleared his throat.

"Micah. I'm a witch, too. And I make things."

Daria's eyes widened, and the bag slipped out of her hands. "A ... a witch. Oh. Oh, that's ..."

"I know you hate magic, Mother. You don't have to pretend." Viv tugged on Micah's arm.

"It's just that it's dangerous, darling. You don't know what it can do."

"Don't call me *darling*." Viv blushed hot, and Sasha stepped in front of her, shielding her from her mother's gaze. "You never called me anything before. And I have enough to deal with right now."

"Enough to ... Is something wrong? Are you sick?"

Viv rolled her eyes. "Nothing you can or want to help with, I promise. Unless you know how to stop a mirror person."

Daria's brows furrowed. "A mirror person?"

"It's nothing. We have things to do right now."

"Of course." Daria drew back and walked around them on

the way out the door, leaving the wool behind, which made Viv feel like a monster. She knew her mother regretted neglecting her. She knew Daria was trying to make it right. It was just so hard to look at her without remembering being young and desperate for a kind face, only for her mother to look past her as though she weren't even there. And her father didn't help at all. He left and found another family to love, never giving Viv a chance. That felt almost worse.

"Sorry, babe," Sasha whispered, and Viv let go of Micah to run her hands over her face.

Micah picked up the bag of wool. "Her hands were shaking."

"Thanks, Micah. I already feel like the world's worst daughter to the world's worst mother. Twist the knife in deeper."

Micah shook his head, looking down at the wool in his hands. "It wasn't that. She was scared. I know what it looks like."

"She's always rabbity around Viv," Sasha said, heading over to a pile of firewood, stone, and clay in the corner. "I'd be, too, if I took her for granted."

Viv sighed and followed Sasha toward the bricks, glad for his unwavering support, but when she turned, Micah was still standing there with the wool in his arms, frowning.

Run-ins with her mother always left Viv disoriented. On the one hand, she had every right to be furious. No child deserved the aching loneliness of her early life, following around a mother who treated her like a ghost. On the other, she knew Daria regretted it, and there was no real way she could make up for it. What should she do, be miserable for the rest of her life? Viv was a sadist, but she wasn't cruel. She didn't think suffering was the same as atonement.

But she wasn't *ready* to forgive her parents. It still felt too raw. With her sickness relapsing almost twice a year, though, Viv feared deep down that if she didn't forgive them soon, it would be too late. It was all a tangle of bitterness and regret, and it made her feel like she'd spent the morning wading through mud.

"Viv?" She jumped at a touch on her arm and turned to see Micah holding an armful of wood. "Do you want to look through my book tonight?"

Viv narrowed her eyes at him. "You're trying to distract me."

"Maybe. Do you want to, anyway?"

"Yes, damn you."

Micah smiled, and Viv caught Sasha grinning at both of them, his gaze fond. "That's all right, then."

The walk back was slower, because Micah and Sasha were burdened with wood and bricks, and Viv snorted when they collapsed in a heap in the spare room. Micah looked at Sasha and smiled, and Sasha patted Micah's face.

"Good dom," he said. "Burly dom. Build up those muscles."

"Oh, f-fuck off."

"Did you just say fuck off?" Sasha sat up. "I didn't think you knew how to swear. Say it again."

Micah made a rude gesture, and Sasha beamed.

They built the rest of the kiln in a few hours, and Micah immediately started moving a lump of clay around in his fingers, kneading it until it was malleable and cutting pieces out of it with one of Viv's knives. Viv lounged on Sasha and flipped through Micah's book, which was full of complex diagrams and recipes in tiny handwriting. There were helpful hints everywhere, from how to arrange sprigs of thyme to summon good fortune to the best way to position a mirror on the wall for scrying.

"Your great-grandmother has to have been the most educated witch on Lukos," Viv said, and Micah blushed, looking away. "I mean it. No wonder your magic is so powerful. These spells ... they answer questions I've had my whole life."

"Do you want to try one?" Micah held up his creation: a perfect, simple model boat, just the kind an eight-year-old would love. "It's a summoning. I thought it was just a fanciful idea, so I always used a string to reel it back, but ... Here, come look."

Viv climbed out of Sasha's lap and sat next to Micah, who showed her a bump in the bottom of the boat. "So you draw two circles around this bump, and you write the name of the kid the boat belongs to. It's supposed to make it so he can call it back and it'll float toward him."

"And how do you call your magic?"

Micah stared at her.

"You don't even think about it, do you? When you cast a spell, it works because you expect it to."

Micah nodded. "But I'd like to see how you do it."

Viv carefully drew two circles, then Timon's name, and called on her magic, letting it rise from her core and enter the boat. She thought of Timon, with his round face and his booming voice despite his youth, and when she looked down at the boat again, the circles were gone. All that remained was Timon's name.

"Perfect," Micah said, taking the boat from her. "If I didn't know any better, I'd say you were a witch."

Chapter Five

The storm rolled in shortly after dinner, thunder echoing in the caves as it drew closer and closer to the Compound. They were all cozy in front of the fire, and Sasha was amused at how much Viv and Micah were *talking*. Sure, Sasha didn't understand half of what they were saying about magic and shit, but it was nice to see her so animated ... and Micah, for that matter. He'd even *smiled* a time or two, and damn, what a cutie he was when he smiled. Sasha was sure that Viv was catching all the appreciative glances he was casting Micah's way, but Sasha couldn't help it. Competence just did it for him, and Micah might be twitchy when it came to things like talking and socializing with people, but was he ever smart when it came to magic and the pottery stuff.

And unless Sasha was really wrong about his wife, she was giving Micah a few appreciative glances of her own. Not only about the magic, either—when Micah went to put more logs on the fire and bent over, Sasha elbowed her and gave her a sly grin when he noticed her checking out Micah's ass. She shrugged and gave him a *Like you weren't noticing* look in return.

The conversation had ebbed for the moment, with Sasha

sprawled on one of the sofas and Viv curled up next to him, cocooned in her usual nest of blankets. Micah was in the chair where Viv usually sat to weave, with her table loom pushed aside so he could see them. He was covered in an old quilt that Viv had made when she was a little girl, patchwork squares haphazardly sewn together, with a few dangling threads. It was one of the few things she'd brought with her when they'd married, and she'd told Sasha it was one of her first magical endeavors: sewing a quilt with comfort and healing magic, so she could wrap herself up in it when she was scared, or unwell, or after one of her bouts of sickness passed and she was left to cry herself to sleep all alone.

Fuck, he wanted to go yell at her parents every time he thought about it. Who the hell ignored their young daughter like that? Instead, he focused on how sweet it was that Viv had offered the quilt to Micah, sensing he might need a dose of that old comfort magic.

Sasha wasn't sure it was working, though. Micah had gone from chatty to withdrawn, huddling in the chair and tensing up like he was expecting to be told to leave or something. Sasha glanced at Viv, but she was reading and so engrossed that the cave could catch on fire and she wouldn't notice.

"You want a book or something?" Sasha asked Micah.

Micah startled at the sound of Sasha's voice—yeah, he'd never met an outside voice he didn't immediately bring inside, like a lost kitten—and gave a slight shake of his head. "No, that's all right." His eyes went to Viv, then to Sasha, and then he looked away, drawing the blanket tighter around himself.

But Sasha figured it out. Maybe he wasn't book-smart or magic-smart ... but he could tell things about people, and right now, he could tell that Micah was lonely. And that was something Viv's magic blankie wasn't going to fix. Spells in thread were one thing—and, hey, he wasn't going to knock it; that blanket had helped him over a few summer colds—but what Micah needed now was the sort of comfort that wasn't magic, just human. He needed to be touched.

Sasha glanced at Viv, then back to Micah. He cleared his throat, thought for a minute how to ask, then gave up and barreled on as he usually did. "Hey, Micah, you want in on this?"

Micah blinked. "What?"

"This," Sasha said, waving a hand to indicate the sofa.

"I'm warm enough," Micah said, but the yearning was there, in his glance if not his words.

"Great, but that's not what I meant." Sasha patted the space next to him. He was in the middle, since Viv was small enough not to take up much room. "Come have some cuddle time, buddy."

Viv sat up a bit, peering over at Micah. "Sasha is good at many things, but he's best at this."

"I'd like to think there are one or two other things I'm equally good at," Sasha said, waggling his eyebrows at her. He play-winced when she smacked him on the arm, then shot Micah another encouraging smile. "Seriously, come on over. You can bring your blankie."

"It isn't a blankie," Viv huffed.

"I don't want to intrude," Micah said softly, and now the longing was in his voice, not just the look he was giving them.

"Can't intrude if I'm inviting you," Sasha said.

"Come over here, already. He won't stop until you do," Viv said. "Believe me. That's how I ended up married to him."

"Hey! I won't lie, sheer perseverance was a part of it, but baby, you know I bring other skills besides that."

"I know. I'm only teasing." She leaned up and kissed him on the cheek. "Micah, come over here."

"The dom says so," Sasha added. He beamed when Micah

stood with the blanket around his shoulders like a cape. Micah took a few steps closer, then stopped.

He looked lost, hopeful, and so very, very wary. Sasha wondered if someone had hurt him, offered comfort and touch and then recoiled or pushed him away.

"Please, c'mon. I'm a cuddler by nature, man. Don't keep me from my favorite job."

"You're ridiculous." Micah sat on the couch, leaving plenty of space between them. He gave Sasha a pained look.

Sasha put his arm around Micah's shoulders and hauled him close. "There you go. See? Want me to play with your hair?"

He was teasing, but only because he didn't expect Micah to agree. But to his surprise, Micah nodded, and Sasha felt like he'd won a prize. "Lie down a little. There you go." Micah slouched, and Sasha reached out to draw his fingers through Micah's hair. It was clean, washed and combed, with none of the grime or tangles he'd had when Sasha first brought him home. It was soft as silk and smelled good. Micah also smelled good.

"See, it's nice, right?"

"It ... is," Micah said, sounding strangled. "Strange. But nice."

"No one's played with your hair before? Really?" Sasha shook his head. "Thought those doms over in Dragan's village were smarter. Guess not."

"No one touches me," Micah said, shifting closer. "I like this, though."

"Like I said," Viv murmured, voice warm, "Sasha's good at this. He's the human version of that blanket I gave you."

"Aw, babe." Sasha smiled at her, and with his other hand, he played with her hair, too. "Damn, living my best life right now, yeah? Two hot doms, and I can *pet* them."

"Sasha," Viv said, but she laughed. "Micah's right. You are ridiculous."

"Very," Micah said, the tension gone from his voice. He sounded almost drowsy.

"Is that any way to speak to the champion cuddler of all of Lukos? Skull-crusher cuddle-monster Sasha?"

"Never say that again," Viv demanded, voice full of her natural dominance.

"The skull-crusher part or the cuddle-monster part?"

"Maybe both of them together," Micah suggested. "And I don't think you could crack a skull."

"Hey!"

"I mean, you wouldn't unless you had to," Micah amended.

"I don't mind a good brawl, but yeah, I try to leave skulls uncrushed. Unless someone hurt you guys. Then it's no holds barred, all skulls crushed."

Micah went tense again. "You don't need to protect me. I'm fine."

"Right now, yeah. 'Cause the cuddle monster's got you," Sasha teased, turning as if he were a monster tackling Micah to eat him.

"What—" Micah yelped and shoved at Sasha's shoulder as Sasha pinned him, but through the spill of Micah's long hair, Sasha could see a smile. "I agreed to the petting, not this."

Sasha shivered at the dominance in Micah's tone, and he immediately sat back. As much as he teased about perseverance and sticking with a plan, he'd never force his attentions on anyone. And he liked how Micah's dominance felt, different from Viv's but equally arousing.

Micah looked abashed as he pushed his hair out of his face. "I didn't mean to make you feel bad."

"Don't apologize. He's just being a puppy," Viv murmured, leaning closer. Sasha noticed she'd marked her place in her book and put it aside, clearly more interested in couch shenanigans than whatever was happening on the pages.

"I didn't ... mind," Micah said, slowly, like he was figuring something out. "I'm just not used to it."

"You wanna?" Sasha tilted his head. "I can definitely get you used to wrestling on the couch."

"Sasha," Viv said with a choked laugh.

Micah looked startled, and then he *blushed*. "I think the, uh. Cuddling. That's good for now." He shifted and pressed up next to Sasha, then peered around him at Viv. "You don't mind?"

"You've seen how much of him there is, right? I'm small. I don't need all of him; I can share."

Sasha was the one shifting now, because it turned out that being discussed like a *thing* was doing it for him. But he concentrated on getting them both in the optimal cuddling positions, so he could pet their hair and provide body heat and all that good, old-fashioned human comfort.

It was strange, really, how easy it was to have Micah on his other side. Sort of like he and Viv had been waiting all along for someone to take that third seat as their own. Huh.

Viv fell asleep there, breathing softly, and Micah was so still that Sasha thought he must be asleep, too. But when he looked, he saw Micah was staring at the fire, eyes open, as if he were trying to make himself stay awake.

Warmth rushed over Sasha, and it wasn't from the fire or the heat of Viv and Micah next to him. It was the same sort of thing he felt when he saw Viv lovingly making him leather gloves to pummel a log with in practice for his fights. Or how she'd looked the first time he'd brought her off with his mouth, the way she'd clung to his shoulders and laughed, calling him "good boy" and saying, "Don't ever stop doing that." He liked this: being there for both of them. If the fire got too low, he'd go out and chop some wood, make it warm again, like he was warm.

"It's okay," Sasha said, his voice as quiet as it ever got. He stroked Micah's hair some more, gently. "You can fall asleep. I'll stay here. It's a comfy couch."

Micah didn't say anything, but whatever lingering tension was in his body seemed to drain away. He melted against Sasha and closed his eyes, and Sasha sat there, stroking their hair and holding them close while the fire burned down in the hearth and the storm faded outside, until he, too, fell asleep.

* * *

Viv woke with an ache in her bones that wouldn't go away, even when Micah made a hot floral drink to go with a breakfast of stuffed snow leaves. The snow leaves were Sasha's: the skin of a white plant that grew in the caves, thick and mildly sweet, which he wrapped around eggs before dipping the bundles in a pot of spiced, boiling water. Micah ate only the egg until he saw Sasha tearing into the leaves as well, and Viv wrapped her healing blanket around herself, trying to focus on the way Micah smiled when Sasha licked his own fingers clean.

"He's a little feral, but he's useful," Viv told Micah, and Sasha beamed at her.

"I thought you foraged in the mornings, though."

"Yeah, well." Sasha shrugged. "You made her breakfast yesterday."

"So he wanted to show off," Viv mock-whispered. Micah flashed her another brief, nervous smile. He was a lot like Zev in that way. Zev's smiles always used to fade quickly, as if he was afraid someone would tell him off for them. When they were young, she'd wanted to hold his cheeks up and *make* him smile, but now he didn't need the reminder. He was quicker to laugh now.

She hoped Micah might get there one day, too.

It had been nice to see him and Sasha together the night before. While Micah took to affection like an abandoned cat in the woods, jittery and uncertain, he'd practically melted when Sasha touched his hair. They were sweet, Viv decided as she got up to work on her weaving. They would do well together if ... if something happened.

She flexed her fingers, and the ache in her wrists traveled up her arms.

"Baby?"

She looked around. Sasha had his hunting gear slung over a shoulder. Micah was working with clay by the table, his brow furrowed, hair falling over his eyes.

Sasha leaned in to kiss her, blocking Micah from view. "Baby, you know I love you."

"Let me guess. You want to fight tonight."

Sasha shook his head. "Not tonight. Half moon, in a week. Aiden's back in the circle, and I have my honor to protect."

"You have honor?" Viv smiled at Sasha's look of mock outrage. "All right. But if Aiden goes for your head—"

"Duck this time. I know: concussions are bad. Yes, ma'am." Sasha kissed her again and turned to head up to the main exit.

"And if you see anyone who looks like me out there, run."

"Toward it or away?" Sasha shouted back, but he was already out the door, letting it thump in place after him. Viv sighed and finally got to work on her loom.

"Why is he fighting?" Micah asked. Viv didn't look up, hoping her aches were just the result of sleeping on the couch. "And what's the circle?"

"Fighting circle. A bunch of people from the Compound get together in the fighting pits and make bets on who's going to win the most matches. It's like wrestling, but you hit people with your fists, so everyone loses a tooth at least once. I had to magic

Sasha's front tooth back in a month ago, actually. And he's terrible at betting, so he always loses."

"What does he bet with?"

Viv fell into the rhythm of her weaving, and so did her words: pausing when she did, picking up when she leaned forward to use the shuttle. "Things we can afford to lose. Don't worry. We'd never go hungry because of a few bets."

"What if he gets hurt, though?" She glanced Micah's way. He was still working the clay, completely focused, and there were strange shapes lined up on the table. "What if someone hates him, and they try to beat him badly enough he can't recover?"

"There are rules. We generally try to fight honorably, here. And no one hates Sasha. He *likes* getting beat up a little." She smiled. "Or more than a little."

Micah stopped, setting down the clay. She could see him jiggling his leg under the table, despite his quiet tone. "About that. Is that something you also like? Giving him pain."

"Oh, I love it." Viv tried not to smile at Micah's bewildered look. "You've never heard of a sadist? Or a masochist?"

"I ... know the words. I was never really told much about dominance or submission in general. It was assumed I wouldn't ..." A shadow of pain passed over his face. "It was assumed I wouldn't need to know."

"Bastards," Viv said, and Micah looked down. "But you know it's normal, right, to give a submissive pain if they want it? To like the way it sounds when they're begging you for it? I couldn't believe how lucky I was to find Sasha. You can work him over for hours, and he'll be happy as a cat in a sunbeam."

Micah was silent for a long moment. "Or a wolf pup in a leaf pile."

"See? You know him already." Viv went back to her weaving. "The first time he asked me to use my magic on him, I was so afraid I'd stop his heart with it that I dropped after the first attempt. I was a mess, Micah. Fussing over him, asking him if he was okay, whether he could feel his fingers—and do you know what that man had done? He came without permission. Right there. First try with the magic."

Micah chuckled, and Viv went into a long story about their first time playing with knives, including the embarrassing part when Sasha made a terrible cooking pun and Viv had to leave him tied up for a minute while she wept with laughter into the mattress. Micah didn't contribute much after that, but he did smile a little more, and she could tell he was listening.

"Thank you," he said, after a moment. "For talking to me."

Viv wanted to press his cheeks together and hold him that way until he admitted he didn't have to thank people for enjoying his company, but she knew that wouldn't get them anywhere.

Sasha came back from hunting with skinned rabbits and no reports of weird creatures in the woods, and Micah scrubbed the clay off his hands so he could make them a meal. Viv lay back on the couch to watch, trying to ignore the aches in her joints and the fatigue slowly creeping over her as Sasha taught Micah how to cook rabbit the way they prepared it in the Compound. The kiln warmed the entire cave that evening, and Micah again went through the uneasy dance of joining them on the couch.

It was like watching a pattern form on a loom. As the days went by, Micah eased into their lives as though he'd always been there. He started cleaning the floors "for something to do" and burned red when Sasha complimented him. He disappeared with some supplies and tools and came back with a little footstool once he saw how often Viv shifted position when she read on the couch, and he used dyes from Viv's storage to paint the creation he was working on at the table—a blue-and-white dragon puppet suspended on strings.

"There are carvings of them, in the village," Micah said, making the dragon soar through the air and open its mouth as though to roar. "You can find rocks on the beach with carvings of a dragon sometimes, but no one knows who made them or when."

"My little cousin Yulia would love that," Sasha said, and Micah handed it to him. "Wait. You're sure?"

"Yeah." Micah was blushing. "It's fine."

Sasha packed up the toy boat and the dragon on his way to the fighting ring, and Viv tried not to let on how tired she was as she waved goodbye. She went to bed as soon as the door closed and heard Micah moving around in the other room, felt the heat of a fire starting.

Micah came in a few minutes later with one of his witch drinks, as Sasha had taken to calling them. Viv grimaced. "How'd you guess?"

"You just croaked those words," Micah said, and Viv groaned, sinking onto the pillows. "But I didn't guess, really. I just wanted to make you something, since you seemed tired earlier. Can I check your forehead?"

Viv covered her face with a blanket. "It's just a cold."

Micah sighed. "Viv?"

Viv could feel herself shaking. She'd thought maybe she was worrying unnecessarily. The early signs had been so much less severe this time, probably thanks to Micah's magical cooking, but no amount of kitchen magic would hold off a relapse for long. She'd just ... she'd hoped maybe she'd skipped it. That, this once, it wouldn't happen.

The bed creaked, and Micah climbed under the covers with her. He looked almost ghostly under the sheets, a dim reflection that could disappear at any moment. He pressed a hand to her forehead, and Viv closed her eyes, as though she could banish the fever through sheer will alone.

"You're hot," Micah whispered. Viv tried to suppress the sound building in her throat, which felt uncomfortably like a sob, but it wrenched out of her without warning. And Micah, who was always so wary, who Zev said wouldn't go out to see him unless he warned him first by ringing a string of signal bells, kissed the spot his hand had touched. Then he drew back, eyes wide. "Sorry."

"I hate this." It came out as a rasp.

"I think I do, too." Micah reached for her hand, even though it was damp with sweat, and took it in his. "Do you want me to go get Sasha?"

"You shouldn't have to. You don't like crowds, and there'll be one, in the fighting pits."

"But you want him here." It was like Micah could read it on her face. Viv wondered if he'd always been so knowing, or if it was some aspect of his magic that gave him the gift of insight. "I would, too."

"He'll be back in a few hours."

Micah lay there a minute, breathing slowly, holding her hand. Then he sat up, letting the blankets fall back. Viv shivered and let go of him to wrap them around herself. The relapses always happened so quickly. It was like a winter storm, brutal and sudden, devastating in its force. She had maybe an hour left before she started spitting up bile.

"Tell me how to find him." Micah was trembling, and his eyes were bright, but his tone was firm.

"You shouldn't—"

"I want to. You need him. Please." Micah was biting his cheek so hard, she wondered if he might be tasting blood.

"All right," she said.

Chapter Six

Micah couldn't stop shaking.

He'd left Viv with enough tea to feed all of Lukos and a circle of chalk he'd made on the floor, recreated from one of the designs in his great-grandmother's book. It was supposed to be drawn into the inside of a shield to "protect friends," but Micah figured it wouldn't hurt to push the boundaries of the design a little.

Viv had been shaking, too. She couldn't seem to keep warm, even though her forehead was burning hot, and Micah kept thinking of his parents, falling ill one after the other, shivering in their own sick. He hadn't realized, until that moment, how much that had affected him.

But this wasn't the same. He repeated that over and over in his mind as he braced himself at the door to the cave, wrapped up in his new coat with his fingers trembling and his breath coming too fast. Viv had been through this dozens of times. She'd survived it then, so she'd survive it now. And Micah had his recipes, his magic. *She* had magic. That had to count for something.

He wished there were a spell that would allow him to communicate with Sasha.

He opened the door. It was almost dark out, and the woods were just visible beyond the field that separated Viv and Sasha's cave from the Compound. Treetops formed a jagged black scar against the twilit sky. That thing Sasha had seen could still be out there, somewhere, wearing Viv's face. What was it doing now? Was it waiting for Viv to die, so it could replace her? Was that what it wanted?

Micah had to move quickly. He couldn't leave Viv alone for long. He dashed toward the entrance to the Compound, which was nothing more than a dark pit in the earth. Sasha said it had been kept unlit to prevent villagers from finding their community, and even after Zev escaped and the secret got out, no one bothered changing it. Micah held his breath as he descended the steps and fumbled toward a distant light far down the stair, away from the entrance.

"Turn left, then right, then right," he whispered, repeating Viv's directions under his breath. "Don't open any doors. Down the stairs. You'll hear them."

Someone came running past him along the dark corridor, and Micah pressed himself to the wall, breathing fast. It took him a minute to recover, and he kept a hand on the wall as he turned left, then right, then right again. He passed several doors and another tunnel, and he smelled cooking food and heard voices through the walls. An entire village was here, underground, like a living organism. Micah started imagining it as a puzzle on his old workbench as he moved, trying to ignore the growing sound of voices.

He staggered down the first set of stairs he found. Someone was at the bottom, sitting with a bottle in their hand, talking to someone else Micah couldn't see. They laughed, and their voices boomed up the stairs.

Micah almost couldn't continue. His tongue felt heavy, and anxiety heightened every sense, making the noises of people and the scent of sweat and stone nearly unbearable. Even his own footsteps sounded impossibly loud, and he rushed past the talking men, terrified they'd try to talk to him, or ask his name, or stop him.

He emerged into a well-lit cave. A circular pit was built into the middle, and in it, two men were striking each other in what looked like rhythmic, timed bursts. One of them hit the other in the jaw and sent him falling back, slipping in the dirt. A woman sitting on the wall surrounding the pit shouted something, and the crowd of people watching let out cheers of excitement or derision. It was like being in the belly of a roaring beast, and Micah wasn't sure he could make himself take another step.

Then the worst thing happened. An older man spotted him and walked forward, smiling. Micah knew he should smile back. His parents had always told him to, at the fire. *Just smile and be polite.* But he couldn't smile when he felt like throwing up, and he stood there frozen as the man peered at him.

"You all right, kid?"

Micah tried to speak. Nothing came out. The man frowned and reached for him, and Micah took a jerky step back. "S-Sasha."

"Uh. You need Sasha?" Micah couldn't even nod. He knew what was coming. The man probably thought he was mad, just like his parents had, just like … But no, Micah couldn't focus on that. He couldn't focus at all. It was too much.

The man withdrew, and Micah clenched his fists so tight he could feel his nails pricking into his palms. Then—thank the gods, there was Sasha, walking through the crowd like a candle flame in a dark forest, blood on his cheek and his brows knit with confusion. When he saw Micah, he turned to say something to the man at his side and hurried over on his own.

"Hey, boss. What's wrong? Thought you hated crowds." Micah couldn't answer. "Oh. Okay. Okay, let's ... go upstairs, yeah? Think we can go upstairs? You need me to help, or—"

"Touching is ... bad," Micah managed to say, and Sasha nodded. "Viv's sick."

Sasha's entire posture shifted, like one of Micah's toys that would turn from a caterpillar to a butterfly when you turned the key. It was remarkable to see on a person—and terrible, too, because Micah could see his own fear reflected in Sasha's face.

"Let's go home," Sasha said. Micah nodded.

It was easier to head back, but Micah still couldn't breathe right. The only thing that made it manageable was that Sasha was with him. Sasha wasn't trying to hold him or carry him or settle him—he was just there, keeping pace, like a wall between Micah and the rest of the world. Micah let himself think of Sasha instead of the crowd, watching how Sasha walked, the sweat on his skin, the blood on his cheek.

When they made it back to the entrance, Micah was shaking, but he didn't feel as sick and miserable as he usually did after he panicked. It was still awful, and he was light-headed and tearful, but he didn't think he was going to throw up or have to crawl into somewhere dark and private until the world stopped pressing down on him. Maybe it was because Sasha and Viv's home *was* that quiet place he needed, and he knew he was almost there.

When they entered the house, Micah's heart clenched at the sound of Viv retching in the other room. The door was open, and he could just see her feet through it. Oh, gods, she was on the floor. What if she was choking, what if she'd hurt herself—

"Aw, baby." Sasha strode to her, and Micah stayed where he was, only just remembering to close the door behind him as Sasha bent down at Viv's side. "Come on, it's okay."

"I fucking hate this. Fuck this, fuck it, fuck everything."

"That's right, baby. Kick its ass." Sasha picked her up. "Gonna wash you off."

"Fuck baths, too."

"Yeah, baths are assholes." Sasha carried Viv to the bathroom, and Micah sat down on the floor. Viv was paler than usual, and her hair was damp with sweat, her gown soaked with it. Sasha gave Micah a look and a nod, and Micah covered his face with his hands, trying to remember, yet again, how to breathe.

* * *

By now, Sasha knew what to do for Viv when she was sick, but that didn't mean he liked having to do it.

Oh, he didn't mind the caretaking. That made him feel good, because while he was more of a masochist than anything, he also enjoyed service—and he *loved* Viv, so of course he was happy to help her with whatever she needed.

The thing he didn't like was that it happened at all. His badass wife, with her magic and her clever fingers and her insatiable appetite for knowledge, should be as strong in her body as she was in her mind. Sasha hated—*hated*—watching her retch and tremble and shake, because he knew how much *she* hated it.

At least when he was tending to her, bathing her or cleaning her clothes or making the broth that was all she could keep down some days, it helped keep his panic at bay. Every time this happened, Sasha would look down at Viv's small body and see the truth: she was fighting for her very life, and the fever was only trying to burn the sickness out of her. But the fever made her miserable and angry. Which in a way was fine: he'd rather have Viv snarling curses as she retched and shivered than just giving up.

So he carried her to the bath, repeating, "I know, sweetheart. Yeah, it fucking sucks." He knew he needed to see to Micah, too, because it was clear that Micah was having some kind of ... *thing* ... from going to find him. There was probably a word for it, and Sasha was proud as hell of Micah for venturing into the pits to get him. But Viv first.

"He found you," she said weakly, shivering in the bath despite the water being hot enough that the room had filled with steam and Sasha was sweating. "He was ... He insisted. I—"

"Hey, shush, you know you can't tell him what to do like you tell me," Sasha murmured, stroking her hair. "I'm glad he did. You know I hate being gone when you need me."

"I didn't realize," she said, leaning back against him. The tub was big enough for both of them, and Sasha was glad, even if he hated how much she was shaking against him. "That it was ... going to be bad."

"Of course not," Sasha said, but he didn't think she was telling the truth. It was all right. Sometimes these sorts of ... mistruths ... made her feel better.

She sighed, and Sasha washed her, holding her as she coughed and gripped him with nails that dug into his shoulders. The pain helped ground him, but without her sexy smile and wicked laugh, it wasn't fun the way it usually was when she hurt him. But he let it settle him enough to finish her bath and dry her off, carry her to the bed and bundle her in furs.

He went to get her something to drink and found Micah mixing something in a pot on the small stove.

"Hey," Sasha said, smiling tiredly. "Meant to tell you, Yulia loved the dragon. And Timon thinks that boat is the coolest thing he's ever seen. They'll want to thank you, but I told 'em to wait a bit. Know how you are about strangers."

Micah glanced over his shoulder. His eyes were shadowed and still too wide, but he gave a slight smile and a nod. "I'm glad they liked them. And that's— Thank you."

"It's all good." Sasha went to the stove and put a hand on Micah's shoulder, gently, not wanting to crowd or push. "Thanks for coming to get me, yeah? I know that must have been hard."

Micah breathed out, slowly, and nodded. "Yeah."

"You okay?"

Micah stirred whatever was in the pot and was silent for so long that Sasha got a little worried. Eventually, though, he nodded again. "I needed someplace quiet. I'm okay. Thanks."

"Sure." Sasha dropped his hand, peering into the pot. "Whatcha making?"

"It's a drink. It was in my book—tree bark with flowers. Um, it's supposed to be good for fevers and for when you need more fluids."

Sasha watched him, the way he concentrated and stirred, measured and checked the temperature. "You're good at this stuff. That your chalk circle on my bedroom floor?"

Micah was too fair for Sasha to miss the flush on his skin. "It was supposed to help while I was looking for you. I don't know if it did anything, but it's for ... protecting a friend."

"A friend, huh." Sasha smiled.

"Yes." Micah glanced at him, and Sasha realized he might have said the wrong thing. "Isn't that— I thought maybe—"

"We are definitely friends, boss," Sasha assured him, giving him a pat on the back. "Viv thinks you're the cat's tits."

"The what?"

"You know." Sasha waved a hand. "Cats need those. Important and, like, super great if you're a kitten?"

Micah blinked at him. "I— Okay. I'll need to strain this. The little flower bits might not be good if she's having trouble breathing or swallowing. Do you have something?"

"Uh." Sasha thought about it, then nodded and found a

piece of cheesecloth. "Viv uses this when she makes her potions and shit."

Micah took it, and Sasha watched him as he strained the mixture into a mug. "Is she ... going to be all right?"

Sasha almost, *almost* lied. Instead, he said quietly, "I hope so. It came pretty quick, this time."

Micah slammed the pot down on the stove. "It's not fair. She's— I've never met anyone like her. Like you. Why do you— I don't *want* her to—"

"Hey, hey," Sasha said, quickly, before Micah could finish that sentence. "She's tough, boss. She survives out of spite, yeah? The Lukoi way. And all the drinks and stuff you've been making? Your witch drinks? That shit's helped, buddy. I can tell."

"But she's still sick," Micah whispered, breathing hard, his hands gripping the edge of the wooden counter.

Whoa. There was clearly some other thing going on here. Sasha put another careful hand on Micah's shoulder. "She is. She's always been sick. But like I said, she's also a fighter. Even more than me."

Micah breathed out, slow and even. "Yeah. I didn't even ask ... Did you win?"

"Actually, yeah. You came to get me before I cleaned my face off, but for once? Wasn't my blood." He laughed, though it was strained, since it was hard to be as happy as usual when Viv was sick. "Won my first fight. Was prolly gonna lose the second, so, good timing."

Micah didn't smile. Instead, he turned to Sasha and said, bluntly, "My parents died of a fever. I tended to them both. They didn't like me. I heard my mother tell my father she wished I'd go away, that I made her feel worse."

Sasha stared at him. "What? *What?* The fuck. I hope your father told her to get a fucking clue." Maybe that was mean to say about a sick person, but who the hell did that? Why did both Viv and Micah, two nice people, get such shitty parents? Time to tell his ma she'd need to adopt another one.

"He said I couldn't help but make it worse. He thought I was sick, too."

"Like, with the same thing they had?"

"No. In my head." Micah tapped it with a finger. "He thought there was something wrong with me, because of how I am."

"Smart and hot and a little twitchy? Ain't nothing wrong with that, believe me."

Micah shook his head. "Sick because of how I get—like how I was when I found you in the cave. I've always been that way."

Sasha tilted his head. "What, brave?"

Micah blinked, and then—oh, fuck, his eyes were filling up. "You really think that. I could barely say your name, and you think— You're wrong. I'm scared of everything."

"Thought it was like, crowds and stuff." Sasha frowned. "I mean, if it was easy for you to come find me, then it wouldn't have been brave. But you did it anyway, so what's the problem?"

"Take Viv her drink." Micah's voice was strangled, but a rush of his dominance made Sasha straighten his shoulders a bit and reach out, accepting the steaming mug. "Tell her I put the honey in."

"You whip that dominance out way less than you should, boss," Sasha said. "Hey, eat something, yeah? Probably gonna need you to make more of these."

Micah nodded silently.

Sasha took Viv her drink and helped her sip the whole thing, relaying the information about the honey even though he probably didn't need to. She did stop shivering as much, and Sasha beamed at her as he put the empty mug on the table by the bed. "He'll make you more of these, I bet. Also, did you know he didn't think we were friends?"

"He can probably hear you," Viv said, bundling back up under her blankets. "And I don't think ... that's what he meant."

She was asleep before he could ask her to clarify.

Sasha went about the rest of his chores, and as he usually did when Viv was down with a fever, that meant he cleaned the house, cooked, and washed the clothes she inevitably needed laundered after she got sick in them. He washed the bedding, too, since he knew she hated lying on dirty linens that she'd sweated into.

But this time, it wasn't just him doing the work.

Micah made her witch drinks and a sachet of herbs and flowers that he said would help her sleep better. He consulted his books and made more weird shit at the stove that smelled like something Sasha would rather eat mud off the bottom of his boot than consume, but he always added honey or maple sugar and instructed Sasha take it to Viv. He made salts to put in the bathwater that he said would disperse in the steam and help her breathe. He drew more chalk circles and heated the bathwater with his magic so Viv didn't have to expend energy to. At a certain point, Sasha realized Micah was washing the dishes, too.

And that's not all he did. He took his book to Viv and read to her while Sasha did the laundry, and he did more laundry so Sasha could read from another book at night. He was the first one up in the morning, and after one particularly bad night when Viv couldn't sleep and coughed up blood while her fever raged, Sasha stumbled into the kitchen, bleary-eyed and exhausted, to find Micah had made *him* a drink, too. It perked him up and eased his headache, but it didn't lessen the fear that overtook him when he saw how badly off his wife was, how the sickness still had her in its grip and hadn't let go.

Sasha found himself unable to sleep, dread a cold chill in his heart, his veins. He loved her so much. He couldn't lose her. She was better than ... anyone. Better than he deserved, probably, a big brawler who lost trinkets beating up people in the pits while she—

"Stop," Viv muttered, cracking an eye open. "I can feel you worrying. Go bother Micah. Give me the bed. You take up too much room, and I'm hot." She gave him a weak shove and a slight smile. "Go get him to settle you down."

"He might not be awake," Sasha protested, getting up. She'd done this a time or two, kicked him out when the fever went into the phase where she was always sweating.

"He is," Viv mumbled, waving a hand.

That was a good sign, really, the sweating. It usually meant the end of her episode was near, and that, of course, was what they wanted. Retying the drawstring of his sleep pants, Sasha went into the other room, intending to sleep on the sofa, and saw that—as usual—Viv was right: Micah was awake.

He wasn't just awake. He was working. Cutting petals off flowers and pushing them into the tiny cloth bags Viv made, grinding things to bits in the mortar and pestle, doing all sorts of things to make up his tinctures and medicines and witch drinks. There were clothes hanging to dry in front of the fire: laundry that Sasha hadn't gotten around to washing.

Micah looked up as Sasha entered, and his look of concentration turned into worry. "Do you— Is she okay?"

"Yeah. Just hot, and I'm a fire on my own, so. Needed the bed." Sasha yawned, then glanced around. "Been busy, boss."

"Just getting ... some things done," Micah mumbled. "Seemed like maybe it would help."

"It is. It's a good sign that she's hot, means she's sweating it out." Sasha thought about what she'd said, how Micah should settle him. "She had an idea. Maybe let me run this by you real quick."

"Is it from the book?"

Sasha grinned and waggled his eyebrows. "Not that book. A different book. A *sexy* one."

"What?"

He laughed. "She's on the mend, Micah. Always is, when she kicks me out. Wants her space, you know, get that sprawl on."

"What does this have to do with sexy books?"

Sasha laughed again. "She thought maybe you'd settle me down a bit."

Micah stared at him. Sasha stared back.

"How?" Micah asked, finally.

"I mean, whatever you like, I guess. You're into that, right? I mean, the whole dom thing."

"Is it— How could I not be?" Micah waved a hand. "I don't know what you mean. I need you to say it."

"Sure. Maybe, I dunno, wanna scratch my back?"

Micah blinked. He looked momentarily disappointed, but then he shrugged, though his face was red. "Okay."

"Yeah?" Sasha beamed. "Great. I'll just lie down on that rug, you climb up and scratch my back." Excellent. This would be a great start. It would help settle him, and probably Micah, too. Viv was smart, even when she was sweating out a fever. Brilliant woman, his wife.

He lay on the furs in front of the fire, head pillowed on his arms, and waited. As he figured, it took Micah a bit to get with the action, but eventually he climbed onto Sasha's back and settled over his hips. He put his hands on Sasha's skin, and as Sasha braced himself ...

Micah scratched his back.

Gently. As if it *itched.*

Sasha laughed. "Boss, I didn't mean— I meant *scratch* it, yeah? Like, fuck me *up.*"

Micah was so still that, if not for his weight, Sasha would think he'd vanished. "I don't know if I can do that."

Sasha was pretty sure Micah could, or at least *wanted* to, because something was getting hard against his ass and that, yeah, that was a good sign. "I bet you can. Try it. Look, if you're worried, this was Viv's idea. You can go ask her, but she'll get pissy if you wake her up."

"I wouldn't," Micah whispered. "Will you tell me if it's too much?"

"If you make it too much, I'll kiss your fucking feet," Sasha said cheerfully. "Go on, please, make me bleed. I could really use it."

Micah's hands were warm on his shoulders, and when he dragged his nails down ... it was good—it was great—but it could be *better*.

"Boss, c'mon, give it to me harder. I can take it. You know how hard Viv does this?"

"Shh," Micah commanded, and ah, there it was. It was like a warm blanket, like being pinned in the ring. Micah scratched Sasha's back again, and it felt good, but it still wasn't *enough*. "Harder?"

"Oh, hell yeah," Sasha mumbled into his arm. "I don't know if Viv mentioned, but I fucking love pain. Make me bleed and I'll, uh. Do something nice for you."

Micah made a sound like a laugh and put his hands at the top of Sasha's back again, and this time, he *scratched*. Then he did it again, and again, and Sasha started to really feel it the fourth time, the sting and drag of Micah's nails making him shiver with want.

"Oh, fuck, *thank you*," Sasha gasped as the pain sparked through him, making him hard and sending all the dark, panicky thoughts to the back of his mind. "Yeah, *yeah,* that's so good, boss."

"Fuck," Micah whispered, "I can't *stop*."

"Don't stop," Sasha said, as turned on by the pain as he was by feeling Micah's cock hardening against his ass. "Seriously, I can take it. I love this shit."

"You do," Micah said softly. "You do, don't you."

"I do, yeah, fuck—" He moaned as Micah went at him, over and over, nails raking his back until it felt like it was on fire. He realized, belatedly, that he was humping the floor, so turned on by the pain he couldn't help himself.

"I've never—" Micah didn't finish that, simply went back to scratching, and Sasha could feel it when the skin tore—and Micah said, in a voice that sounded halfway between arousal and panic, "You're bleeding."

"Thank you," Sasha moaned, pressing against the floor again. He turned his head, and the sight of Micah—fuck.

Micah's eyes were bright, his hair wild around his flushed face. He was breathing fast, but he had this look, a feral grin, and he was staring at Sasha's back, rocking his hips and rubbing his cock against Sasha's ass. "It feels so good. How does it feel so good to hurt you?"

"Probably better fuck me," Sasha managed, because if Micah kept talking in that hot-as-fuck dom voice, he was going to come in his pants.

Micah went still, which was only all right because it meant Sasha could really feel the scratches on his back. "I can't. Viv—"

"Boss, you don't know my girl and how dirty she gets when she's feeling it. She'll like hearing you rail me. C'mon, I got a tight ass, and you feel like you have a big cock—"

"I *can't*." Micah pressed his hands to Sasha's back, ran his fingers from shoulders to hips.

"But you want to," Sasha said, pushing his ass up in encouragement. "She won't mind, I promise, yeah? I wouldn't do it if she would."

"I need to ask her," Micah said, sounding torn.

"Can't if she's sleeping. Won't wake her up." Sasha bit his own arm, trying to channel his arousal back into pain. "Okay, well, if you don't want to fuck me—"

"That's not— It's not that—" Micah made a frustrated sound and scratched him again.

"Okay, I get it, s'fine," Sasha slurred. He was so fucking close to coming. His back was burning, and gods, he wished Micah would fuck him or maybe ask Sasha to rail him instead— that'd also be fine. He just needed to come and have someone tell him he did well, took it like a good sub. "Get the salt. From the kitchen. Get it, rub it into my back."

"You want me to rub salt on your back? Your back is ... it's bleeding."

"That's why I want the fucking *salt*, man."

Micah swore softly and climbed off him. Sasha watched him go, biting back a helpless whimper as he saw the sizable erection tenting out Micah's pants. "I can't believe you're cocked and ready and I'm so fucking here for being a dirty slut for you, and you're not gonna fuck me."

Micah returned with the salt, and his eyes narrowed, and then he *put his foot on the back of Sasha's neck* and said, in a voice so full of dominance it made Sasha's breath catch, "I said *no*."

Sasha felt it, then—not going under, but close enough that the salt would probably get him off, because damn, did Micah have a hell of a tone of command when he chose to use it. "Sure, sorry, just ... please? The salt. Something. I need it."

Micah straddled his hips again, and Sasha watched him, certain the need was plain on his face. "How do I do it—just pour it on you?"

"Fingers, use those. They should be wet—" Sasha moaned as Micah stuck his own fingers in his mouth and sucked on them.

He almost asked again for Micah's cock in his ass, because if Micah fucked him with salt on his back? Sasha would go under so hard he wouldn't come up for a week.

But then Micah paused with his fingers in the salt. "Are you going to scream?"

"Fuck *yes* I am."

"Don't. She needs her sleep." Micah shifted and then, before Sasha could figure out what was happening, he felt cloth in his mouth—Micah's *shirt*. Micah had shoved his shirt between Sasha's teeth. And before Sasha could process that, Micah rubbed his salt-covered fingers on Sasha's back, on his scratches.

There was a half second of quiet, and then the pain came. It was beautiful, hot, like a fire sweeping over him. It was so much, so inescapable, that Sasha fell into it and didn't ever want to come back out. He screamed around the gag, and it made a lot of noise anyway. A rush of intense, mind-numbing pleasure followed on the heels of the pain that didn't end, the salt a burn and the pleasure a wonderful, delicious undercurrent. He came in pants, fucking out his orgasm against the furs.

When it was over, he was panting and weak and so fucking happy he could melt into a puddle there on the floor. He watched as Micah climbed off him, took the salt pot back to the kitchen, and wet a cloth. Sasha made a noise and shook his head.

"Let me feel it, yeah?" he slurred, blinking up at Micah. "You're so hot. Thank you. That was fucking amazing. You liked it?"

Micah's cock was still hard, and he turned away. "I— Yes. I'm glad you feel better."

"Do you?"

Micah nodded, but he didn't turn around.

Sasha got up, wincing as he realized how messy his pants were, but whatever, that had been great and he'd really needed it. He was so relaxed it was hard to make himself talk. "You want me to take care of that, boss? Would love to, if you want."

"I— No, just. Check on Viv."

Sasha sighed, but he was too under to argue. He went up to Micah, wanting to hug him, but all he did was say, "I really needed that. Thank you."

"You're welcome," Micah said, still not turning around. "I ... would like to be alone."

"Sure," Sasha said, agreeable and sleepy. "If you're sure. We could just, y'know. Cuddle."

Micah gave a wild laugh, and then he left, quickly, going to the bathing room. Probably to get off, which Sasha really wished he could help with, but instead he went into the bedroom and cleaned himself, changed his pants, and climbed into bed with Viv.

"He scratched the fuck out of me and rubbed salt on my back," Sasha said, when Viv blinked her eyes open and gave him a *Well?* kind of look. "I came so hard I saw stars."

She smiled. "Good. Did he have fun?"

"Yeah, but he ran off before I could make him come. A shame. I saw what he's packing in those pants, babe, and it's nice. Not me, obviously, but a damn good size. Wanted to get my mouth on it, but ..."

"He's not ready for that, maybe." Viv yawned. "I'm feeling better, but I think you'll have to sleep on the couch tomorrow."

"Sure, babe. I know how it goes." He turned and smiled at her, smoothing her hair back. "He was making you stuff. Those drinks. Flower packets and stuff. It was cute."

"Good. Let me see your back."

Sasha rolled over so she could see, proud as he always was when he took pain well. Viv's fingers were warm on his back, and Sasha smiled in pleasure as she examined the scratches.

"He did a good job," Viv murmured, kissing his shoulder.

"I'd like you to hold me for a bit. Until I get too hot and need you to go away."

Sasha laughed, rolled back over, and drew her close. "Oh no, how could I possibly." He kissed her head. "I think it's helping, yeah? His witch drinks."

"He's helping in a lot of ways," Viv murmured. "I like him. I like that ... when this is over ... you might have someone to give you what you need."

"You do that, babe. And you're getting over it, yeah? Lasted less time, this one, didn't it?" Sasha stroked her hair, the panic present but at bay for now since he was so wonderfully under and sated.

"That's not what I meant," Viv murmured, sighing, "and you know it."

Sasha shook his head. "Yeah. But, baby? No one gives me what I need like you do. No one is *you*. No one could ever be you."

Viv smiled, something sad in her expression, but she said nothing—just curled up and pressed her face to his chest.

Sasha thought he heard something—a door, or a stumble, something that might suggest a person was moving about. It was probably Micah, heading back from the bath, and Sasha was drifting into sleep with his wife in his arms, content and happy ... pretending he didn't know what she was trying to tell him, what she meant by *when it's over*.

Chapter Seven

*N**o one could ever be you.*

Micah sat on the couch, clasping his hands between his knees. He couldn't keep doing this. He'd fooled himself, for a while, thinking that he could be useful, that Viv and Sasha seemed to like having him around. And Sasha had certainly been eager, writhing deliciously under Micah's dominance. But in the end, Micah wasn't Viv. Viv and Sasha were mates, the kind Micah used to dream about when he was young, and Micah couldn't complicate that.

He would leave Viv the book in the spring. That would help. But first, he would need to make it through autumn and winter without making a mess of things.

It was odd. Micah hadn't even considered the sexual rules of the Lukoi in the village until now. They all abided by them—no kissing or oral sex with anyone who wasn't their mate, no sex between unmated dominants and submissives—but Micah had always felt strangely removed. The restrictions hadn't applied to him, because no one expected him to find a sexual partner. And the thought of kissing Sasha or Viv didn't make him feel like less of a Lukoi or like he'd be doing something wrong. It made him feel jittery, excited. Viv and Sasha were more important than rules set down by strangers centuries ago. And that was frightening to realize.

He hadn't been afraid when his parents fell ill. He hadn't thought they might die, so it had been a shock that left him numb and lost, going through the motions until grief could set in. But he knew better now, and he understood what Viv feared —she'd told him that her sickness had been survivable so far, but it wouldn't always be. A day would come when the fever didn't break. And Sasha would be devastated, because she was his person, the only one he could love so deeply.

Settling Sasha had been thrilling, a feeling of raw power like the roar of a new fire, but it wasn't love. Or maybe it was for Micah, but not for Sasha. Not for Viv.

Micah wasn't the kind of person to sit in his feelings. He tended to avoid them, especially the unpleasant ones. But that was a habit left over from his parents—and why would he listen to people who treated him like a burden, instead of the way Sasha and Viv treated him? Or Zev, who never questioned Micah's need for quiet, who understood the fear of a crowd, even if it wasn't so strong for him.

He'd let his parents control him for a long time, Micah realized. Even after they were gone. He'd treated himself the way they had, like he and his love for crafting were shameful, to be hidden away. He'd isolated himself in the mountains when he could have just made the rules for visitors clear and gotten to know his neighbors slowly, on his terms.

But Viv thought making beautiful things was worthwhile. Sasha thought he was brave. Who else might have thought that, if Micah hadn't listened to his parents?

He needed to remember the *right* voices, this time. He opened his great-grandmother's book to the precious blank pages in the back, reserved for new recipes and designs. Some of his designs were already there, written small, to save precious space. He found a quill and ink and found a margin where he squeezed in the words:

I can make beautiful things.

I'm not broken.

I'm brave.

He kept his handwriting close enough to his grandmother's careful hand that it would be hard to tell the difference. It felt ridiculous at first, but writing it in this book was like turning it into a design or a spell. He couldn't take it back. He couldn't say it wasn't true. And he could remember it on those days when his parents' voices were too loud.

He stared down at the empty patches of paper and thought of Viv and Sasha. He didn't know if the twisting, burning feeling in his stomach was love, but he did know he wanted to do something for them. Viv hated being helpless—Micah could relate to that. And just because she fell sick didn't mean she should isolate *herself*, either. It hadn't escaped his notice how much time she spent at home. Maybe he could help with that.

He found a slate in the weaving room. As in all of Lukos, paper was something precious here, used for preserving finished words, not practice. Most people used birch bark or slate for that, and slate could be washed clean. So Micah started sketching, scribbling furiously while laundry steamed in front of the fire and tea sachets cooled in the basin by the kitchen.

Viv's fever broke the next morning. She was grumpy, kicking Sasha out of bed again and complaining about the way the mattress made her back ache, but she was able to keep down more broth and tea, and she let Sasha dress her so he could take her into the living room. She saw the slate on the table, and Micah grabbed it before she could look too closely.

"It's a surprise," he said. "I think."

"What's a surprise is how quick this fever eased," Viv said.

She was wrapped in half a dozen blankets, and she looked too thin and too pale, but at least she was sitting up and giving him a wry smile. "I'm usually out for weeks. Thanks for the help, witch boy."

Micah could feel the blush on his face. "Oh. Well. I mean."

"I said thank you. Don't be rude." Viv poked him with a foot.

"You're welcome."

"*There* we go." Viv lay her head back on the pillows. "Maybe tomorrow I can go outside. Lie in the sun. I feel like I need it."

"I can carry you out now if you want, baby," Sasha called from the stove, where he was heating up one of Micah's tarts. Viv made a face, and Micah guessed what she meant: she didn't want to have to be carried. He thought of the scribbled sketches on the slate, half-formed ideas of a moving chair, and blushed deeper.

"Thanks for settling him last night, by the way," Viv said, poking him again. "I should've told you it's not a problem. I trust you with him."

But I'm not you, Micah thought. "He's. Um. Very enthusiastic."

Viv smiled, shifting in her blankets until she was half leaning against Micah. "I know. Doesn't he take pain well? Free up your lap, Micah. I want to sleep on you."

"Bossy," Micah muttered, moving the slate. But he didn't mind, not when Viv settled down with her head on his thighs.

"Mm. Pet my hair."

Micah gently stroked her hair, and Viv fell asleep almost immediately, curled up like a snow cat in a tree. Micah glanced at Sasha, who was watching them fondly, and then looked away.

Sasha was just setting plates of tart on the table when the knock came on the door. It was light, more like someone was brushing the surface than tapping it with their knuckles, but the voice was loud enough that it echoed.

"Vivian? Vivian, it's your mother."

"Oh gods, it's a nightmare," Viv murmured, and curled in tighter. Micah looked from Viv to Sasha, who was staring at the door.

"Vivian, let me in. Please."

Vivian covered her ears, and Micah lay a hand over hers. "Sh-she isn't well. She doesn't want visitors today."

"She needs her mother," the voice said, and Sasha's face, usually so amicable, closed up tight like a trap. "Please. Open the door."

"Not a chance," Sasha said. He got up and locked the door. "She'll talk to you when she wants to. Don't push this on her."

"I'm her *mother*."

"You want her to say she forgives you, because you don't wanna feel bad anymore. She can't handle that shit right now. Go away."

There was a breathless silence and then a rustling sound, which gradually faded. Micah sighed and looked down at Viv, whose face was pink.

"Why does she always have the worst timing?" she whispered.

Micah stroked her hair again, and Sasha stomped away from the door, coming to sit next to Micah. He picked up Viv's legs so he could drape them across his lap, and Viv rolled to the side, her pale hair falling over her cheek. Even wan and weak from fever, she was beautiful.

"You're kinder than me," she said. "I would have cursed more." Sasha huffed.

"That ain't me being kind. I get she wants to mend fences, but it's just her fence she wants to mend, not yours."

"I understand why she did it," Viv whispered, while Micah

stroked her hair out of her eyes. "I never knew my siblings—they died before I was born—but the last one ... the fever took them in one day. Suddenly. Like a wind running through the cave. One day they were here, and then they weren't. Sasha's mother told me. Then I came around, and Mother looked at me like she wanted to brick me up in my room. And she did, in a way. She bricked me up in her mind, so it wouldn't hurt."

"But it hurt *you*," Sasha said. Micah agreed. He'd blocked himself off from the world, sure, but he couldn't imagine doing that to someone else. Especially a child. It unsettled him to think that his parents had effectively done exactly that to him.

"And she knows that. I don't know what I want. I can't expect her to, I don't know, crawl over hot coals or something to prove how much she's suffered. I'm just not ready yet."

"She isn't, either, if she doesn't respect that." Micah hadn't meant to intervene, but the words came out anyway, and Viv looked up at him, her gaze sharp.

"You're right. Maybe that's why."

Thankfully, no one came to the door again.

Viv slept most of the day, lounging on Sasha or Micah, mumbling half-real words in her sleep. She ate a little, and when the bed had been stripped and remade, the linens washed and hung by the fire to dry, she bossed Micah and Sasha into sitting on the mattress with her.

"I need pillows," she said, tugging at Micah on one side and Sasha on the other. "Since I'm not a furnace anymore."

Which was how Micah ended up sleeping in the bed with them that night, Viv swinging a leg over his while she lay her head on Sasha's chest.

Slowly, she improved. Sasha did take her out to the field the next morning, and Micah spent a few minutes looking at the steps leading up past the door, mentally running over the sketches already filling his brain. It was always like that before he came up with a new design, every day bringing a revelation that subtly changed his plans. He lay in the sun with Viv while Sasha picked herbs that had been cleverly planted in the field— it turned out that the grasses above the Compound were all hardy plants that could be eaten. For all that Lukos was a harsh, dangerous place to live, it wasn't barren.

A few nights later, when Viv was finally eating something other than broth, there was another knock on the door. This one, at least, wasn't Viv's mother.

"Sasha! Sasha Sasha Sasha!"

Sasha grinned and opened the door to a young boy and a girl who were hopping on their toes. They peered around to look at Micah, who blushed as the boy waved.

"We wanted to give your toymaker a thank-you," the boy said. "For the magic boat."

"And the *dragon*," the girl said. "I'm gonna be one. I'm gonna breathe stone and scream at people."

"Hey, good on you, Yulia."

"There are maybe other letters, too," said the boy, who must have been Timon. "If he wants them."

"I'll—I'll write you b-back," Micah said, and Timon grinned. His smile was almost exactly like Sasha's.

"Mom made you mittens!" Yulia shouted, and Micah smiled nervously. He never knew how to act around kids, even if he liked making toys for them. But Yulia didn't seem to mind. The two children spent a while talking excitedly to Sasha and then pattered off, leaving Sasha with a pair of mittens and several sheaves of birch bark.

"For you," Sasha said. Birch bark paper was made out of the inner layers of birch trees, which grew everywhere in Lukos, and it looked as if the kids had only just started to learn how to write, based on the misspelled words and occasional intervention from an adult hand. Micah set the mittens on the table and looked at the first pages.

"'Dear toymaker,'" he read. "'I loved the dragon. Can you make it spit rocks? I deserve it because I've been good and I help Mama with preserveveveveveves. I love you. Love Yulia.'"

"Yulia's a terror," Viv said fondly. "I say give it to her."

"I don't think I can make a puppet spit rocks. Here's Timon: 'Dear toymaker, I like the boat. How do you make it move? Nan says you're a witch. Did you know Aunt Viv is a witch? She is. She cured Nan when her hands were hurting. I like witches. I will be ten one day. I will count to ten for you.'"

"Smart kid," Sasha said. "What are the other ones?"

Micah shuffled the letters. "From ... other kids, I think. This one is from a boy who wants a doll, because he's getting a little sibling soon. This one wants ... Oh, a sword is probably a bad idea. Maybe a blunt one? And this is a little girl who just says she's five and that I don't need to give her a boat, but if I did, she'd let me ... marry her mom. Oh no."

Viv laughed. "Looks like you're getting popular, Micah. You don't have to make anything for them, though."

There was a lightness in Micah's chest, bubbling up every time he looked at the misspelled words so carefully scratched into the birch bark. "No. I want to. No one told me what they thought of the things I made, before. I don't think they knew they could, because I lived so far away. I'll need glass for the doll's eyes, though."

"Glass is easy," Sasha said. "There's a glassmaker at the other end of the Compound. She's always saying something about the ground being good for it?"

"It is!" Micah smiled. "There's this kind of sand you find on the beach near the rocks that's perfect, and you can even color it if you know how."

"You two need to meet," Sasha said. "Di can talk for hours about things like *sediments*."

Micah thought he might like that. People in the village knew how to make glass—it was time-consuming, but it was an old skill left over from the empire, and they'd held on to it—but they weren't usually interested in making anything that wasn't practical. And if he could meet Di on his own terms, not in a crowd, maybe it would be okay.

He looked down at the messages in his hands, written by kids who *wanted* impractical things, who called him *toymaker*, and blinked tears out of his eyes.

"Yeah," he said. "Yeah, that would be good."

* * *

Viv was itching to weave again. The worst part of a relapse—beyond the fear that the fever wouldn't break, the vomiting, and the sweating—was boredom. It always took her ages to recover, and she couldn't stand being idle. But the most she could manage was a lap loom, so she grumpily made squares of cloth while Micah muttered to himself and scratched marks on the slate he'd started carrying around.

He was up to something. She knew that much. He kept looking at her when she was trying to weave, and at one point he carved little wheels out of scrap wood, fidgeted with them so much they broke, and tossed them in the fire.

"You know, they usually work better when they aren't on fire," she said.

"At least they'll keep us warm." Micah pushed the slate away, looked at his whittling knife, and sighed.

Well, that wouldn't do. Viv knew how to handle frustrated doms—after all, she was one. "Put that down. We're going outside. Sasha's chopping wood, and you can help."

"Don't see how that'll fix this ... thing I'm working on," Micah said, even as he got up from the table. For all that her dominance didn't affect him the way it would Sasha, he was very agreeable and didn't seem to mind being bossed around. "Do you want me to carry you up?"

Viv almost asked whether he'd be able to. He was a skinny man, without the bulk most Lukoi favored, and he didn't give off the impression of someone who could lift more than himself. Viv had figured a few swings of the axe would be enough to wear him out, but if he wanted to pick her up, too ... "Why not?"

She expected him to offer her his back, but Micah stepped in front of her and lifted her into his arms. She could feel muscles moving as she swung an arm around his shoulders, and she realized that they were broader than she'd thought—she was just so used to Sasha, everyone else seemed diminutive in comparison.

"We should make this a ramp instead, maybe," Micah said as he pushed open the door and headed up the stairs. His gaze was flicking back and forth, as though he was measuring the stairway. "It'll be easier to go up and down."

We, he'd said. For all that Micah still inched around them, sometimes, *we* slid off his tongue so easily.

It was a cold day, even with the sun shining, but Sasha was stripped to the waist and gleaming with sweat as he chopped wood on a stump a little ways out. The woods were close, and Viv couldn't bring herself to look at first, wary of what strange creature she might see lurking in the shadows.

When she turned her gaze to the trees, everything looked normal.

Micah set her down in a patch of herbs she liked to use for spells, and Sasha grinned at them both. "Come to watch?"

"Came to help, actually," Micah said, and oh my, he was already stripping off his coat. He offered it to her, and she draped it over her shoulders while he started pulling off his shirt.

She raised her brows. So he *did* have muscle.

"Nice" Sasha said the quiet part out loud, as usual. "Where'd you get those?"

"I hunt when I need to," Micah said, going pink. "And a kiln needs wood. Give me the axe."

"Sure thing, boss, whatever you say."

This had to be Viv's best idea yet. She lay back in the sun while Micah's muscles bunched and sweat gleamed on his bare chest as the axe came down again and again, the crack of wood echoing over the field.

Sasha whistled as Micah tossed the split wood into the pile. Then, as Viv had expected, he picked out a heavier log. "Three strokes," he said, and Micah stood back, hands on his hips, as Sasha swung the axe.

"You can throw your weight around if you want," Micah said, as Sasha triumphantly added the new pieces to the pile, "but it'll tire you out."

"Yeah? Wanna bet? How many do you think you can do?"

"Oh no," Viv murmured. "Don't *compete* over wood chopping, what an *awful* sight that'll be."

"I don't have anything to bet," Micah pointed out.

"Okay. Winner gets the girl."

"Excuse me?" Viv picked up a clump of herbs to throw at Sasha. "Winner gets the *girl*? What does that mean?"

Sasha gave her his best winsome puppy expression. "I don't know, a kiss?"

"Micah, destroy him."

"I don't think you can give people away as bets," Micah said.

"Winner gets a present," Viv said, before this could spiral out of control. "And *I* decide what it is."

Micah shrugged. "Fair."

"Aw, Viv, I love your gifts."

"I said destroy him, Micah."

It was exactly what Viv had hoped for. Sasha threw himself into the competition full force, hauling wood and grunting when the axe came down. Micah seemed wary at first, but then he started smiling when Sasha tried to dig at him, and when he split a log that could have been big enough to be a base of its own, Sasha whooped and clapped him on the back so hard he almost fell over.

Viv was exhausted, she hadn't slept through the night in over a week, she'd only eaten one meal that wasn't broth all day, and she was so happy she could have lain there forever.

By the time they ran out of wood, Micah and Sasha were both sweating heavily and breathing hard. The trees behind them were a glorious blend of gold, red, and yellow, and Viv wished she could freeze that moment somehow, hold it close so she could examine it on cold days when winter made the world go white.

"So who won?" Micah asked, panting. Viv realized, belatedly, that she was supposed to be keeping score.

"Me," she said. "Obviously."

Micah actually laughed, and even Sasha stopped to take it in, grinning. Micah had a nice laugh. "And what's your reward?"

Viv gestured to both of them, and Sasha, of course, flexed. "I think ... I deserve to see what Sasha looks like when you fuck him, Micah."

Micah's smile faded, and Viv wondered if she'd gone too far. "Oh, but. He's your husband. I wouldn't want to ..."

"You're our Micah," Viv said, and Micah blushed a deep red. "Do you want him? No beating around the bush, remember? We agreed to be straightforward with each other."

"Y-yes."

"Is it the mating thing you have, in the village?"

"No." Micah looked away. "That's not ... I don't follow those rules."

"And I bet you both need to be settled. Sasha always needs to go under after ... after I've been unwell. You should put him there."

"You're so good to me, baby," Sasha said.

Micah blushed even deeper. "I ... wouldn't want to get between you ..."

"That's an image." Sasha winked.

"But you aren't," Viv said, because she knew Micah needed to hear it. "I wouldn't ask if you were. Besides, it's my victory, and I think I could use another show."

Micah ran his hands through his hair and closed his eyes for a moment. Then, to Viv's surprise, he nodded.

"All right," Sasha said, and wrapped Micah into another one-armed hug. "Winner takes it all."

Chapter Eight

Sasha was having a pretty great day.

His girl was feeling better, enough to come lie out on the grass and be bossy. Micah wasn't wearing a shirt, and damn, he had a fine figure under those clothes, didn't he? Who knew all that toymaking would get you so buff?

The weather was cool but sunny, and they had enough wood now for a week or more, thanks to Micah's help *and* his competitive streak. Viv being appreciative of their work was also awesome, and now Sasha was going to get more of Micah domming him for Viv to watch? Damn, he was a lucky man.

First, though, they had to do a few things. He and Micah carried the wood into the cave while Viv sunned herself a bit more and collected some herbs, and then they had to eat, because they'd worked up an appetite. Sasha ate two bowls of stew, half the loaf of bread Micah had made the day before, and one of the leftover tarts. He had four mugs of cold water, too, and by the time he went to wash off the sweat and grime, he was already anticipating the rest of their evening.

As Sasha left the bathroom, the look Micah gave him was both hungry and uncertain. Sasha nearly pulled him in for a kiss, but he figured he should wait until they were all naked and in bed. "Make that bath fast, boss," Sasha said cheerfully.

Micah's eyes narrowed, and he *smirked* at Sasha. "Are you trying to dom me?"

Sasha almost knelt right there. Damn, that was hot. "Nah, I'm tryin' to hurry us up to the part where *you* dom *me*."

Micah, to Sasha's shock and delight, touched him—a quick pat on the shoulder, but it was something. "Be patient."

"Ain't real good at that, boss."

"Try to learn," Micah said with a heated look, before he went in to take a bath.

Sasha needed a minute after that. By the time he wandered into the bedroom, it was to find Viv already sprawled in the chair across from the bed, looking far too pleased with herself.

"You plan this or something?" Sasha asked, going to his knees in front of her when she beckoned him over. She wasn't entirely recovered, but there was color in her face again and her eyes didn't look so shadowed.

"No more than you did," she retorted, tugging at his hair. "Cutting wood without a shirt."

"It was warm! I didn't even know you'd be coming outside!" Sasha laughed, grinning at her as she pulled his hair harder. On his knees, he was about the same height as she was, and it was easy for her to lean in and kiss him. Except she smacked him instead. And that was just as great.

"Sasha," she admonished.

"I mean, I *hoped*," he admitted, and she laughed and then *did* kiss him, soft and sweet, even as she yanked his hair hard enough to tip his head back.

"You need a haircut," she told him, ruffling his hair after she was done pulling it—hopefully just for the moment. He really did like that.

"Probably," Sasha agreed. "Or maybe I should grow my hair real long, like Micah's."

"Mm, let's not. I like Micah's hair the way it is, and I like yours a little less wild." She ran her fingers through his damp hair, making him shiver. "This is all right with you?"

"Um, yeah. You've let doms fuck me up before. And fuck me. And that one time, Annalee, remember her? She made you come like a—"

"Sasha," she chided, shaking her head. "It's different with him. You know that."

"Yeah," Sasha agreed, leaning in for another kiss. "I know."

It *was* different with Micah. He wasn't merely a friendly dom who liked to hurt the biggest pain slut in the Compound. He was ... special. He was in their lives for more than sex or dominance. He made tarts and bread and tea and drinks to make Viv feel better. He'd mended one of Sasha's shirts without anyone asking. He made toys for Sasha's niece and nephew.

He was the person who should be on that third cushion.

Before Sasha could say anything about that, there was a sound of someone clearing their throat. Sasha turned and saw Micah standing in the doorway, looking uncertain. His long yellow-blond hair was wet but combed free of tangles, and he wore nothing but a towel wrapped around his waist.

"Damn, you really are jacked," Sasha said, with an appreciative once-over of Micah's muscular chest and arms.

"He says every thought in his head," Viv said.

"I've noticed." Micah drew in a deep breath. "I need to ask. Is this really ... all right?"

"Yes. I wouldn't have offered if it wasn't," Viv said. "Nothing will ever happen in here that we don't want. Though, honestly, there isn't much we've done that Sasha *doesn't* like."

"What's the point of being a masochist if I don't want it all?" Sasha shifted on his knees and glanced at Viv, who nodded—

and then he stood up. If Micah wanted him to kneel, Micah could make him. Even the thought of it had his blood running hot.

Micah still looked a little … something. It was hard to read his expression.

"Hey," Sasha said, suddenly worried they were pressuring Micah into this. "You know *you* don't have to, right? I mean, it'd be awesome, but we're not gonna make it, like, a rule that you have to fuck me up and fuck me, promise."

"Sasha, you're not making the rules here. I am," Viv chided, enough dominance in her voice that Sasha bowed his head, even if he didn't kneel again. "He gets excited," she said to Micah. "There's the expression *topping from the bottom*, yes? He tries that, so you have to get him worked up enough that he goes quiet." Her voice was warm with affection. "Or gag him."

"Those are two of my favorite things, talking and being made to be quiet," Sasha agreed.

"But he's right," Viv continued. "If you don't want to be with us like that, you don't have to."

"I want to," Micah said, and fuck, there it was again, his heavy dominance that made Sasha swallow hard. "If you're sure."

"We are," Viv said. "Sasha, go get your toys. Pick three. Not the really scary ones, please."

Micah's eyes went wide, and Sasha didn't miss that his dick—which Sasha was *really* eager to get a look at—was getting hard, tenting out the towel. Sasha grinned and dashed over to the trunk in the corner, humming while he sorted through the toys they kept there. He picked up a cane, a leather flogger, and his favorite: a flogger Viv had spent hours on, weaving heavy, thick, thorn-covered briar branches together with leather.

"I said, not the scary ones." Viv sighed. "I should have known you'd go for that one."

"*I* don't think it's scary. I think it's fucking awesome," Sasha told her, reverently raising the flogger and kissing it.

Micah made a noise, and Viv laughed, stretching out on the chair. "All right. Give him the— Not that one, Sasha. The other one. But how about this: put the handle in your mouth, and crawl."

"Fuck," Micah said.

"Pretty much, right, boss?" Sasha, feeling like he'd won every match in the ring on fight night, went to his hands and knees, stuck the flogger's handle in his mouth, and crawled toward Micah. He could feel the urge to be hurt rising like a tide, and while what Micah had done for him before, with his nails and the salt, had been nice, just *thinking* about what Micah could do with that arm strength and the floggers ...

"You don't have to be naked," Viv said, and Sasha was confused—the hell he didn't—until he realized she was talking to Micah. "But if you're wearing nothing but that towel, you might as well be."

Micah blushed, which was, frankly, adorable, and then shrugged and unwrapped the towel.

If he hadn't had a flogger handle in his mouth, Sasha would have whistled. That was a great dick, and the thought of being fucked with it was making him want more than just pain. It would all get mixed up together soon enough, though.

"Are you warm enough?" Micah asked Viv, and Sasha felt a rush of affection for him.

Viv laughed. "I'm getting warmer."

Micah took the flogger, and Sasha stayed on all fours and stared up at him, waiting and eager. Micah gave it a bit of a flick, and the sound of the tails made Sasha's mouth water.

"Sasha, stand up so I can show him where to hit you," Viv said.

"Anywhere, buddy."

"Hey," Micah said sharply, giving him that look again, the same one as when they were outside the bathing room. "I don't want to gag you, but I need to listen."

Sasha got to his feet, nodding, ready for whatever as long as he got that flogger on his back sooner rather than later.

"Sasha's a pain slut," Viv said, as if that were new information, "so he'll like it if the tails wrap around his shoulders or go too low—but you shouldn't do that. It can be dangerous, and *Sasha, do not talk.* Just turn so he can see your back."

Her dominance settled over him, and the thought of both of them topping him at once was so hot, Sasha stayed quiet so they'd get started quicker. He turned, and Viv quirked a brow at him when she saw his cock was already hard. He shrugged. What did she expect?

"You want to hit him on the back. Think of it like a square: between the shoulders, to the hips, and never on the back of the neck or on the spine *no matter how much he begs for it.*" She raised her eyebrows when Sasha grinned at her. "Most people like a warm-up. Sasha gets bored. Try a few hits on the bed, there."

Sasha watched Micah draw his arm back and bring the tails down. The blow wasn't very hard—it'd barely fluff a pillow—but it was a start.

"He really can take it hard, but it's more fun not to give him what he wants immediately."

"Sadist," Sasha said fondly.

"That's right. Try some more," Viv urged, and Sasha could tell she liked this, using her dominance to show another dom how to hurt him. Usually the others they played with already knew the basics, and Viv didn't get to show off and be so bossy.

Sasha stood by, quietly dying as Micah whipped the bed instead of him. He was getting into it now, his muscles moving smoothly as he struck harder and with more and more confidence.

"That's good," Viv praised. "Okay, Sasha. On the bed. We'll do the leather flogger and the cane, and then, if you're very well-behaved, I might let him use the thorn flogger."

"I call it the briar bitch, and I *love* it," Sasha told Micah. "Use that, put salt on me after? I'll melt into a puddle."

"You'll do that anyway by the time we're done." Viv's voice sharpened. "The bed, Sasha. Lie flat so Micah can practice."

"I would fucking love to." Sasha took a flying leap onto the bed, so eager he was almost panting into the bedding.

"It won't bother the scratches?" Micah asked.

"Hell yeah, it will!"

Viv sighed. "He'll like it. I promise, you'll think it's too much and he'll just beg for more. Sasha!" Her voice went heavy with dominance again, probably because he was humping the bed.

"Babe, I can't help it. Turns out you two talking about me like I'm a thing is really doing it for me."

"Everything does it for you," she said, sounding only a little exasperated.

"I'm starting to see that," Micah said. "You'll tell me if it's right?"

"You'll know," Sasha promised, smiling into the bedding in anticipation.

"I was asking Viv," Micah said, but he, too, sounded like maybe he was smiling, and that was a hell of a thing, wasn't it? This was clearly a great idea for everyone.

"Keep the strikes where I told you. Don't bother with a warm-up—he's been a good boy; we'll let him take it hard from the beginning. If you want," Viv added. "It's a torment if it's too light, but he likes that, too, even if he says he doesn't."

Sasha would have protested, but she was right, and he was desperate to feel leather hit his back. It'd been a while.

Micah's hand gripped his hair, pulling his head up. Micah was leaning on the bed on one knee, giving him a stern look. "Tell me if it's pain you don't like."

"Haven't invented that yet, boss. But we can try and find it. Sounds awesome. I'm game if you are."

"He really is just ... like this, isn't he." Micah pushed Sasha's head down again, not hard, exactly, but the casual firmness of the pressure made Sasha wonder if Micah had ever fully let his dominance out. His own need for pain and submission became harder to satiate if he went too long without, and he had a feeling it was the same for doms. And sadists, for that matter. Viv was always eager to fuck him up once she recovered from one of her episodes.

"He really is. Now, I want my prize, so get to it, please."

There was a breathless moment of silence, and then—finally—the flogger fell on his skin. Sasha hadn't known what to expect. Part of him did think that Micah might start the way he had when he'd hit the bed ... but no, he laid the leather straps perfectly across Sasha's back. It was so delicious, Sasha moaned.

"Already?" Micah snorted.

"Pain. Slut," Sasha reminded him.

"Mm, harder, please," Viv said, and the only problem with the position Sasha was in was that he couldn't turn his head and see her. "Sasha, stay still, or I'll have him tie you up and use the flogger with the fur straps."

Damn it. "Okay, okay. That was great, boss. You can't hurt me, really."

Micah said softly, "Oh, I think I can," and Sasha's eyes closed as lust shuddered through him, making his cock swell and press down into the bedding.

Before he could say "Great, show me," Micah struck him again. And then again, and again, the leather falling rhythmic and so fucking good on his back, stinging against the fading traces of the nail marks.

"Oh, that's so good. Look at him—you have him writhing already," Viv said. "He takes it so well, doesn't he?"

"Yeah," Micah said, his voice heavy with dominance. "He does." He wielded the flogger again, and Sasha closed his eyes and drifted on the pain, which was starting to pull at him, drag him closer to that perfect place where it was indistinguishable from pleasure.

"Can I—harder?" Micah asked, and Sasha nodded as Viv laughed and said he could. The next few strikes made him buck, grabbing at the headboard. "Tell me how it feels, Sasha."

"It feels like ... I'm ... the luckiest bastard in Lukos," Sasha managed. A particularly hard strike landed on his upper back, and he shifted, trying to get the tails to hit high on his shoulder.

Micah stopped. "No. That's not how you get what you want."

"You're doing pretty good for being new at this," Sasha mumbled, forcing himself to be still. "Isn't he, baby?"

"He certainly is. Do you want to try the cane next? Sasha likes that on his ass, his upper thighs. It's a different kind of pain."

Sasha lay there, relishing the throb in his back, as Viv instructed Micah in how to use the cane, the flicking motion that would produce the most sting. Listening to Viv tell Micah how to hurt him was almost as good as the flogging, and anticipation was making him hump the bed again.

"I didn't know people could like pain this much," Micah said, and Sasha shivered as he felt the tip of the cane move over his back, gently tap-tap-tapping on skin sensitized by the flogger.

"Most people don't," Viv said. "But Sasha always has. Then again, there could be others in his fight ring. That would explain why they do it."

"One or two, maybe, but I think I'd win," Sasha said, idly wondering if there was some way to arrange a competition for *Best Pain Slut in Lukos*. He'd love some official recognition of his talents—who wouldn't?

Then Micah brought the cane down on his skin, and before long Sasha was lost again, moaning into the bed.

"Doesn't he have a nice ass?" Viv asked.

"Should fuck it later," Sasha mumbled into the pillow.

"It really is hard to make him be quiet, isn't it," Micah said, but he didn't sound like he minded.

He laid stripes on Sasha's ass, his upper thighs, and even— under Viv's careful instruction—on the tops of his shoulders. The bright flash of pain there did shut Sasha up for a bit, because if it were something he could roll around in, he would.

"I cane him a lot," Viv was saying, distantly, as Sasha luxuriated in the sensation. "It's less effort than the flogger—you can see that, right?"

Sasha had a faint, unwelcome thought that she was showing Micah how to do this because of what she'd said a few nights ago—*When this is over, you might have someone*—but then Micah caned his upper thigh harder, and the flash of pain blanked out his mind.

Micah was breathing hard by the time Viv told Sasha to roll over, and he looked—ah. His cock was hard, and he was bright-eyed and flushed, staring at Sasha with the cane gripped tight in his fingers.

"About that thorn flogger," Sasha said.

"I want to *bite* you," Micah said, and Sasha blinked at both the words and Micah's voice, full of dominance, want, and *hunger*.

"I'd love that," Sasha said, stretching out on his back. "Sure. Go for it."

"Put your arms above your head, Sasha. Go on, Micah. Bite him, scratch him, do whatever you'd like."

Micah put the cane down and climbed onto the bed. His eyes immediately went to Sasha's cock, which was flushed and hard against Sasha's stomach.

"I know, right?" Sasha grinned, reached down, and gave his cock and balls a quick jiggle. "Seriously impressive equipment. You can tell Viv how lucky she is, if you want."

"I'm so sorry. You're going to have to bite him *very* hard if you want him to not be impressed with his own dick."

"I'm impressed, too," Micah said. "If we're being honest."

"The two of you." Viv was smiling. Sasha noticed her hand was between her legs and flashed a grin at her. "Hand off your cock, Sasha. That's not yours until we say it is."

"She's so hot, right?" Sasha sighed and put his hands up again. "Have at me, boss."

Micah pushed his long hair out of his face, crawling catlike over Sasha. "Where does he like it, Viv?"

"Where doesn't he? I bit his balls once—gently, but he almost came. And he likes teeth when you suck his cock, but don't bite that. He's not lying; I do appreciate it."

Being talked *about* instead of *to* was a thing Sasha hadn't known he was into, but goddamn, was he ever. Micah looked like he wanted to grip Sasha's cock, but then he pushed at Sasha's knees to spread them open. He touched Sasha's inner thigh. "Here?"

"Fuck, oh, god, yeah," Sasha moaned. "Definitely, definitely there."

Micah's hair tickled as he bent down, and his breath was so close to Sasha's cock that Sasha gasped and his cock twitched.

Micah didn't need any warm-up for biting, either. He went at Sasha's thighs like he'd been dying for the chance. The pain was unreal, so beautiful he could get lost in it: the slow, inexorable closing of Micah's teeth on his skin, so very close to breaking but not quite. Micah's hair brushing against Sasha's cock might have been enough to make him come—and he almost did when he heard a soft gasp from Viv that meant she'd gotten herself off for the first of what would probably be many times.

Micah stopped at the sound and looked over, then said, "Oh."

"Please, don't let me distract you," Viv said, and Sasha smiled up at the ceiling as Micah went back to biting him.

Sasha fell into a haze of lust and pain, with Micah crawling over him, biting him, using his nails and scratching. It was even better than the cane, because Micah was warm on top of him, all lean muscles and his hard, wet cock dragging against Sasha's skin as Micah bit Sasha's chest, his arms, the sensitive part of his inner arm that really *was* one of the most painful places.

"I bite him there a lot," Viv was saying. "It drives him crazy."

It was doing both with Micah, too—Sasha was thrashing so much he almost bucked Micah off the bed, and Micah made the sexiest growling sound and tossed his hair—*tossed his hair*—in a way that was somehow primal and hot, forcing Sasha down with his hands on Sasha's shoulders.

"Stop that. Stay still. Let me hear how much it hurts," Micah said, voice dark, and Sasha had to squeeze his eyes shut so he didn't come. He was under enough from the pain that getting off without permission was almost unthinkable, but also, he *wanted* Micah to make him come.

He wanted Micah to fuck him, either like this, with that gorgeous wild-eyed stare, or with Sasha on his hands and knees so Micah could rake his back with his nails while he made Sasha come on his cock.

For now, though, he gave Micah what he wanted, crying out when Micah bit his way across Sasha's chest to his other arm, so hard that the skin *did* break, and Sasha's shout was loud enough to echo in the cave as he kicked his heels against the bed.

Viv must have come again—hell, maybe two or three more times. Sasha was losing track. The only thing he could concentrate on was the pain.

Micah patted his face, and Sasha dragged his eyes open, too far gone to smile or quip.

"Good job, Micah," Viv said warmly. "You put him under."

Micah was looking at him like Sasha hung the moon, which was great but weird, since Micah had done all the wonderful, painful, gorgeous work. "You're so beautiful," Micah said, and yeah, he was probably in top space, the way his breathing was fast and his eyes overbright. "I've never— It's so beautiful. What pain does to you. I did this to you. And you like it so much."

Before Sasha could think about replying, Micah leaned down and kissed him.

For all the pain that came before it, the kiss was one of the sweetest Sasha could remember. He let his eyes close, fell under completely, and kissed him back.

Micah had never felt this way before. The closest he'd come was when he finished a complicated design, the moment of satisfaction when it all came together under his touch. Except it was that moment extended, a buzzing in his mind and under his skin. He ran his fingers over a mark he'd made with his teeth on Sasha's arm, and Sasha shivered. Micah had done that.

"I want to fuck you," he said. He wanted more than that, though. He wanted to keep Sasha like this forever, to never go back to the woods where his old kiln lay in a heap of ashes, to stay here and cook breakfast and make tea and build a moving chair for Viv. He wanted everything, and for this brief, lovely time, he could imagine it was possible.

"Yeah," Sasha said, and the dreaminess in his voice made Micah think he was under. He wriggled, canting up his hips. "Please. Make me feel it, yeah?"

Micah pressed a hand to Sasha's belly, holding him down, and turned to look at Viv. She had her hand under the front of her gown, which was folded up around her hips in a waterfall of soft fabric, and she was smiling at them both with a fondness that made Micah's chest ache. "Is there something I can use?"

"Aw, no," Sasha said. "I don't need—"

Micah shot Sasha a look, and he went quiet, which made Micah's dominance flare even hotter than it already had.

"Bottle in that bag over there," Viv said, gesturing. "I can show you how."

"I know." Micah hurried to the bag hanging up on a hook by the door, reluctant to give up touching Sasha even for a moment. "I'll make him a toy, I think. Like I used to make for myself."

"Oh, fuck, that's so hot, I'm going to die."

"No, you aren't," Viv said, as Sasha whined. "Hush."

Micah would have blushed if he weren't riding the crest of his dominance, which felt like a physical pull, now, like the magic that Viv talked about drawing from her core. He found the bottle and brought it to Sasha, who parted his legs eagerly, gaze fixed on Micah. His cock was hard, flushed, and Micah resisted the urge to slap it—he'd try that next time.

Next time. Yes. There would be one. Hopefully.

Micah got onto the bed and moved Sasha the way he wanted, not bothering to give him orders. Sasha seemed to like the manhandling, though, and when Micah trailed a finger over his hole, Sasha made a soft, needy sound.

"I had several toys." He probably didn't have to work Sasha

open too much, but this was his first time fucking someone else, so he wanted to do it right. Oil slipped onto the sheets, and Sasha groaned as Micah pressed a finger inside. "Glass. Treated wood. The glass one had ridges. Took me six tries to find the pattern I liked."

"I'll build you a glass oven," Sasha said, and Micah smiled.

"Should probably make a bigger one for you. How much is enough, Viv?"

"You can tease him until he cries, but let's not be cruel today. He should be ready for you, if you're slow."

"Yeah, yeah, go however you like," Sasha said, and he really must be under if he wasn't begging Micah to fuck him immediately. Micah leaned down to kiss his belly, next to the head of his cock.

"Keep your arms above your head." Micah slicked his own cock, and when he pushed inside, slow and careful, Sasha was so tight and hot Micah had to stop to brace himself. Sasha tossed his head, clearly struggling not to move, and Micah pressed farther in. "You're being good. So good, Sasha."

"Don't need glass," Sasha murmured, which was the best compliment Micah could imagine right then. He tossed his hair out of his eyes and drew back, just a little, before thrusting hard. Sasha rocked on the bed, and fuck if that wasn't as hot as the pressure around his cock, the dominance surging in Micah's body.

Micah fucked Sasha until he heard him make a sound midway between a moan and a gasp, and then he tried that same move again, and again, going harder until sweat slicked his back and Sasha was making wordless sounds, clenching his hands tight above his head. Micah felt wild, white-hot, like a star hurtling to earth from the night sky, and he was taking Sasha with him. He reached for Sasha's cock, and Sasha squeezed his eyes shut, jaw clenched.

"No," Micah said, dominance heavy in his voice. "Look at me when you come."

"Fuck." Sasha's eyes flew open, and he came in Micah's hand, shaking apart beautifully as Micah fucked into him. It was too much, too perfect, and Micah drew out before he could break apart himself, panting hard. Sasha stared up at him, eyes blown dark and lips parted, and Micah didn't look away as he came over Sasha's stomach. Sasha was breathing slow, blinking at him like a snow cat before the fire, and Micah leaned down to kiss him one more time.

"Viv should win more often," Sasha whispered when Micah pulled away. Except Sasha's whisper was still loud enough to fill the room, and Viv snorted behind Micah's back.

"Yeah," Micah said. "Chop more wood tomorrow, right?"

"Lukos is gonna be bare, boss."

Micah laughed and sat up, twisting around to look at Viv. She was still reclining in her seat, her gown rumpled and her hair slightly messy, and she cocked an eyebrow. "The phrase you're looking for is *thank you*."

That probably should have grated on his dominance, but Micah was riding too high to care. "Thank you, Viv."

"Yeah," Sasha said. "Thanks."

Micah patted Sasha on the knee and slipped off the bed, looking Viv over. "Do you need anything?"

"I came already," Viv said, a little smugly. Sasha laughed.

"Yes, but ..." Micah jerked his head back at Sasha. "You can always use him, too."

"I might. Help me up?" Micah took her arm, and Viv turned away from him, lifting her hair away from her neck. "Help me *out*?"

Oh. Micah undid the button on the back of her collar. There was a line of flat buttons covered in cloth, and he worked them free one by one. When the gown fell to the floor, Viv turned to look at him, and Micah, impulsively, kissed her. He felt her smile under his mouth before she kissed him back, and she reached up to tuck his hair behind his ears.

"You two are so fucking cute," Sasha said, in that sleepy, dreamy voice. Viv smirked at him, and Micah helped her onto the bed, trying not to stare at the curve of her legs, her breasts, the way she'd filed her nails into a point. She'd probably done that for Sasha, and Micah wanted desperately to see her scratch lines down Sasha's back, to send him under.

"I need a pillow," she said, looking at Micah pointedly as Sasha rolled to the side. It took Micah a minute to realize she meant she wanted him to be the pillow, and she settled at last with her back against his chest, his arms around her waist, as Sasha crawled lower on the bed.

"Sasha's very good at this," she said, as Sasha moved between her legs. He kissed her thigh, and Viv took Micah's hands in hers, drawing them up to her breasts. "You can touch them, you know."

Micah was almost too distracted by the way Sasha looked at Viv, worshipful and soft, but then he ran his fingers over Viv's nipple and she drew in a slight breath, and he looked at her, instead. She was so expressive, but her face seemed more open, now, and when she grabbed Sasha by the hair and pressed his mouth to her cunt, her lashes fluttered in a way that made Micah think of the little flowers that grew near the mountain and rustled in the wind. If he were to make her something beautiful and impractical, it would be that. Flowers, moving at the turn of a key, until they flipped over and became something else —a spiked crown, like the ones the witches used to wear.

She would look lovely in a crown.

He kissed her as she came on Sasha's mouth, cupping her small breasts and running his hands down to where Sasha was gazing up at her, glassy-eyed and loving. She came twice like that, shaking slightly the second time, and when she pushed Sasha away, his mouth was wet and he looked utterly blissful, lying at their feet.

"And now the bed's ruined again," Viv said, but she didn't sound remotely put out about it. Sasha smiled at her, and since he was under and Viv was stroking his hair, Micah got up to fetch a cloth.

They slept on the couch that night, as no one felt much like changing the bedding and it was easier to gather the clean blankets and make a nest near the fire. Micah fell asleep on Sasha's left side, Viv on the other, and as he drifted off, he could hear Sasha humming to himself, voice soft against the crackle of the flames.

Chapter Nine

The next morning, Micah was scrubbing out the stove when he heard Sasha open the door to go out foraging, then bellow something incoherent and thunder up the steps. Viv, who was still asleep on the couch, muttered and covered her head with a blanket, but Micah shook ash off his hands and warily crept to the door.

Where Sasha was wrestling with a white wolf, foraging basket lying forgotten on the ground.

"Zev!" Sasha ruffled Zev's fluffy fur, which was shinier and glossier than it had been the first time Micah saw him running past his cabin, and Zev barked at him. There was a sling around Zev's back, complete with a bow, a quiver, and a small bag, and he was dancing on his paws in the way Micah used to see Dragan's pet wolves do when they wanted people to stop hugging them. Sasha let go, and Zev shook himself out, shifting seamlessly from wolf to human. He drew his fur, which was shaped like a cloak, around his shoulders with the fur against his skin and pulled a wrap out of his bag. He fastened it around his waist for the sake of modesty.

"Hi, Sasha. Hi, Micah." His long white hair hung in a braid

over one shoulder, and Micah saw that the clasp for his cloak had been carved to look like a wolf's head, mouth open in a smile. "I wanted to check in. How's Viv?"

"Tired!" Viv shouted from inside.

Zev smiled warmly. "I don't want to interrupt your preparations for winter, but I needed to check on Micah. Is it okay if we talk for a minute?"

"Sure," Sasha said. "Lots to talk about, eh, Micah?" He winked, and Micah felt his cheeks burn as Zev raised his brows in surprise. Micah looked down and pushed past him, heading up the steps.

"Make something for Viv for breakfast," he said, letting his dominance slip out a little, heavy and sharp.

Sasha straightened up, but he was still grinning. "Whatever you say, boss."

"Boss?" Zev whispered. Micah ducked his head and bumped shoulders with Zev, who bumped him back and started walking across the grass. "Okay, we definitely need to talk."

Micah didn't say anything until they were a good ways from the entrance to Sasha and Viv's house. It was strange, walking with Zev after so long with Sasha and Viv. "We had sex last night."

Zev shrugged, then stopped. "*Oh.* Shit. I forget, sometimes, what that means to people from the village. So you're mated?"

Micah felt like his face was going to burst into flames. "Not really. I don't ... I'm not ... I know everyone else follows that rule. I know it's the rule that helped us survive. But I tried that a long time ago—you know, courting a mate—and it didn't work out. And Viv and Sasha feel like ... They're different. The rules don't fit them."

Zev gave Micah a curious look. If he was cold, with his chest and legs mostly bare in the autumn breeze, he didn't show it. "You know I didn't grow up with those laws, Micah.

I'm not going to judge you. I guess I'm just surprised it happened."

"I'm allowed to be interested in people. Other people are allowed to be interested in me." Micah was surprised by the harshness in his tone, but while Zev blinked a few times, he didn't look upset or disappointed.

Zev was quiet for a few seconds, watching a cardinal hop across the grass. "Are you interested in them?" Micah turned away, and Zev's voice went soft, gentle. "Are you?"

"They're already mated," Micah said. "I just fell into their laps, and ... I'm not them. I can't be Viv to Sasha, or Sasha to Viv. They invited me into their bed, but I can't be their mate."

"Why not? And do you want to be?"

Micah looked out over the wide field. There was mist rolling over the grass, and the sea beyond was hazy and indistinct. "What I want doesn't matter. It's just how it is. Sasha said there would never be anyone like Viv. Viv was telling him ... he shouldn't be alone, if she dies, and he made it clear no one could replace her."

Zev crouched down, picking an herb and trailing his fingers over the spiky leaves. "Dragan's first mate died, you know. Elena's mother. We talk about her, sometimes, when he misses Elena or when he's cleaning one of her knives. I'm not a replacement for her, either."

Micah twisted to look at him. "But Dragan loves you. That's different."

"Not really. You can love more than once in your life, Micah, or more than one person at a time. The love Dragan has for me isn't less because he loved his first mate. Elena's love for Aleks isn't less because she loves her other mate, the one she told us about in her last letter. Viv can be irreplaceable and you can be loved as well."

Micah groaned. "She is irreplaceable. She's clever, and she's kind, even if she doesn't admit it. She doesn't think I'm broken, but she doesn't act like that's a big deal, either—it's like it's a given, like everyone should feel that way."

"They should. There's nothing wrong with who you are, Micah."

Micah glanced at Zev. Zev understood. The man who raised him—his captor, more like—had taught Zev to be afraid of himself, terrified that the wolf inside him would make him violent and wild. That only his captor could tame him. Zev had told Micah how difficult it still was to banish that voice from his head.

"I'm starting to get that," Micah said. "I think ... I think I do want to be their mate, Zev. It would be so nice. I want to cook for them. I want to build things that make their lives easier. I want to enjoy the way Sasha looks at me sometimes, like he's happy I'm around. But if they just want me because I'm convenient ..."

Zev got to his feet again. "Have you talked to them about this? Sasha needs things spelled out sometimes—otherwise he'll assume. He'd apparently decided we were friends way before I knew it was possible. And Viv likes things to be straightforward. She spent so long trying to analyze her mom, you know, to figure out if she really loved her or not, that she doesn't do well with uncertainty."

Micah kicked at the grass. "I don't know why her mom treated her that way. It doesn't make sense."

Zev looked uncomfortable, his shoulders going tight, gaze drifting to the side. "Evgen told me a little. I mean, he was a monster, so he might've just been talking shit about them because he knew I liked Viv, but ... it was really sad, Micah. Sickness runs in her family, on her mom's side. It skipped her mom, but her mom's first kid was sick for three weeks before he died. Everyone still talks about it. It was like a piece of her died, too. She was making a scene, Evgen said, constantly coming to him about it. He said he had to kick her out of the house once—she wouldn't leave, because she was pregnant and was so afraid it would happen again. Then it did, but it didn't take three weeks that time. It was sudden. One day she had a daughter, then she didn't. Happened like that with the third child, too."

Micah struggled with pity. Children were precious. It was devastating to lose one, let alone more. But it was worse to neglect the children you had. "That's no excuse for how she treated her."

"No, it isn't. But I think the experience broke something in her. When Viv and I were kids, her mother acted like she didn't even have a daughter. Viv was always running after her, and then, after a while, she stopped trying. She started healing people for supplies of her own, and when I asked about her mom, Viv said she was just a woman who lived in her house. Her dad had left when Viv was a baby—has another family now. Sasha was the first person who looked at Viv and saw someone worth fighting for. He told her he loved her after courting her for three days."

"I can believe that."

Zev lay a hand on Micah's shoulder, and Micah felt a surge of affection for him. He, too, had been neglected, but here he was, opening his heart for other people, giving them a chance. Being vulnerable. "If you love her—or Sasha, or both—you need to tell them. They need to see you're willing to fight for it. Not physically. I mean face the difficult part of love. The part that requires giving someone the chance to see who you are. They might say no. It might hurt. But if it's real, you need to take that risk."

Micah sighed heavily. "I wish I could be like Sasha. He always has his heart on his sleeve."

"Sasha's a rare one. The rest of us have to trudge through

the bracken while he's stomping about on clear ground. So." Zev grinned. "Tell me about last night."

Micah blushed and pushed at Zev's shoulder, and Zev pushed back, as playful as he was in wolf form. "It's nothing."

"Nothing, huh? Well, tell me about nothing."

Micah rolled his eyes and walked off, and Zev followed him, laughing as a cool breeze stirred the trees, making golden leaves twirl about them like gentle rain.

* * *

Sasha was humming as he went about preparing some tea, and Viv watched him from where she was working at her loom, wondering if she should say anything.

She felt better. Not back to full strength, but she was clearly headed that way, and it was a relief. In the midst of the fever, there was always that horrible moment where she thought, *This is how the others felt, only they never got over it,* and despite her firm admonitions not to, started wondering if this would be the time it took her, too.

Then the fever would break and she would sweat, and clarity would return along with her usual determination: *I won't give her the satisfaction of dying yet.* Macabre, perhaps. But it helped. After all, she *was* Lukoi. Spite was the main reason they were all still here, whether villager or Compound-dweller.

"I wonder what he's working on." Sasha set the tea to steep and wiped his hands on a towel. He went over to the table where Micah had set up his slate and tools. Peering down, he said, "Doesn't make much sense to me. Is he, aw, making you a throne? That sounds about right." He picked up the slate. "I don't know what these arrows mean, though."

"Sasha, put that down before you erase something." He

wouldn't mean to, of course, but his hand was almost the same size as the slate itself.

"Yeah, good point, babe." Sasha returned the slate, then picked up a curved piece of wood and blinked at it. "Snow-Walker has a chair with a bottom like this. I thought it was strange, but it turns out if you sit in it, it moves back and forth. Maybe Micah is making one of those."

"Sasha," Viv said, shaking her head fondly. Her husband's curiosity was just part of who he was. "Remember how I don't like when you pick up my tapestries and ask what they are, before I'm done with them?"

"Yeah, yeah, artist's mystery and all that." Sasha put the wood down and went back to the stove to pour the tea into a mug. He added a bit of honey and brought the drink to her. "Here you go."

She smiled and took the tea, sipping it and eyeing him. He was wearing a shirt, but it was loose enough that she could see the marks on his shoulder from Micah's teeth, and she shivered remembering last night, how good it had been between them.

"Kneel here for a minute," she urged, and she barely needed any of her natural dominance to make Sasha do so. She laughed, setting the tea aside and running her fingers through his hair. "Someone's awfully agreeable today."

"Aw, come on, you know I'm always agreeable," Sasha said, leaning into her touch. He chuckled. "Probably a little more so today, though, yeah. Can't lie, last night was fucking *awesome*."

She laughed and tugged on his hair. "It was, wasn't it? The two of you together were quite something."

"Right?" Sasha beamed, as he should. He'd taken quite a lot. "And next time, he can use the briar bitch, some salt, *really* get me going."

"You are insatiable," she teased, patting the side of his face. "But do you think there will be a next time?"

Sasha looked confused. "I mean, sure. Why wouldn't there be?"

Viv sighed. She loved Sasha with all her heart, but he was one of the most easygoing people she'd ever met and tended to think people were less complicated than they were. Which wasn't necessarily a problem, since they wouldn't be married otherwise: he'd seen her as desirable and appreciated her talents, when others thought she was strange and best avoided due to the tragedy of her family line.

Being so reliant on strength for survival meant the Lukoi had little tolerance for perceived weaknesses. Sasha was one of the few who didn't see Viv's recurring health episodes as a point against her. He wouldn't see Micah's need to avoid crowds as anything other than part of who he was, either. But for people like Viv and Micah, that sort of attitude was the exception, not the norm.

"Micah's people, when they have sex, it usually means they're mated for life," she said.

Sasha shrugged. "Not like I want him to leave. And you don't, do you? I thought you liked him."

"I do like him," Viv assured him. "I like him a lot." She did. It was surprising how seamlessly Micah fit with them, like a thread in a tapestry that both brightened and complemented a design. Micah could keep up with Sasha without adding to her husband's chaotic energy, and his intensity for his work was well suited to Viv's own. He was thoughtful and kind, and his dominance didn't keep him from letting Viv boss him about a bit, which was a plus.

"Then what's the problem? Did he say there was a problem? Did I do something wrong?" Sasha looked crestfallen.

He loves Micah already, Viv realized. Of course he did. Sasha gave love like flowers gave pollen in the spring—as if there were no other choice, as if he had an unending well of it to share. And Micah, despite what he might have been taught, was an easy man to love. She was headed that way herself.

"You were wonderful, and you know it," Viv said, leaning over to kiss the top of his head. "But we've had others join us before, and they didn't stay."

"Yeah, I know, but they weren't *Micah*," Sasha said, like it was obvious. "He's not, you know, just for sex."

She snorted. "That's what you're for."

Sasha grinned up at her. "Damn right, baby." His smile faded. "Do you think he really doesn't want to stay with us?"

Viv was careful when she answered. "I think he does, but it might … take him some time to admit it. And if he chooses to leave in the spring, we have to let him."

Sasha's dark gray eyes glinted. "But if he wants to stay, and we want him to stay, why would he leave?"

She thought for a bit, petting his hair and then reaching once more for her tea while she tried to put into words what she meant. "Your heart is as big as you are, Sasha Black, and that's why I love you. But people like Micah, like me, it … sometimes it's hard to believe we can have what we want. Sometimes we don't trust it."

"Is that why you turned me down the first three times I asked you to marry me?"

"You asked three times on the fifth day you were courting me," Viv pointed out. "I thought you'd been hit in the head in the fighting ring too many times, honestly."

Sasha, unbothered as ever, knocked the side of his head with his fist. "Sasha Skull-Crusher, baby."

"More like, Sasha Too Stubborn to Let a Crushed Skull Stop Him."

"That's a mouthful, baby." Sasha leered at her. "Know what else is a—"

She clapped her hand over his mouth and laughed despite

herself. "I know. If we do get to keep him, Micah, I'd love to see if he could take all of you."

"Bet you guys could if you took turns. Mmm, now *that* is ... not what you wanna talk about, huh."

She'd rather talk about that, but no, they needed to talk less about the sex and more about the emotions. "I don't know if Micah considers us mates or not. I would think someone who lives apart from the villagers might not follow all their customs. Either way, of course I'd like him to stay. But you need to understand that he might not want to."

"We want him to, though, right?" Sasha glanced up at her. "I mean, I do, if that's what you're asking."

Viv nodded. "I figured, but it's good to hear. I do, too. I suppose what I really wanted to tell you was that he might not want to. And I know, if he leaves, that will hurt you."

Sasha could take any amount of physical pain you dished out, but the thought of losing someone he loved inflicted mental anguish that had nothing to do with his biological need for submission. He lowered his gaze and turned his head, the same way he did whenever she tried to talk to him about her illness.

Sasha could handle her episodic relapses. He did so with love and affection, for which she was forever grateful, but he couldn't handle any discussion of her death. Every time she brought it up, he did the same thing: shut down, tried to change the subject. Losing Micah would hurt like that, in the way that made him afraid.

"He wants to stay, though," Sasha said after a moment. "I know he does."

Viv sighed. Sasha was as stubborn as any Lukoi. "I think so, yes, but that's not ... it may not be that simple."

"Well, yeah, but ..." Sasha shook his head. "I guess we'll have to convince him, that's all."

"He was hurt like I was hurt, Sasha. Someone—maybe more

than one person—treated him like he was broken. It takes time, after something like that, to understand that not everyone sees you that way. It took me time, with you."

"Not nearly as much time as we have until spring," Sasha said, indomitable as ever.

"You were very persuasive," she agreed, petting him again. "But even if he loves us, he might still want to leave. This might be too much for him. My point is, it's up to him to decide, and we have to respect his answer."

"Sure. I'd never want someone with us who doesn't want to be, but Viv, he's ... It's like he was always supposed to be here, you know?"

She nodded. "I do." She took longer to fall in love than Sasha, but she could feel the stirring of it, deep down. "I hope he stays with us. Part of that, too, is that ... as I told you before, I'd like you to have someone, wh—if I don't recover from the fever, one day."

"You got better so much faster this time, though. See, that's another reason why Micah should stay—"

"Micah has to want to stay for *him*," she interrupted. "Not because you like the pain he gives you, or because I like his magic and his healing drinks, or even because it helps to think you'll have someone to love when I'm gone." She reached out to turn his face toward hers. "He's more than that, and I think if he knows how we feel about him, he'll want to stay. People like to be useful, appreciated ... but we should love him for more than what he gives us."

"Well, yeah, but that's just how he is. And I told you, no one could replace you, not ever," Sasha said, brows drawing down.

She rubbed her thumb over the lines on his forehead, smoothing them—a frown looked as out of place on Sasha's face as a snowstorm in summer. "I would want you to be happy, Sasha. If you can't accept that you'd have someone else to love when ... when I'm gone, then I don't know that Micah *should* stay. Because losing me will hurt you both, and if you couldn't find comfort and love in each other, it'd just make him feel abandoned all over again."

"I wouldn't do that, but I don't—I don't want to think about it, because you're not gonna die. You're gonna be just as badass as you always are." He turned, pressing his face into her shoulder. "I hate when you talk like that."

I know, so I don't, even though I think sometimes I need to. "I know. I've beaten the odds this long, and here's hoping I'll keep doing it. But we can't pretend, Sasha. Micah deserves to know, if he stays with us, that it might not be three forever. And that might not be okay with him. It might feel easier to leave and avoid ... being left."

"I don't think he's gonna look at it that way, baby, because you know what? I never did."

"Yes, I know that, but you're not *him.*" Viv gave his head another pat. They were talking in circles, but at least she'd gotten through what she wanted to tell him. That having been abandoned by the people who were supposed to love him, Micah might choose solitude over the pain of losing someone who *did.*

"So we should just tell him all this. And ask him." Sasha turned to peek up at her, one cheek still pressed to her shoulder. "Isn't that how this shit works?"

"For you, apparently it is." Viv laughed. "But yes. I think it's a good conversation to have, while I'm feeling better and everyone is ... as settled as we get, I suppose. Even you, though I'm not sure how long that will last."

"Eh, just pinch my bruises and smack me on the back. It'll be fine for a bit." Sasha leaned up on his knees and kissed her. "And maybe after we have the serious talk, I can watch you ride his face. You know. Since you're feeling better." His grin was wolfish.

Speaking of wolves ... Before she could say anything to what was, honestly, an intriguing suggestion, the door opened and Micah and Zev came back inside. Zev was smiling, and Micah looked wind-tousled and flushed but relaxed.

"I brought you something," Zev said, reaching into his bag. He pulled out a bundle of raw wool wrapped in twine and handed it over. "Mira sent it, to thank you for the herbs you sent with me last time."

Viv smiled and took the bundle, then stood to add it to the basket next to her spindle. She was pleased that she could get up so quickly and with only a little bit of dizziness, using Sasha's shoulder for balance. "I have some more for her. Here." Feeling more stable now that she was on her feet, she went to the kitchen and found the supplies she'd set aside to send to the village's healer.

Zev took the herbs and tucked them into his bag, then accepted a mug of cold water to drink. He smiled at Viv and Sasha both, and when it turned sly, Viv knew Micah had told him what happened. "My mate asked after Micah, to make sure he had somewhere safe to spend the winter. I'll tell him that he does."

Sasha looked as if he was about to say, *He'll be here for the rest of his winters, forever,* so Viv hurriedly responded, "Yes, tell Wolf-Breaker he's in good hands."

"So I hear," Zev said, laughing.

It was good to hear him laugh, to see his pretty blue eyes free of their old fear and wariness. He even hugged her, and she hugged him back tightly and gave his braid a tug. She hoped Micah would find a home here, with them, just as Zev had found one with Dragan in the village.

Sasha was right, she realized, as Zev took his leave after

hugging Sasha and Micah. Maybe a conversation was all they needed, to make it clear that they wanted Micah here not just for the winter, but for good. It would be up to him, of course, but he deserved to know he was wanted, loved. If she had learned anything from a lifetime of illness, grief, and loss, it was that you shouldn't wait to tell someone the important things, because you never knew when it might be too late.

* * *

Micah almost wished Zev had stayed. It would have helped to have someone he could look to when he fumbled for his words or couldn't find them at all. But Zev had a mate to go home to, and Micah had ... he had Viv and Sasha. Sitting there. Sasha covered in bite marks that showed over his collar, and Viv in a gown patterned with stars and clouds.

"I'm making you something," Micah said, after the silence stretched too long. It was the wrong way to start, he knew, but he couldn't think of anything else to say. He grabbed his slate and shoved it at Viv.

"Oh," she said, staring at his scribbles.

"It's a chair that moves," Micah said. "On wheels. You'd have to turn the wheels yourself, or someone else could—those two, on either side, not the little one in the back—but I think if they're bigger they won't be hard to move, and you can wear gloves so your hands don't get dirty. And there's a guard here so your dress doesn't catch. We'll need to test it, so it might look different when it's done, but I know you hate being carried everywhere, and you should be able to get around when you want to."

Viv was silent for a long, long moment. "What about this, here?"

"Uh, I was trying to figure out if you could use a crank and a chain to make it move instead of moving the wheels directly, but it would make the wheels snap off, so ...”

“Those were the things you kept throwing on the fire? Models of it?”

Micah rubbed the back of his neck. “Maybe.”

“You’re so fucking smart,” Sasha said, and Micah looked down. “I can help. I’m good with my hands. And the glass-blower can make, like, metal from that weird rock she’s in love with.”

“She isn’t in love, Sasha. She’s just passionate.”

“She calls it her baby.”

Viv gave Micah a knowing look and handed the slate back to him. “I love it, Micah. I can’t wait to see it when it’s done.”

“I’m not good at words,” Micah blurted, and Viv lay her hands in her lap, head slightly tilted. “Making things is easier. I can ... tell people how I feel, that way.”

“And what does it mean when you build someone a moving chair?” Viv asked.

“I don’t know. Same thing it means when I make them tea or do the laundry or ...” He was rambling, because he didn’t want to say it. Saying it would make it real, and making it real meant he could be hurt again. “In the village, you cut your hand when you mate someone, and you give them a vow. I think I’m ... the kind of person who makes things. And we haven’t known each other long, but I would like to ... keep making things, for you. Both of you. If you want.”

“Babe, is he proposing?” Sasha whispered, which of course Micah heard. Probably even Zev heard it. Micah wanted to laugh, and by the smile Viv hid behind a hand, so did she.

“Are you?” she asked.

“Because that’s not fair. We were gonna do that,” Sasha said. “Or I was. What we do here is, basically, I take you to the fighting pits and tell everyone how hot and smart you are, and then I beat up anyone who wants to court you instead. It's great."

"Or," Viv said, "we do it our way. If that's what you're asking, Micah."

"Is that something you want?" Micah asked. He felt like he'd tripped off the edge of the world and was spiraling dizzily out of control. "You want to mate—marry—me? I know I can't replace either of you. Sasha, you said no one could be Viv—"

"Of course not." Sasha looked genuinely bewildered. "She's Viv. You're Micah. You can't be each other; that's impossible."

"He means there's room for you here," Viv said. "With us. The space you fill isn't mine, or Sasha's—it's yours. We want you because you're Micah."

Micah sighed and covered his face with a hand. "That's ... a lot."

"We'll remind you, if you forget," Sasha said.

"Remind me of what?"

"Why we like you." Sasha sat next to him on the couch and hauled him in with an arm around his waist. "You're hot. You're smart. You're a witch, and can I just say being a husband to two witches is probably a record? I should get a statue. And you're a good guy. You make kids toys even though you're not big on the whole ... people thing, like Viv heals people's cats and stuff. You and Viv, right? People were fucking shit to you, but you came out nice. Who wouldn't want you?"

Micah covered his face again, and Viv leaned over to pat his leg. "I know. It's like that, with Sasha."

"I can't believe I'm glad my house burned down," Micah said, and then he was laughing, all the stress and pent-up emotion bubbling out of him. Sasha hugged him close, Viv squeezed his knee, and Micah leaned his head against Sasha's shoulder. "My parents' voices are still pretty loud sometimes. You know, the ones saying I'm not ... normal enough."

"We'll tell them to fuck off whenever you want, boss." Sasha kissed him, and Micah reached up to tug his hair, thrilling at the way that made him moan into Micah's mouth. Micah turned to Viv and pulled her in as well.

"But there are some things we should talk about," Viv said, and Sasha's brows knit together. "I've been getting sick less often than I usually do, but what you saw before? It'll happen again. And there might be a day when my body isn't strong enough to fight it off."

Micah thought of his parents, the way the blood pooled to their backs when they died, the strange, inhuman look to their skin as he dragged them outside for the pyre. One day, he might have to see Viv like that. He might have to see Sasha like that, if he were injured on a hunt or fell sick.

"Anything could happen to any of us," he said. "When you love someone, isn't it ... isn't it expected, that you might mourn them one day? I've hidden away from being hurt before. I'd rather risk it. You and Sasha, you're worth it."

Sasha closed his eyes for a few seconds, then looked at Viv. "Yeah. He's right. We'll just have to risk it."

"Okay." Viv smiled. "Never let it be said a witch of Lukos is a coward."

They sat there together for a few breaths, until Sasha inevitably broke the silence. "So. Am I gonna go fight people for Micah, or ..."

"How do witches do it?" Micah asked.

Viv shrugged. "Same as everyone else, I guess. But maybe we should make our own ritual. We exchange rings, in the Compound. We can get you one."

"Or we can make one. Something to represent all of us."

Viv tugged at Micah's hair. "I love it. We'll get some supplies from the glassmaker, and we can decide on it together."

Chapter Ten

That night, Micah slept in Sasha and Viv's bed.

He woke up with Sasha's arm around his waist and Viv's hair in his mouth. He'd learned that Viv tended to roll to the edge of the bed, and Sasha woke at the slightest sound. They danced around each other in the morning, and Sasha kept sneaking him sly smiles and practically *begged* Micah to pull his hair on the way to the kitchen.

Micah was still drifting on the knowledge that *they like me, they want me, they want me to stay* when Viv put on her hooded cloak and announced that she was going to see her mother.

"What?" Sasha, who was cleaning one of the vents carved in the ceiling while Micah held the ladder, nearly tumbled off. "I thought this was a good day, Viv."

"It is. And it'll still *be* a good day." Viv adjusted her cloak. "But since we're all confronting things, I suppose I can't put this off any longer. It's about time I figure something out: why do you think Mother always comes here when I'm sick?"

"She does?" Micah frowned. "How does she know?"

"That's my question. I've let it slide, because it's easier to avoid unpleasant conversations. But I'm done avoiding. If she's keeping an eye on me to the point that she knows when I'm sick, I want to know why. This can't keep happening. So I'm going to the Compound to ask her. Sasha, you'll come with me, yes?"

"I can come with you, too," Micah said, as Sasha descended the ladder.

Viv shook her head. "I'd rather have something nice waiting at home." Micah's cheeks went hot. "This feels like we're starting new, doesn't it? All of us. I want to do it right."

Micah understood. If he could talk to his mother and father again, even if only to tell them they were wrong and that he *was* worth it, that they'd wasted their chance as parents, he'd do it. Viv needed this. But she also needed to know she had people who loved her.

"I'll make you something."

Viv kissed him, and then Sasha, not to be outdone, kissed them both. Micah understood the Lukoi rule saying only mates could kiss. There was something thrilling there, now: a promise. *She likes me. She wants me to stay.*

Sasha helped Viv into her boots, and Micah watched them go.

Then he closed the door and turned back to the house— their house—and got to work.

He cleaned the bedroom and changed the linens. He made another tart, grinding nuts into a paste and slicing fruit into the shape of a rose. He drizzled maple syrup over the whole thing before placing it on the fire. The air went sweet, and he thought of his old house: the giant kiln, the cluttered shelves, the bed shoved into the corner like an afterthought. He touched the letters he'd received from the kids in the Compound, now with his toy designs in the margins. He had space here, and quiet when he needed it, but he wasn't lonely. Not anymore.

When the tart was cooling, Micah decided to gather herbs to make their clothes smell fresh the next time they were washed. It was an old trick from his great-grandmother's book, and he stepped outside just as dusk started to fall over Lukos.

The sun was an orange spot on the horizon as he began stuffing herbs into a bag. The plants were abundant, growing between little spiky flowers that had nuts Micah's great-grandmother wrote could stave off hunger in a pinch. Even if all the deer fled Lukos, they could still survive. It was amazing how an island an ancient emperor thought was a death sentence had so much potential for life.

He wandered amid the drifts of fall leaves with the scent of herbs on his fingers, taking his time, and barely realized that it had gotten dark. He turned back to the house, swinging his bag, and stopped when he saw a figure slumped at the steps leading down to the cave. Their cloak fluttered in the breeze, and their hair was pale yellow, their hands grasping at the earth.

Viv.

Micah wasn't thinking. All he could focus on was Viv, collapsed on the ground, without Sasha, falling ill so soon after her last fever. He went to his knees next to her and reached out to touch the delicate wisps of her hair.

A pale hand grabbed his wrist with the speed of a striking snake, and Micah shuddered as the creature, stinking of moss and earth, looked up at him with Viv's face.

"You're not Viv," he said.

"Vivian," the creature said. It grabbed at Micah's shirt. "Vivian. My baby. I need to protect her. Where are you keeping her?"

Micah trembled with revulsion. The voice wasn't Viv's. It was lower—a woman's voice, but without Viv's usual tone or dominance. "What do you want with her?"

"She's in danger," the thing said. Its mouth was a black hole with no teeth, no tongue. "They're all in danger. My babies. My girl. So weak. I can protect her. Make it stop."

"Viv's in danger?" Micah winced as the grip on his wrist tightened. "What do you mean, babies? Are there more of you?"

The thing tilted its head, and Micah fell back as it tried to climb over him, fingers solid as stone. "No. No, no. I saved them. I can save her. You are a witch, too, aren't you? I sense it in you. Power. As strong as the one who is of me. Strong as blood. As fire. Let me eat of you, witch, so I may have my Vivian."

It tried to shove its fingers into Micah's mouth, and Micah pushed at it, calling on the warmth of his magic. He dragged at it, and fire sprang up in the creature's hair, which changed from pale gold to the tangled gray of moss. It screamed, an inhuman shriek like the cry of a hawk, and tried to beat the fire out.

Micah called more fire, and the shredded bark that was the creature's dress burst into flame. He called on it again and again, over and over, until the creature's wails died out and it collapsed in a pile of charred bracken at his feet. A wind rolled past him, and he heard another shriek, in the woods.

Where the creature was waiting for Viv.

Micah sat at the steps of their house, his gaze fixed on the distant trees, as moss and twigs burned like a signal flame beside him, sending smoke into the darkening sky.

The last time Viv set foot in her mother's home, she'd been nineteen.

She'd just married Sasha, who had stood in the middle of an empty fighting ring, waiting for someone to challenge him for the right to her hand. It happened sometimes that a person didn't have any challengers, but there were usually friends who playacted at it, throwing a few punches to make the lovers appear desirable. Viv had been surprised that Zev hadn't challenged Sasha—they were friends, after all, and he was there when Sasha announced his intent to marry her—but she learned later that he'd been afraid Evgen might order him to win. At the time, though, the lack of challengers stung, and Viv had snuck into her mother's home to retrieve her things while her mother was out hunting, rather than risk having to talk to her.

Then she'd gone to Sasha's family home, which was a larger cave system in the Compound, and hugged her favorite quilt close while Sasha's family fussed over her and Sasha held her, showering her with so much affection she felt dizzy.

She suspected Micah felt the same, now. It was a rush, being loved after such a long drought, and she knew he would inevitably wonder—as she had—if he could ever reciprocate properly. For the longest time, Viv had worried that Sasha had gotten a bad deal, ending up with someone who grumbled in the mornings and was unused to casual affection. But she'd been wrong. Micah would understand that, too, in time.

Now she was heading back to the house where she'd lived largely alone for most of her childhood. The house where Sasha, already big and loud even as a child and nursing a broken finger, had rushed in, demanding to see "that scary witch girl who fixes people." It was close to the Compound's entrance, near the cave where Zev used to live with the old headman, and Viv stared at that cave for a moment as she stood at her mother's door.

Sasha leaned around her to look. "Don't think anyone's living there now."

"I wish I'd realized it earlier," she said. "What Evgen was doing to him. How he was controlling him."

"You were a kid," Sasha pointed out. "You didn't know."

That's what everyone said. They hadn't known Evgen was

forcing Zev to fight his battles in the pits. They hadn't known Viv spent most of her childhood alone. But they must have suspected. They saw the signs. They just didn't want to admit it.

Just like Viv didn't want to knock on her mother's door.

She rapped on the wood. The sound echoed in the cave, and she heard footsteps, the sound of something scraping against cloth. She reached for Sasha, and behind her back, out of sight, he held her hand as Daria opened the door.

"Vivian." It was unsettling, how alike they were. it was like looking into a mirror twenty years in the future: they had the same sharp nose, the same blond hair, the same narrow face and wide eyes. But there were more shadows under Daria's eyes, and her expression always looked tight, wary, like she was being hunted. "You're pale. Are you well?"

"Is that a joke?" Viv had meant to be as civil as possible, but the frustration pushed out of her like a blast of errant magic. "You know I had a relapse."

"A ... I'm sorry, what?"

Viv squeezed Sasha's fingers tight. "A relapse, mother. I was sick. Again. As always. The way I am once or twice a year now. Like I've been since I was a baby."

Daria's brows knit. "I thought it stopped when you married Sasha. You never said—"

"I didn't need to say ..." Viv took a deep breath. "Mom. You know I've been sick. You had to know. You've been coming by every time, trying to get me to open the door even though—as you're aware—I'm never really in a good place to walk to the door, let alone when I'm sick. How do you know? Do you track me? Check when I visit the Compound? When I do spells for people and when I stop?"

Daria was silent. Her face had gone white, and she clutched at the doorframe, fingernails digging into the stone.

"Well?" Viv felt like she was fifteen again, begging her mom to do anything, say anything, for it all to make sense. *Why do you hate me? Why didn't you give me away to someone else?* But, as before, Daria offered no answers. Just silence and that strange, tight fear behind her eyes.

"I've never come to your house," she said. Viv frowned, but before she could speak, Daria reached for the door. "Go home, Vivian. If it upsets you so much, the next time you hear me? Don't answer."

She tried to shut the door, but Sasha grabbed it before it could close. "What do you mean you never came?" Viv asked. "I heard you. We heard you."

"Go home. You clearly don't want me around. I know I made a mistake—"

"A mistake?" What did her mother think was a mistake—treating Viv badly, or bringing her into the world at all?

"But this needs to end. Go. You have your own family now. A better family."

Viv felt anger boiling inside her. "And you don't want to be a part of it. You never did. You never cared. You never fought for me like Sasha did, like Micah, like Zev. It never mattered to you if I lived or died."

Her voice echoed in the face of her mother's ringing silence. Daria stared at her, and there was something new in her expression, a deep, aching pain that grated against Viv's outrage.

"I lost you before you were born," Daria said. Sasha only had a moment to get out of the way before the door shut with a resounding thud.

"Fuck you," Viv said. She kicked the door, cursed, and beat her fists against it instead. "Fuck you!"

"Oh, Viv." Sasha reached for her, and Viv turned into his hold, grabbing him around the shoulders. She held him for a minute, breathing into his neck. "She doesn't deserve you. Let's go home, huh? Bet Micah's got dinner ready for us."

"Why did I think I'd get anything out of talking to her?" Viv started off down the corridor, shame making her blush hot. "It never works. It ends like this every time."

"She knows how to piss you off."

"Yeah, she's a real expert at ..." Viv came to a stop. "You're right. She said that to get me angry. Why? Why did she want me angry?"

Sasha looked lost. He always did when Viv analyzed her mother's motivations. He didn't have a family he needed to second-guess—his clan was as straightforward as he was.

"Before she said that about me leaving, she said she didn't come to see us when I was sick. That she never came to our house." Viv started walking again, looking at her feet. "Why would she tell such an obvious lie? But if she was telling the truth ..."

"Someone else was at the door," Sasha said. Viv suppressed a chill.

"Every time? Every single time I've been sick since I've lived with you?"

Sasha shrugged. "I don't know. Who would want to do that? Someone your mom doesn't like? Someone who doesn't like you? That'd be a short list, baby. I don't know anyone who doesn't like you."

"Thanks, Sasha. But I can name one. We just met her." She groaned. "I don't get it."

"Let's go home and have some of Micah's witch tea, and maybe it'll make more sense." Sasha took her hand again. "And then you can use your magic on me. Or teach him, so you can shock my nipples, right, and he can shock my ass, and then you can get the briar flogger."

Viv snorted. "Making you cry sounds a lot more appealing than trying to figure out what Mother meant."

"See? That's what I bring to the table," Sasha said, gesturing to himself. "Perspective."

He had her laughing by the time they made it up the steps out of the Compound, and Viv was wondering if he didn't deserve another night of torment for turning a miserable situation around. He was whistling as they made their way slowly across the field, taking time to stop when Viv needed a rest. The wind stirred Sasha's hair and made Viv's cloak billow, and it wasn't until Viv smelled burning moss and green wood that she suspected anything was wrong.

She saw Micah before he saw them. He was standing in front of the entrance to their cave, a ball of magical fire in his hands, staring at the woods. When Sasha called out to him, the fire disappeared, and Micah ran for them, grabbing at Viv's cloak.

"Get inside." His voice was frantic, more so than Viv had ever heard before. "Get inside now. It's out here. The thing with your face, Viv, it's back."

Sasha didn't hesitate. He grabbed Viv, who was used to him hauling her around, and Micah, who squawked indignantly as he was slung over Sasha's shoulder, and ran down the steps to the door. They tumbled inside, and Sasha slammed the door shut, locked it, and shoved a board across it before Viv could even speak.

Then he flicked a rude gesture at the door for good measure, which would have made Viv laugh if she weren't sitting on the floor next to a terrified, panting Micah. She turned to him and lay a gentle hand on his chest, and he looked at her, eyes wide.

"Tell me what happened."

It came out in a rush. When Micah explained how the thing tried to climb him—wanted to eat him—Sasha actually growled, but Viv's mind kept circling back to what it had said to him when he was questioning it.

"It said it had babies," Viv said. "It called me by name."

"And it wanted us to open the door," Micah added. "So, I mean, if we keep the door shut …"

"We'll starve," Sasha said, voice hard. "We're not done preparing for winter. If you can set it on fire, I wonder if I can beat it to death."

"It'll come back," Micah said. They were still sitting in front of the door, and Micah's breathing hadn't slowed. "It was in the woods. You can kill it, but it comes back."

"It wasn't me," Viv said. Sasha and Micah turned to look at her. "That thing, it wasn't me. It wasn't wearing my face."

"What do you mean?" Sasha asked.

"It's my mother." Viv shuddered. "That thing is wearing my mother's face, not mine. It probably had my mother's voice. You said the voice was wrong, didn't you, Micah? That's because it was hers. Her voice. The voice we hear every time I'm sick."

"The voice asking you to open the door," Sasha said, too quiet.

"And Mother said not to open the door to her anymore, when I spoke to her just now. She said it wasn't her coming here." Viv felt cold, distant from her own body. "She knew. She knew it was out there. She knew what it was. What it wanted."

"But how?" Micah reached for her, and Viv leaned against his chest. She started kicking off her boots, and Sasha took them off the rest of the way for her.

Viv thought of her mother. The way she'd always locked the doors when Viv was sick, keeping her in her room as if she were something ugly that had to be pushed out of sight. How tense she'd been when Viv began using magic, how she'd tried to discourage her, told her it was dangerous, unlucky. But then …

"When I was ten, I made a fire in the kitchen," Viv said. "Out of that … violet light I give off, sometimes."

"Oh, yeah, that's the best, Micah."

"Hush," Viv said, poking Sasha with a foot. "When the fire was out, she said that I needed to keep it in a circle next time. I used to think she knew to tell me that because she had relatives who were witches, but …" Viv didn't want to say it. "But maybe I was wrong. Maybe that thing out there … it's hers."

"You mean she's a witch?" Sasha scowled. "After she gave you so much shit for it?"

"Why would she make something so violent? Because maybe it said it wanted to protect you, but the way it moved, how it came after me? I don't trust it." Micah wrapped his arms around her as though protecting her from the thing that waited in the woods.

"I don't know. Maybe she didn't want it to hurt me. It was talking about babies, wasn't it? What if … what if it … I don't know. It's all conjecture."

Micah sucked in a sharp breath. "Maybe there's something in the book. Something to fight it or protect us."

It was worth a try, in any case, and it was better than sitting on the floor. They moved to the couch, where Micah grimly set down the most beautiful tart yet, then opened up his great-grandmother's book.

"There's a section here called 'When Needed,'" Micah said, flipping through the pages. "I always thought it was her being nice, you know, giving her descendants ways to deal with their emotions and stuff. Like wanting to feel better or safe, or giving yourself more energy. Learning to ask for help. But if they're spells …" He tapped one. "This might work. It's a door."

Viv looked down at the page. The door was flimsy, sketched to look like three twigs held together with string. There was no reason to believe it would ever stand up, let alone stop anyone from coming in. But the note below it was clear: *Only invited guests can enter.*

"It's a pretty easy spell," Micah said, skimming through it. "We just need some wood, string, and salt. Make a line of salt around the entrance to the house, and nothing can get past it unless we invite them in."

"But is there anything to fight the creature?" Sasha asked. Micah shrugged and flipped through the pages.

"I don't know. It's all metaphors. Making light. Laughter. Speaking the truth. An extra pair of hands?"

"Wait, stop there." Viv held Micah's hand before he could turn the page. The "An Extra Pair of Hands" page featured the drawing of a small clay doll, but there was a shadow stretching from it, impossibly long.

"'When needed,'" she read aloud. "'How to make a shadow. Tell it who you are in the dark, and it will do what you need. It is your shadow. You cannot hide the truth from it, or it will twist your words ...' Micah, how did you not know your great-grandmother was a witch?"

"I thought she was being metaphorical! But we shouldn't do this, Viv. It sounds dangerous. If you have to tell it who you are in the dark ... that probably means you have to say something you don't like. Your true self, without hiding."

Viv nodded, running her hand over the image of the doll. "I wonder if other witches knew this spell."

Sasha looked at the door. "Like your mom. You're saying she made some shadow thing?"

"Maybe. Everyone said she was inconsolable when my brother died. Maybe she wanted help."

Micah closed the book. "So she made a shadow. And now it wants you. It thinks it's protecting you." They sat there for a long time, staring at the book with the witch symbol etched into the cover, before Micah stood up. "All right."

Viv saw the same look in his eyes that he had when he was working on a new design, his mind whirling like a storm. "Micah?"

"We know what's out there, now," he said. "We know why it's here. So I think, between the three of us, we can probably ... What's the right way to say this, Sasha?"

"Kick its ass?" Sasha asked, grinning. Micah smiled back.

"Yeah. Kick its ass."

Chapter Eleven

Sasha spent the next few days being the most bossed-around submissive in Lukos.

His wife and his … husband, really; they'd make it official soon enough … were in the throes of intense witchy shit, and for it to work, they kept sending him on errands.

"Sasha, we need, hmm. A pile of twigs?" Viv looked at the scribbles Micah was making on the slate. "Yes. Twigs."

"Cool. Twigs. I can do twigs." Sasha went outside, gathered up more twigs than they could possibly need, and brought them in.

The twigs were fussed over and discussed, and then Viv decided they needed some of the weeds that grew near the Compound entrance. Sasha went to get those, then did the washing for the week, since Micah and Viv were mumbling together on the couch, poring over the book.

He didn't understand most of what they were talking about —sigils and poppets and strings, doorways that weren't supposed to open, circles of salt—but every now and then, he'd smile, seeing how engrossed they were and how, when they looked up in surprise to eat the meal he'd made for them, they both had the same faint, glowing violet light in their eyes.

Sasha didn't mind. He knew they were figuring out something important, and he didn't feel as if he wasn't helping just because he was sent on errands instead of muttering over a book he didn't really get. He wasn't a witch, and he didn't mind being their errand boy.

The problem wasn't the various and sundry tasks they were setting him. The problem was the way they would take their frustrations out—or, more to the point, how they wouldn't.

Micah, while working on a complex ... thing ... for the spell, asked if Sasha would kneel, gagged and with his hands behind his back, so Micah could pull his hair. Sasha agreed, because that seemed about the best thing ever as far as tasks. He let Micah fit a strap in his mouth, knelt eagerly ... and then was mostly ignored, except for a few times when Micah would get irritated at whatever he was doing, make a disgruntled sound, and reach out to give Sasha's hair a quick tug.

Eventually, Viv needed him to go and get some moss, so he had to stand up, take out the gag, and go outside again.

"I don't understand what this means, about sending the puppet through the doorway," Viv said when Sasha deposited an armful of damp moss on the table to join the other various and sundry items he'd been sent to collect.

"Can't help you there, babe," he said, waiting expectantly. "But if you need to work out some frustration, I'm here for that."

Viv scratched his back and smiled distractedly at him, and Sasha shivered until she gave him a smack on the side of the face that wasn't hard enough by far.

Micah walked by to show her something, and he pulled Sasha's hair as he passed. He always gave Sasha a look when he did it, though, as if he was still not sure that he *could*.

The problem was, by day two of fetching a thousand raw ingredients—and some things he had to go searching for, like twine and beads and glass—Sasha was so desperate to be properly hurt he couldn't see straight. The casual hair pulls and slaps were awesome, but Viv and Micah were ... distracted when they did it, and while Sasha understood *why*, logically, his masochism didn't.

On the third day, when they were trying to make puppets of moss, twigs, and twine do ... something—he wasn't sure exactly what you *could* do with the world's least cuddly doll—he realized he was in a bit of a state.

"Okay, hang on for a second. Your submissive has something to say," Sasha said, facing them with his hands on his hips. "And that something is, I'm glad you're working hard, but I've spent three days half-under, and you're gonna need to put up or shut up, as we say in the fighting pits."

"What?" Micah frowned. "Is— Are you all right?"

"Um, no, I'm not all right! The hair pulling, the smacking— it's so fucking great, but you gotta give me *more*. I'm dying here." Sasha was whining, but he couldn't help it. "I'm happy to let you take your frustrations out on me, and I know we're trying to fix this whatever-it-is, but ... help a guy *out*, yeah?"

Micah and Viv glanced at each other, and then they looked guiltily at Sasha.

"We didn't mean to ignore you," Viv said.

"We didn't," Micah added, and he looked devastated, which ... no.

"No, no, that's the thing, see?" Sasha waved his hands. "You're not. That's what I'm getting at. I love helping, and if helping means 'Fetch stuff and get your hair pulled,' that's the best, right? But I'm pretty worked up; I can't lie."

Viv smiled, walked over, and twisted his nipple. Sasha

hadn't been wearing a shirt for days, in the hopes it would help convince them to see to him properly. "Our submissive needs us, Micah. I suppose a break couldn't hurt."

"No, no, baby, it *should* hurt. C'mon, stop teasing."

"It would probably help clear our heads." Viv was smiling, that grin of hers that meant he was going to get what he wanted, and then some. "Micah, do you want to do a little magic practice? I should show you how to use it on Sasha."

"Oh, fuck, *yes,* you should," Sasha agreed, his cock half-hard just at the thought. "Micah, the best thing about magic is how you can use it to make me scream."

"And to heat baths," Viv said dryly. "But yes. Also that. Go strip and lie on the bed, Sasha. I'll give Micah a few pointers before we join you."

Sasha gave a whoop and lifted her up, kissing her soundly before returning her to her feet. Then he grabbed Micah, who made a strangled sound and grabbed wildly at Sasha's bare shoulders. He laughed when Sasha kissed him, too, and then shook his head when Sasha set him down again.

"That you can just *do* that," he said, and Sasha winked at him, then hurried to the bedroom before either of them changed their mind.

He could hear the low murmur of their voices as Viv explained the electrical magic and how she used it. Sasha, eager to feel said magic, shucked his boots, socks, and pants and climbed naked onto the bed.

When Viv and Micah entered, they had matching expressions of dominants up to no good, and Sasha grinned.

"You're—already?" Micah shook his head.

"I'm a simple man, boss." Sasha put his hands under his head and bucked his hips up, showing off his hard cock. "I'm gonna get hurt by both my doms? What do you expect?"

"Smack his cock, Micah. He likes it," Viv said. "And he deserves it."

"Does he?" Micah smiled, moved over to the bed, and reached out ... and slapped Sasha's cock sharply enough that warmth blossomed in Sasha's belly.

"Hell yeah, he does." Sasha breathed out, trying not to beg for more. "You know what you could do?"

Micah grabbed Sasha's hair. "Make you be quiet and take what we give you, then thank us for it?"

"That sounds about right," Viv murmured.

"Fuck, boss, that was *so hot*," Sasha breathed.

Micah smiled, then chased it off as if he was trying to be a serious dominant instead of an adorable one. He smacked Sasha's cock again, and Sasha's grin turned into a choked moan.

"You have to tell me if this is too much." Micah put a warm hand on Sasha's chest. "The magic."

"I will," Sasha promised. "But it prolly won't be."

Micah shook his head and closed his eyes, and Sasha drew in an excited breath as Micah's hand began to grow warmer on his chest.

"That's good. Think about lightning," Viv suggested.

There was something like a spark, and Sasha gasped. "That's it, yeah, fuck."

Micah's eyes opened, and he stared at his own hand, lifting it slightly off Sasha's chest and drawing in another breath. There was an arc of light, faint violet, and Sasha felt the shock run through his whole body, electric and hot.

His cock twitched, and he arched up toward the pain, toward Micah. "That's so good."

Viv appeared next to Micah, with the gleam in her eyes that had Sasha moaning *before* she added her hand, and her power, to Micah's. Together, they called on the ancient magic, charging the room's atmosphere like a storm. When their combined efforts made the lightning arc all over his body, Sasha shouted and thrashed, grabbing the mattress as his cock swelled even farther.

"The two of you are gonna wreck me, and I'll love every fucking second," Sasha vowed as Micah pressed on the fading bruises from the bites he'd left on Sasha's upper arm.

"Of course you are. Because you're the biggest pain slut in Lukos," Viv said, patting him on the face—without magic—before she tweaked his nipple, pinching it hard between her fingers *with* magic and sending more waves of delicious pain through him.

"Biggest and best," Sasha agreed, shivering as they worked him over. Viv had asked him, once, to describe how it felt. He didn't have the words for it, not really. *It feels like if the tip of a knife was on fire and cut you without making you bleed,* had been the best he could come up with.

"Can he take it on his cock?" Micah asked.

"Yes," Sasha said. "Yes, *yes,* fuck yes he can."

"Yes, but keep it quick, light—we don't want any permanent damage," Viv said, and Micah laughed.

Sasha's eyes were squeezed shut, his whole body tense as he waited for the shock to rush over his dick. He loved this, lying there hurting for their pleasure, being the center of their sadistic attentions. Those magic twine-twig-puppet things were lucky as *fuck.*

Micah's fingers brushed over Sasha's cock, leaving hot electric pulses in their wake, and Sasha nearly came. Viv shoved her fingers into his mouth, and he sucked on them desperately as Micah continued to torment him with surges of magic.

"This is fun," Micah said, sounding a little surprised.

"Mmph," Sasha mumbled around Viv's fingers, nodding. It was definitely fun.

"Is there something you'd like to see, Micah?" Viv asked, dragging her damp fingers over Sasha's cheek, smiling fondly at him when he beamed up at her.

"You riding his face," Micah said, and that was so ... unexpectedly *dirty* that both Sasha and Viv blinked at him. He shrugged. "I'm new at this, but I have an imagination. I like to watch you feel good, Viv. I like watching you use Sasha."

"Absolutely on board with this plan," Sasha agreed. "Get up here, babe. Put that sweet cunt on my mouth."

"Oh, I suppose you've been good," Viv said, and started to take off her clothes.

She was gorgeous naked, all that power and intelligence in her slight frame, those perfect breasts and thighs that made him wish he knew how to write fucking *poetry*. "Damn, we're lucky, aren't we, boss?"

Micah's voice was soft when he answered. "Yes. We are."

"You could use the magic on his thighs while you suck his cock, if you wanted to try that," Viv said, climbing onto the bed.

"I think I ... do, yeah." Micah shifted to the end of the bed as Sasha eagerly spread his legs to give him room.

"And you should definitely try this sweet snatch at some point," Sasha said cheerfully. "She tastes so fucking good."

Viv sighed. "Sasha, we have talked about that word. Luckily, this will keep him quiet." She paused. "Or, at least, it'll just be sounds, not words."

Viv settled over him, and Sasha took her hips in his hands, drawing her down so he could bury his face between her legs. He loved doing this, and the way she ground her cunt against his face made it hard to breathe—so that was a bonus.

Then he felt the tickle of magic against his thighs and moaned into Viv's sweet cunt as Micah licked up his cock while sending waves of pain through his fingers into the bites on Sasha's thighs.

"Oh, he likes that," Viv gasped, riding his face a little faster —hell, he might be ready to hurt at a moment's notice, but his girl could come like a pile of kindling in a fire when she was into it.

"Mm-hmm," Sasha agreed.

Micah didn't say anything, simply sucked at the head of Sasha's cock. Sasha licked Viv's clit with frantic need, wanting to feel her come on his face, wanting more of the shocks on his thighs, wanting more of Micah's mouth, of *everything*.

Micah couldn't take all of him yet, but that was all right. It'd taken Viv some time, too, and she'd gone about deep-throating him like a personal challenge. But Micah was doing a damn good job, driving Sasha wild with the licking, the sucking, the gentle glide of teeth. He was still using the magic, too, sharp shocks of pain that made the pleasure all that much better.

Sasha felt Viv's lovely thighs go tense, and she cried out and rode his face harder, coming in what might be a personal best time, hell yeah. Sasha worked her with intent, licking her and sucking gently, knowing she could get overstimulated and wanting to get her off as many times as he could before that happened.

"You look so good sucking him, Micah," Viv said, voice breathy.

"I want to ride it," Micah said, in a low, husky tone that Sasha wanted to hear forever.

Viv gasped and came again, probably because the thought of Micah on his cock made Sasha grab her and pull her down on him even more firmly. He was dizzy with the taste of her, the lack of breath, Micah's magic, and the sweet, delicious suction on his cock.

After Viv shuddered through her second orgasm, she lifted up slightly so Sasha could drag in a deep breath. He took the opportunity to say, "You want that, boss, you better, uh, ease up there. Wanna give you a good ride, yeah? Keep doing that, and it'll be too quick."

Unfortunately, his warning resulted in them both pulling away from him. Viv climbed off, sweaty and flushed, and Micah sat back and stopped everything he'd been doing. Sasha whined, but he watched eagerly as Viv handed Micah the oil.

"His cock is a lot to take," Viv said, and Sasha beamed. "He can get you ready first, or I can."

"Yeah, whatever you want, boss." Sasha would have agreed to anything, really, to get Micah on top of him, riding him hard. "Just, please, scratch me up some more, maybe smack me around a little."

"If you earn it," Micah said, his dominance giving Sasha delicious shivers. "I can do it myself, though. I've used my fingers before."

"Let me," Viv murmured. "I'd enjoy it."

"Sure," Micah said, and he was only blushing a little. "If you want."

Sasha really was the luckiest guy in Lukos, wasn't he? "You should kiss me while she gets you ready for my cock," he said. "Taste our girl. She's so sweet."

Micah tossed his hair back in that casual, sexy way and climbed up, leaning over Sasha on all fours. They kissed, and Micah licked Viv's taste from Sasha's mouth while Viv positioned herself to prepare him for Sasha's cock.

Sasha could tell when Viv started working Micah open, because he gave a soft gasp and bit at Sasha's lip ... which Sasha didn't mind in the least. He let Micah kiss him, bite him, do whatever he wanted. Micah's hair was in his face, and he was rocking back on Viv's fingers, eventually unable to keep up the kissing as he threw his head back and gave a gorgeous, drawn-out moan. "Fuck."

"She's got some great fingers, huh? She milked me once, got

me off so hard I almost passed out." Sasha's cock throbbed, but he enjoyed the view, Micah writhing and Viv behind him, murmuring as she fucked him with her fingers.

"She—yeah, she does, fuck," Micah gasped. He grabbed hard at Sasha's shoulders, digging his fingers in. "I think I'm ready."

"Mm, so do I," Viv said. "Let me get him slick for you."

Sasha had to grab the bedding again as he felt Viv's hand, slick with oil, slide up and down his cock.

"Be good, and don't come until Micah gives you permission, Sasha."

"You know it, baby. Climb on up, Micah. Can't fucking wait to feel you."

It took a bit for Micah to get into the right position, but watching him squirm as he found the perfect angle was hot as fuck, especially with Viv lying on the bed gloriously naked, rubbing herself while she watched.

Sasha felt the head of his cock press against Micah's hole, and he forced himself to stay still as Micah worked himself down on it. Micah had to stop a few times, stroking his own cock once to relax, and by the time Sasha's cock was mostly in, they were both sweat-damp and breathing hard, loud in the quiet of the room.

Micah's thighs were just as lovely as Viv's, especially when he started to raise and lower himself on Sasha's cock. Then he did the hottest thing ever. He smacked Sasha on the stomach and said, "Talk, Sasha. Tell me how good it feels."

Someone asking him to talk? Fuck, this day was basically perfect.

"It feels fucking amazing, boss. You're so tight, so fucking hot around my cock. Do you like it? Ride it just like you want— make me work for it. Yeah, fuck, you're so gorgeous," Sasha babbled, while Micah threw his head back again and moaned as he stroked himself, sliding the last few inches and taking Sasha to the hilt.

For a breathless moment, Micah simply sat there, adjusting to the fullness. He scratched his nails down Sasha's chest, hard enough that Sasha yelped with pleasure.

"Oh," Viv murmured, and shuddered hard beside them.

"Even getting our girl off. You are talented, Micah—you got sex magic," Sasha breathed, and Micah's smile was a quick flash over his handsome face before he set about riding Sasha in truth.

"Sasha, tell Micah how much you like this," Viv said, propped up and watching, clearly taking a break. "Having your big cock used for someone else's pleasure."

"Damn, baby, but I love it when you get dirty," Sasha praised. "And fuck, yeah, use me. Ride me hard, boss. Feels so good."

Micah wasn't chatty, but he was loud, making all kinds of sounds as he fell into a rhythm. He'd stopped stroking his cock, but it was still hard as he bounced on Sasha's dick and scratched the fuck out of Sasha's chest. When the magic flare came again, Sasha twisted the bedding in his fingers and had to close his eyes.

"Better ... be careful, 'm close, it's too fucking good—"

"No. You'll wait," Micah ordered, dominance as sharp as the sting of his nails, the burn of his magic. He stopped the magic, and before Sasha could whine and beg him to go back to using it, he yanked on Sasha's hair. "And look at me. I want to see you."

Sasha opened his eyes and almost came at the expression of intense pleasure and concentration on Micah's face. "Lookin' good up there, boss. Wanna smack me?"

"Yeah," Micah breathed. "I do."

Sasha helpfully turned his head to the side, and Micah slapped him, again and again, and then went back to scratching up his chest. He alternated between the two until Sasha was a goddamn mess, begging to come, heels digging into the bed as he fucked wildly up into Micah's tight, hot ass. "Let me come, please, fuck, please. Wanna do it for you, wanna come for you—"

"Yeah, yeah, go on—" Micah was gasping, shivering, almost as far gone as Sasha by the time Sasha grabbed his hips, hard, and thrust up one last time to come inside him. Micah, the clever, wonderful bastard, somehow knew to lean down and *bite* the second his release washed over him, and the pain sharpened the pleasure almost unbearably, making Sasha shout as his body released.

He was under so far that it took a moment to realize Micah had climbed off and was now kissing Viv. Sasha turned his head to watch, and his cock gave one last twitch and a final spurt of come at the sight. Micah was still hard, though, and Sasha felt like maybe he hadn't done well enough. "Boss, hey, let me suck you," he mumbled.

"No," Viv said. "That cock riding looked like so much fun, I want to try it. Micah?"

"Oh." Micah sat up, hair disheveled and sweaty, and nodded. "If you— Yeah."

"Her cunt feels as good as it tastes," Sasha offered, though he wasn't sure that came through, since he was yawning when he said it. Hell, who could blame him? Had any sub in the history of the world been worked over as well as he'd been? After the foreplay of the last few days, this had been unbelievable.

"What about," Micah started, then cleared his throat. "That is, are you ... Should I— What about ..."

"Oh, gods, he's so precious," Sasha laughed.

Viv gave him a smack on the flank while Micah lay down next to Sasha. "It's fine. I figured out a contraception spell years ago, since I've never been interested in children and the herbs most people use often run out by the end of winter."

Micah nodded, looking intrigued, like he wanted to ask what the spell was. But then Viv climbed on him and kissed him, easily taking his cock. That put a stop to any theoretical magic questions—understandably. Sasha knew how good it felt to be inside Viv.

Micah was gasping, his eyes wide as Viv began to move on top of him. She smiled at Sasha, who propped himself up on an elbow to watch. "Play with her tits, Micah, she likes that," he suggested.

Instead of being annoyed at a submissive telling him what to do, Micah took the direction like a champ and reached up to cup Viv's breasts, stroking them, rubbing his thumbs over her nipples. "You're beautiful," Micah said, his eyes fixed on her face.

"I know," Viv said, and Sasha laughed, happy to watch them find their pleasure together. She leaned down and kissed Micah sweetly, then sat back to keep working herself on his cock. "So are you. Let me show you how to make me come." She took Micah's hand and guided it to her cunt.

Micah clearly liked learning new things, because it only took him a few tries to get the pressure and rhythm down. Viv eventually left him to it and leaned back, bracing herself on his knees with her body arched beautifully.

"Look at your cute tits bouncing. I love that. Isn't it great, Micah?"

"Yeah," Micah managed, strangled, like he was trying to wait for Viv to come before he did.

"She's gonna come on your cock, and it feels fucking *amazing*, boss," Sasha said, because hey, Micah hadn't told him to stop talking, had he? "She goes all tight, and it gets even wetter, and—"

"Sasha," Viv admonished.

"Sorry, sorry, it's just kinda funny to watch you two being all dommy-doms and 'Oooh, who's gonna come first.'"

"Neither, if our submissive doesn't stop trying to be funny," Viv said.

"Trying? I'm offended." Sasha was not offended. "Can I touch you? One of you? Both of you?"

"No. You had yours," Micah said, because apparently he was going to keep domming Sasha—and that was great, too. "Watch and keep your hands to yourself."

Apparently Viv also liked it when Micah dommed Sasha, because she came right after that. Micah moaned, bucking up hard enough that some of their mountain of pillows fell to the floor.

Sasha couldn't help himself. "Told you so, didn't I?"

It wasn't clear whether Micah heard him, because he took Viv's hips in his hands—he was so gentle with her, it made Sasha's heart swell—and arched up into her, clearly at the end of his patience. He was quiet when he came, but his whole body shook, and when it was over, he pulled Viv down to kiss her, flailing one hand out to find Sasha's and squeeze it.

Sasha squeezed back, turned, and wrapped them both in his arms. "That was so hot, I can't wait to do it again."

They both smacked him for that, but it barely counted. He appreciated the effort, though.

As they lay there, tangled together on the bed that was now theirs, Sasha could feel himself drifting into sleep ... but then he heard Micah murmur, "I think I already love you both."

"Yeah, well, I *know* I love you both," Sasha said, eyes still closed. "So I win."

Micah sighed.

Viv laughed, the soft sound that always made Sasha's heart thrill to hear it. "I love you both, too, but Sasha, there's no winning involved."

Sasha drifted off, thinking she was wrong. There was a winner here, and it was definitely *him*.

Chapter Twelve

They built the door at noon on a day when the weather was quiet, without so much as a breeze. Micah had mixed sand with salt and walked around the entrance to the cave while spilling the mixture over the grass. It didn't matter if the wind blew it away later—what mattered was that the circle had existed. The ground, Viv told him, would remember.

Micah felt like his brain was stuffed full. Viv was a font of ideas, and their experiments had taught him more than he'd learned since he first moved to his great-grandmother's cottage. He knew that there were different types of magic and that witches from the old empire practiced one of the oldest types. Viv thought their magic was inborn, like having brown hair or your mother's eyes, but it worked better if you had something to channel it.

"There's magic in everything, in a way," she'd said. "We bring that magic out, and the magic in us makes it stick. That's why there's all this ritual."

The salt spilled in a perfect line as Micah walked backward around the entrance. Sasha had already built the doorway, which was just a flimsy frame of sticks and twine lying flat on the ground. Sasha stood on the other side of it, watching Micah.

When the sand-and-salt line reached the door, the frame lifted off the grass, standing straight up. Micah caught his breath, staring at Sasha through the open frame.

"Give it a try," Micah said, and Sasha walked toward the door. When he reached it, he cursed and fell back as though he'd slammed into a solid wall. He held out a hand, pressing it against the open air.

"That's a hell of a wall," Sasha said, grinning. He checked the air next to the door, but his hand wouldn't pass through. "Good job, boss. Let me in?"

"You're always welcome, Sasha." It was important to make that distinction, so Sasha didn't leave at some point and find himself unable to get back in. Sasha stepped through the door, beamed, and spent a few seconds hopping in and out. Then it was Viv's turn, though she spent a half hour testing every inch of the circle for weakness before she let anyone welcome her inside.

"Baby, get in here. There's literally a shadow mirror thing out to get you," Sasha said, walking back in with her.

"Yes, but have you noticed it only calls at night or in the woods? If it's a shadow, I think it needs shade. During the day, this field is as good a protection as a spell."

"Maybe we need to test it," Sasha said, looking toward the woods. Micah knew he was itching to hunt again—and he needed to, if they were going to have enough supplies for the winter—but they couldn't risk it until the shadow creature was destroyed. "We can go inside if it gets too close."

"Fire helps." Micah eyed the woods. He wondered if it was out there now, watching them, waiting for dusk to fall. He didn't like the idea of seeing it again, but it might be necessary to ensure the spell worked. "I'll stay, Sasha. In case you need backup."

Sasha lit up as if Micah had just told him to strip down and brace for the cane rather than wait till dusk to watch a creature slither out of the woods. He went down the stairs with Viv and came back alone, carrying two mugs of water, a basket of food, and a blanket.

"Picnic," he said, setting the supplies on the ground in front of the door. "My sister and I used to do this with our cousins. Underground, obviously, because we had to keep ourselves secret from you all in the village, but there's this cave that opens up to the beach, yeah? So we'd go and stay all night telling stories, trying to scare the shit out of each other. It was great."

"You have a big family, then?" Micah took one of the mugs and uncovered the basket to find nut bread, seasoned chicken, and a jar of spiced jelly.

"Yeah. Two aunts, five cousins, Inessa, and Nan. Mom wanted kids, but she wasn't all that into having a husband. She had a hunting accident when I was a kid, and we all moved in with my aunt Bell, 'cause Mom had it up to here with us and she had just one arm. You should meet Bell. She'd love you."

"I can't imagine growing up with so many people." Micah stretched out in the sun. "Or parents getting help with their kids. Maybe that's what mine should've done. Gone to someone else."

"Should've brought you to us, boss. We're loud, but we're all right."

It was strange, picnicking with Sasha, talking about their families as if they had nothing to worry about but the usual challenges of life.

They watched the sun fall over the horizon, painting the sky a glorious orange and red. It was calming enough to dull the edge of Micah's nerves, and he let himself lean against Sasha's shoulder as shadows slowly spread across the field.

"Wait for it," Sasha whispered.

Dusk settled over Lukos, and the darkness deepened as stars shone through gaps in the clouds. Sasha tensed and stood up, and Micah followed his gaze to a figure gliding across the grass. It headed toward them, moving faster than a deer, than a snow cat, but it didn't seem to be running. It was like it was sliding over ice, and when it came close enough for its pale hair and smiling face to be visible, Micah was on his feet next to Sasha.

The shadow person stopped at the door. It tilted its head, so like Viv's, and slid a hand over the invisible barrier.

"Witch boy," it said. "Human. Let me in. Let me see my Vivian."

"Not a fucking chance." Sasha's voice shook, and he was clenching his fists, muscles strained tight.

The creature stroked the air again, tenderly. Lovingly. "Let me in. I need my Vivian."

"She isn't yours," Micah said.

"Yeah," Sasha snapped. "Daria."

The creature tilted its head to the side again, but it moved too fast, too far, with the crack of rotting wood. "I know that name. It is of me."

"So she did make you," Sasha said. Micah had never seen him so angry. "But Viv isn't yours. You'll leave her alone."

"She isn't safe," the thing wailed. "I need to find her. Please. Please let me in."

"No," Micah said, then froze when he heard Viv's voice behind him.

"Stay out, shadow." She was standing at the top of the steps, wrapped in a shawl, glaring at the creature.

Then it saw her. It keened, and its mouth opened wide, wider, wider still, the blackness inside stretching and cracking the lovely, delicate face. Teeth formed around the edge of the hole, sharp and curved, and its limbs twisted until it was on its hands and knees, crouching like a spider with its pale hair wild around the pit of its mouth.

"Vih—Vihv—" It writhed, hands contorting, throat undulating as if a nest of snakes was squirming under its skin. "Vivian!"

"I said *stay out*," Viv said, and the creature slammed into the barrier. It was thrown back, scattering bits of moss and twig, and flew at the door again. Its teeth snapped, and its gaping mouth pulsed as it howled like the wind over the hills in winter. Micah felt sick. Sasha was rocking on his heels, fists up, gaze flicking over its distorted body.

Then it started to dig, and Micah staggered back, pulling on his magic. Fire fell over the creature, and it howled again, covered in dirt and grass, teeth extending until they reached out of its mouth like an insect's antennae testing the air. Micah called another flame, and violet lightning arched from Viv to sear the creature's body. Leaves and lumps of rotting tree bark fell to the ground, and Sasha kicked the burning shell to pieces.

"Sasha!" Viv's voice was harsh with dominance. "Get inside!"

Sasha hesitated, and Micah saw it: another figure emerging from the woods. Sasha made it to safety just as the creature scuttled toward them, already contorted beyond recognition and wailing Vivian's name.

They ran. Sasha grabbed Viv on the way down the steps, and they locked and barred the door while the creature howled on the other side of the barrier.

"Fuck," Micah whispered, stumbling to the bedroom. "Fuck. Viv. Viv, we need to kill that thing."

"We'll use the puppet spell," she said, then squeaked as Sasha grabbed her, dragging her to the bed. "Sasha!"

"Babe, I don't ever wanna see that shit again."

"It's okay. We'll kill it. We have … we have a spell." But even Micah could feel the hesitancy in her voice.

"That spell you made, with the door." Sasha spoke into Viv's chest, his voice muffled. "It'll hold up?"

"Of course." Viv tugged at his hair, and he looked at her. She kissed him softly. "Even I can't dispel it. Micah cast the spell, so he's the only one who can break it."

Sasha was quiet for a moment, brows lowered. "So that thing out there … we can't make it go away."

Viv looked stunned. "What?"

"It isn't your spell. Or Micah's. It's your mom's. What you just said—doesn't that mean she has to break it?"

Viv and Micah stared at each other as horror sank like a weight in Micah's belly. He hadn't thought of that. What if Sasha was right?

Viv took a shaky breath. "Well, we can't exactly convince *her* to help. We'll have to find a way on our own."

"But if that's how the magic works," Sasha said, but Viv interrupted him, stroking his hair.

"It doesn't matter. We have the three of us, and the book. We can do this on our own. It'll have to be enough."

* * *

Sasha Black was a lot of things.

He was a submissive, a masochist, and husband to two witches—or would be, soon enough. He was a brawler, a friend, a nephew, a son, an uncle. He was strong, and he'd won the log-flipping contest three years running before deciding to give someone else a chance at it. He wasn't the smartest person around—that was definitely his wife and his husband. But he was smart enough, and handy, and he could and would carry just about anything for anyone. And while he didn't win every one of his bouts, he always had a good time.

One thing he wasn't, was a liar.

He also wasn't a coward. Sasha would do anything for Viv—and Micah—and if they needed Daria's help to get rid of that *thing* that was trying to take Viv away ... then Sasha would make that happen.

He knew Viv wouldn't want him to go see her mother, much less ask her for help. But the more Sasha thought about it, the more he was convinced that the ritual they were planning wouldn't work unless Daria undid what she'd done. That thing in the woods—while it wasn't Daria, exactly, it was her fault it existed in the first place.

And Sasha believed in taking your responsibilities seriously. If you made a magic twig shadow person that wanted to eat your daughter, you fucking dealt with it when the time came. If Viv couldn't tell her mother that, that was fine. Sasha could.

And he *would*. He'd stood up for Viv before, in the pits, and even though no one challenged him, Sasha hadn't cared. He'd felt proud, standing there with his chin raised high. Now he would fight for Viv. For Micah. For the life they were making together.

The part where he'd have to lie to her and Micah, though, that part sucked. Sasha had always been a terrible liar. When he was little and he'd broken something—he broke a lot of things, especially before he'd gotten a handle on his strength—he never could blame someone else for his own accidents. Even when one of his cousins *tried* to take the blame, Sasha wouldn't let them.

But it was of the utmost importance that he tell a lie now, and do it well enough that the people who knew him best believed him. He waited until a few nights after their initial attempt at destroying the ... thing ... and found them poring over the magic book, cuddled up in blankets in front of the fire. The weather was rapidly turning colder, and winter wasn't far away. They needed to be able to gather supplies to see them through until spring, so Sasha knew he had to convince Viv's mom to show up and own up when they did the ritual.

I promised to fight for you, so I'm going to. It made it easier to tell the lie, thinking about it that way. That this was the fight he should have had in the ring, because Viv should have had a line of suitors challenging him for her.

"Hey, so, you guys seem to have this pretty much in hand," Sasha said, going for casual, bouncing a bit on his heels. "And when it's all done and we're rid of evil twig creatures, we'll need to make those rings."

Viv and Micah both smiled at him. Good. That was a good start. "We will," Viv said warmly, kissing Micah's hand. "That will be a much more enjoyable ritual to plan, I think."

Micah nodded, blushing. Aw, they were so cute. This was what he was going to protect.

"So, this ritual'll be pretty intense, yeah? And as fucking hot as that threesome was, I know you both need to keep your energy up, so I figured instead of whining to be beat up and fucked, I'd just go for the first and fight a few rounds tonight."

There. That sounded believable, didn't it?

"I don't want anyone to hurt you," Micah said, eyes narrowing. "Anyone other than us."

Oh, shit. Possessive dom Micah was hot as *fuck*. Sasha told himself to stay firm. "Aw, it ain't even close, boss. Promise. It's mostly me ducking a lot and shooting the shit with the others, and, you know, maybe winning a few supplies."

Micah glanced at Viv. "The thought of anyone else making him bleed isn't— I don't like it."

She patted him on the arm. "I know, but trust me, it's not

the same. It's good for him to work off some energy. You'll see. That first fight after winter, he's always so excited for it."

"Yeah, and this might be one of the last chances until then. 'Sides, boss, I gotta go brag about my hot new husband," Sasha added, making a note to do that the next time he really *did* go to the fighting pits. He wanted to brag about Micah. Who wouldn't?

"It's okay, if you want," Viv said. "Just don't be gone too late. We all need to conserve our energy, even though I know you have a lot of it." She gave Micah another reassuring smile. "It'll help him focus, and you know we're all going to need to do that, for this to work."

Micah sighed and nodded, and he looked abashed as he kissed Sasha goodbye. "I'm not trying to tell you not to do something you enjoy. I just feel ... like you're *ours* to hurt."

"I know, and I'm really into protective Micah, but I promise getting punched by Andrei isn't the same as you scratching the fuck out of me, yeah?" He gave Micah another kiss. "Nothing in the world could replace either of you."

Micah smiled and smoothed Sasha's hair back—it was slightly less wild, since Viv had recently subjected both him and Micah to haircuts. "Good luck, then. If that's what I should say."

"Thanks." Sasha grinned and hurried over to Viv, kissing her soundly. "I promise I won't lose anything important."

That, at least, was true. He was trying to get something *back*. Something Viv needed and couldn't ask for.

Sasha left the cave and headed toward the pits, just in case Micah came after him for some reason. Then he doubled back and made his way to Daria's door. He knocked, his posture as tense as if he really were about to fight someone.

It took a few more knocks before the door opened, and there was Daria. She did look like Viv, but a tired, wan version. Sasha felt some sympathy for her, since he knew what she'd gone through, but he remembered he was here to fight for Viv. Time for the handshake or whatever later, when this was over. Just like in the ring.

"What is it," she asked, though her tone held none of Viv's dominance. There was a slight note of panic in her voice when she said, "Is it—Vivian?"

"Yeah, kinda. She's fine," he added, and Daria wasn't fast enough to hide her flash of relief. "But I gotta talk to you. Can I come in?"

He half expected her to say no. But to his surprise, she nodded and stepped back to let him in.

The place where Viv had grown up wasn't nearly the luxurious spread they had now. But it was closer to other people— not that Daria really interacted much, as far as he could tell— and it looked homely enough. Quilts that resembled a few that Viv brought with her when they married. Wool and a spindle by the fire. And on the hearth, three trinkets that looked like children's toys, with dried flowers around them.

"One for each of them," Daria said when she caught Sasha looking. "My children."

There was a conspicuous blank space next to the crudely sewn stuffed rabbit, a ball made of leather, and a clay cup with initials marked on it. The blank space was for Viv. Sasha wondered what Daria was planning to put there, then made himself turn around and not think about it. It didn't matter, because there wouldn't be the need.

"I have to tell you something," Sasha began, then faltered. He'd thought so hard about how to convince Viv and Micah that was leaving to do something that wasn't this that he hadn't worked out what to say to Daria. "It's about the thing that wants Viv."

Daria's expression was Viv's at her most inscrutable, and as much as Sasha wanted to sound firm, it was hard to make the words come out right.

"You did something," he said. "To try to help her. I think that's what you were doing, anyway, but it didn't work. You're a witch, aren't you?"

Daria turned away, but she didn't say no, so Sasha kept pushing.

"They know what it is, Viv and Micah. Micah's our husband," Sasha added proudly. "He's a witch, too, like Viv. From the village. He makes toys. And he's smart, like Viv. She's so smart, you know. She can figure anything out—"

"Say what you came here to say," Daria said tightly. Her hands were clenched into fists.

"I came here to say that if you want to ever know her, the great, amazing, talented woman that she is? If you want to have any kind of relationship with her—"

"She's *dying*, don't you understand that?" Daria whirled on him, her eyes, so like Viv's, bright with furious tears. "No matter what you and your witch husband try to do, she's going to die, and I'll put her token up on the mantel and that will be the end of it. "

"We're all gonna die," Sasha said. "Someday. But Viv ain't goin' anytime soon, not if me and Micah have anything to say about it. He's making her a chair with wheels, so she can move around when she's feeling bad. He makes her witchy drinks. I'll fight the world for her. She's not dying. She just gets sick sometimes."

"You are a fool, and you know nothing," Daria whispered. "Go have your time with her. This is all I can do."

"No, it ain't," Sasha tried to gentle his voice. Maybe that would help. "The thing that's after her, the—the shadow thing? It's you."

Daria froze, and then her face crumpled and she started to

cry. She covered her face with her hands, and Sasha heard one loud sob before she choked out, "I know."

Sasha nodded. He'd figured she did. "I think you pushed Viv away because you were afraid of how much it would hurt to lose her, like it did with your other children. Micah, our husband, he thought it would be better to leave, too. Before he got too used to being with us."

Daria didn't say anything, but she was looking at him now, so that was something. Sasha barreled on, as he always did, even when the chance of success looked dim. "Viv told me we couldn't make him stay. We could tell him we love him, we could show him, we could—uh. Show him, yeah. But it was up to him. He had to choose it. And he did."

"What does that—"

"No, listen," Sasha interrupted. "That's the key, you know. Choice. Choosing something. It ain't easy to say you're sorry, but sometimes, it ain't easy admitting you want something, either. 'Cause some people, when they want something, it just gets taken away. Like you, your children."

Daria winced, and Sasha continued, relentless. "You gotta choose to help her, Daria. If you want her to know you, if you want to know *her*, that's what you gotta do. Maybe one day the fever gets her, takes her before she's a cranky old lady ordering whippersnappers to beat me up or whatever, but ... that's not anyone's choice but Death, I guess, when he comes for her."

"He's been trying," she said. "If I could have made her better, I would have. I would have made them all better. I should have them here, but I have nothing. There is no choice I can make, not anymore. Go away."

"No. Because this is worth it. Viv's worth it. She thinks you hate her, you know. Or that you resent her. It's kinda the same thing, after a while. I don't think you want that."

"You don't understand anything. I do want that. If she hates me, she won't ... she won't let me in. She can have more time." Daria was crying again. "I want you to leave."

"I will, but let me tell you why I'm here. On the new moon, we're gonna do a ritual, right outside our house. You know where that is. Right, so, we're gonna call that thing, the shadow creature. Micah and Viv think they can fight it, destroy it. But I know, and you know, that won't work. The only person who can face it, who can get rid of it, is you."

Daria turned from him, staring at the hearth, the mementos for the dead. "I can't."

Sasha raked a hand through his hair. It turned out, fights you could win with your fists were much easier. "You have to. You made this thing to keep her safe. I get it. To keep them all safe. And it didn't work, and I'm sorry, because you lost them and that's awful. I can't even imagine."

"No," Daria said. "You can't."

"But I know Viv, yeah? This awesome daughter you have. She's a fighter. She's full of dominance and smarts and spite, and she ain't gonna go down without slinging everything she's got at this thing that wants her. You should be proud of her."

"I am proud of her," Daria whispered. "That's why she has to keep hating me. Keep living. Keep the door closed."

Sasha sort of wanted to hug the woman, even though she'd probably throw a punch. "You have to be there. You have to undo what you did. If not for you, do it for her. You love her. I know you do."

"I— It's too late. It's been too late for years, and I can't—I can't take it back."

"That ain't what I'm sayin', Daria. Of course you can't take it back, but you gotta try to fix it. What you did. And you can start by helping her."

"Doing one thing isn't going to fix it," Daria told him, not bothering to wipe her eyes. But oh, she looked— There was something so sweetly, achingly desperate in her expression, as if she wanted to believe that she *could* fix what she'd done.

Sasha nodded. "No. But one thing can lead to ... another thing. You can't change the past, but you can change the future. You could have one, with Viv. Come with me. Talk to her. Hear what they have planned, and—"

Daria was shaking her head before Sasha could finish. "I want to, but I'm—I'm too— I know what it is, that thing in the dark. I would give it myself if I could. I have tried to, begged on my knees for it take me instead—"

"It ain't *about* that," Sasha said, in a voice far too loud for the indoors. He didn't feel bad about it, though. She needed to hear this. "It ain't about you, Daria. It's about Viv. If you want a daughter who, yeah, gets sick a few times a year but knows how to live her life and take care of herself, who has people who love her more than the *fucking* moon or whatever people say, then you step up. I stood in the ring for her, you know. Not a single person challenged me. But I'd fight everyone, anywhere. You should fight, too. Come fight this with us, and maybe you can be in her life. Maybe not. But at least you can try. She's worth that. You know she is."

There was a second where Sasha thought maybe she'd say yes, let his impassioned speech sway her to go back with him right now to figure this out. But he saw the moment she shut down, the moment she lost her courage and gave up.

"I can't. Tell her to ignore it. Bar your door, don't listen when it speaks, and never let it in. And, Sasha? Never come here again. Tell her that, and your witch man, too. This door is forever barred to you, and you are not welcome."

It was what you said in the Compound when you disavowed someone. But Sasha didn't care. Instead, he drew himself up to his full height and put his hands on his hips. He wasn't a dominant, but he was a man who loved someone who needed their mother. "Fight for your daughter, Daria. Fight like I will. Fight like Micah does. Fight like *she* does. New moon, at the clearing, near midnight. End this for her, and see if you can't find something else to put on that mantel. Stop living in the fucking past, and own up to what you did. If you can't, you'll lose her. I promise you that."

"I lost her a long time ago, Sasha Black," Daria said, voice empty and vague. "And there's nothing I can do now but leave her be. Maybe one day you'll understand that, or she will."

"You're wrong. I'll leave now, but you be there at the new moon. Show up for her. Even if it doesn't work, you'll have done that. No one fought me that day in the ring, but Viv married me anyway. Sometimes, showin' up is what matters. Do the right thing. It's the only chance you're ever gonna have."

With that, Sasha turned and left. Daria said nothing, but he could feel her eyes on him all the way to the door, and when he closed it behind him, he thought he heard the sound of something breaking against the wood.

Then Sasha headed for the fighting pits. Maybe someone would want to go a round or two, because he couldn't go home like this. He had to work some of his frustration out, the adrenaline rush and the disappointment that maybe Viv had been right all along and her mother really had decided she didn't matter.

But every time he pictured Daria's face, the trinkets on the hearth ... he became more certain that wasn't the case at all, and that Daria's problem wasn't that she didn't care, but the opposite. She cared so much she thought the only way to save her daughter was to make her hate her, so the dark shadow couldn't take her away. It wasn't the way Sasha would do it, or Viv, or Micah. It was something that only made sense to someone lost in pain—that instead of confronting and conquering the terrible thing she'd made, Daria would try to make Viv hate her so she'd never open the door to her mother's voice.

In Sasha's experience, hate never made anything better. All it did was make more shadows, create more monsters in the dark. It was time for this to end, for the sun to come out and chase all those monsters away for good.

Chapter Thirteen

The new moon used to be exciting for Viv. When she was first learning magic, she kept a chart of the moon's phases, which she followed through the vent in the living room ceiling. She learned that some spells—those for fertility or harvest—were reversed if she cast them on the new moon, while illusions always felt stronger and light was easier to conjure. She would make herself midnight dinners and sit in her room with rows and rows of spell ingredients, testing each one. After she married Sasha, he used to stay up with her, cooking supper for both of them and then sitting with her while she worked.

Now the sight of the waning moon made her stomach clench, and she woke up in the night, going over the components of the spell she and Micah had planned. Sometimes the thing from the woods would come to the door and she could hear it crooning her name. When that happened, she would get up and go to her loom, where Sasha and Micah would find her in the morning.

On the morning of the new moon, Viv finished stitching the new coat she'd made for Micah. It was black at the shoulders, but it gradually bled blue, and she'd sewn glass beads into the hem and sleeves. When Micah put it on, he sparkled like a night sky, and Viv leaned back to admire the picture he made. He was still scrawny, like the lanky forest spirit he resembled when they first met, but he was brighter now, happier, quicker to smile. It was like uncovering an abandoned cup and polishing it to a shine, only to find it was something else—a crown or a bangle. Something beautiful that had always been there, hidden away.

Sasha had his own coat, which was red with gold accents, with leather patches on the shoulders. He and Micah moved quietly around the kitchen as Viv buckled her own cloak over a flower-patterned dress. None of them looked like they were preparing for a midnight ritual—more like a walk in a cave garden, where plants crawled over the domed lights and vents that kept them alive.

The last component of their spell was still cooling in the kiln, but around dinnertime, Micah got up and came back with it: a doll made of clay, faceless and featureless, its limbs connected by string. He set it down on the table, and Sasha stared at it like it was going to jump off and start rattling toward the door.

"What's the point of the creepy doll, again?" he asked.

"It's a simulacrum," Viv said. "To make our own shadow selves—controlled ones—that can bring the shadow thing here and fight it, we're supposed to ... touch the doll and tell it something true about ourselves."

"Something unpleasant," Micah added. "I mean, the truth is, sometimes."

"Not always." Sasha gestured to Viv and Micah. "I can say lots of true things about both of you that are pleasant as fuck."

"Yeah, but this is a shadow," Micah said. "Shadows are for things we'd rather hide."

They all looked at the doll in silence. Viv wondered how her mother had done it. *When* she'd done it. She knew the headman had turned her away, and it wasn't like her husband supported her. She'd probably cast the spell alone. With no one who could keep her honest, or protect her, or care if it all went wrong.

Then she'd left Viv to fend for herself. She hadn't warned her. She hadn't prepared her. Viv had to figure everything out on her own.

But not anymore.

Micah picked up the doll, and Sasha gathered the candles in their stone holders. Viv pocketed bags of salt—a last resort, in case Micah's spell failed and they had to make a run for it. Then they climbed the steps to the door and went outside.

It was a windy night. The trees in the woods beyond the field creaked and groaned, and the sound of their branches rustling made Viv think of the sea, waves rising and falling as they beat against the shore. Sasha looked around as if he was expecting the thing to already be there, then set the candles down in a line a few paces away.

Micah lit the candles. They sputtered and flickered but didn't go out, and Viv shivered as Micah set the faceless doll on the grass in front of them. Beyond the candles, just a few paces away, was the spell-door. "Remember," he said. "Tell it the truth."

"I don't have magic, though," Sasha said. "You're sure I should be part of this, boss?"

"Yeah. It'll work as long as one of us goes first."

Sasha didn't look so certain. He kept looking toward the magical barrier, and Viv pulled her cloak tighter around her shoulders. If this didn't work, she wasn't sure what she'd do. She couldn't let that thing keep her from going out at night. It couldn't paw at the door every time she fell sick. But she felt like Sasha had been right—maybe it needed something Viv couldn't provide.

It was no good dwelling on what might happen, though. Viv went to Micah, who was watching the doll, and urged him around to face her. "Can't stop thinking, either, can you?"

"Not a chance," Micah said, smiling as she wrapped her arms around his neck. His smile disappeared quickly, but it remained in the way he took her waist in his hands, rocking as though they were dancing. He looked like he was humming, but Viv could only hear the whistle of the wind and the roar of the trees.

"We should get married both ways, I think," he said. "Sasha can offer to punch people—even if I'm still not sure about that—and we can have rings, and then we can go to Dragan and make our vows."

"According to your rules, you should've done that when you kissed us the first time," Viv pointed out.

Micah shrugged. "We're witches. We make our own rules." He leaned down for a kiss, as if to punctuate the sentiment. "I know it's weird, because there's a thing out there that wants to kill you, and we're about to do this ritual we've never tried before, but I'm happy. I'm glad to be here with you, Viv."

"And I'm glad you're here, Micah."

"Micah Black," he said, and Viv raised her brows as Sasha turned from his vigil by the door. "I'm still Fire-Keeper in the village. It was my great-grandmother's name, and I'll always cherish it. But I'm here, too, and with you ... with both of you ... I think I'd like to be a Black."

"Nan's gonna cry," Sasha said, and Viv squeaked as he crushed them both in his massive embrace. Micah looked at her from where his face was pressed to Sasha's chest, and they all laughed.

Then they heard the voice.

"Vivian?"

Viv shivered. Sasha let her down, and she smoothed out her

hair, bracing herself for the contorted, inhuman creature—only to see her mother standing on the other side of the magical door, one hand on the barrier.

She wasn't the shadow. She didn't move like it, too fluid or too jerky by degrees, and her face wasn't smooth and unwrinkled. When she opened her mouth to speak, there wasn't a black pit inside, and her eyes were sad, wary.

"Mom."

"This is a powerful spell," her mother said, running her hand over the barrier. "I doubt I could force my way in."

"What are you … What are you doing here?"

Sasha shifted on his feet. "Viv. Babe. I asked her." Viv whirled on him, hurt stinging in her chest, and Sasha took her hands. "I know you're mad. I'm sorry. I knew we needed her help, and I knew she would just hurt you if you went to her. So I went."

Viv took a deep breath. She didn't like that Sasha had talked to her mother without her. But he'd only done it out of necessity. She couldn't hold it against him, not when she'd probably have done the same in his shoes. "All right."

"I might … need to be let in," her mother said, and Viv looked at Micah, who was frowning, teeth worrying at his lower lip.

"Go ahead," she told him, and Micah nodded.

"You can come in once," Micah said, and Daria stepped through the door. Viv braced herself, panic rising—what if she was wrong, and the thing had taken another form? But it was still her mother standing in the grass, looking at them like a hunted deer before the bow.

"I don't know what I can do," she said softly. Viv suppressed the urge to shout, *Anything, anything is better than the nothing you've given me before.* But it was Micah who spoke, stepping forward to kneel before the doll.

"We're calling it here," he said, and Daria flinched when Micah placed a hand on the doll. "You know what this is."

"That's dangerous," Daria said. "You can ... you can call something you can't send back."

"Only if we lie." Daria winced again, and Micah looked at Viv. "It's midnight. I think we can start now. Do you want to, or should I?"

"I will." Viv stepped away from Sasha and knelt in front of the doll. She placed both hands on it, feeling the smooth clay under her fingers. "My name is Vivian Black."

The doll twitched under her hands, and the wind picked up, making the candles flicker.

"I let myself think my sickness was a death sentence," Viv said slowly. This was the hard part, the part she never said aloud. "But it isn't, though there isn't an easy answer. I'm going to have to ask for help, even if it makes me feel weak to do it." She glanced at her mom when she said the last part, but Daria was staring at the woods, her arms wrapped around herself. "And I'm angry. It's easier to be angry than to confront why I'm hurting. To admit that I'm still that kid, sometimes, who just wanted my mom to love me."

Daria's hands tightened on her arms, and a wind moved outward from Viv, racing over the grass. When it passed the door, it rose into the shadowy shape of a woman Viv's height, standing straight and still.

Viv moved out of the way, still kneeling, and Sasha got down on his knees next to her. He touched the doll, and it shivered, limbs rattling.

"I guess there are some fights I can't win," he said. "Doesn't mean I shouldn't try anyway. I'm not as brave as Micah and Viv. Sometimes I think if I don't get in the ring, then I can't lose. But I can. And that's fucking terrifying."

Again, a wind made the candles sputter, and it formed into the shape of a man who looked vaguely like Sasha.

"Fuck," Sasha said softly. "Even my shadow's hot."

"Oh my gods, not the time," Viv whispered, reaching for his hand. She knew what it took to say the unpleasant part aloud, in front of everyone. For Sasha, who just wanted people to be happy, that was probably harder than the rest.

Micah knelt next to Sasha and touched the doll. It trembled. "Okay. Okay. I'm not broken. But I ... listened to my parents. I believed them, even when I thought I didn't. I hid from other people, and I hid from myself. I hated the part of me that's not like everyone else, because their voices became my voice. Sometimes I might still think like that. Sometimes I might forget and think I'm not enough."

"But you are," Sasha said, and Micah glanced at him, that lovely smile flashing across his face even as the doll twitched and the wind blew, coalescing outside the barrier to make a shadow Micah.

"Mom," Viv said. Daria looked away. "Mom, it's your turn."

"I shouldn't have come," Daria whispered, and Viv boiled with anger that even now, even at the last hour, her mother would rather wallow in silence.

"Fine. We'll do it ourselves." Viv looked at Micah, and Micah raised the doll. All three shadow figures looked toward them, and Micah swallowed.

"Go find the thing that wants Vivian," he said, "and bring it to the door."

The shadows drifted away toward the forest, blending with the dark until Viv couldn't see them anymore. For a long minute, nothing moved—even the wind had died, leaving them in an unsettling silence—but then there was a flicker, and a lump of shadow writhed across the grass, coming closer. Daria took several steps back.

It was as though the shadows they'd summoned were fighting a wolf. The shadow creature howled and twisted, clawing and biting, and the shadows fought back, their darkness writhing over a lump of bracken and twigs shaped like a woman. Their own shadows weren't made of stone, twig, or moss; they could move fluidly, swiftly, adaptable and powerful. Viv wondered what would have happened if any of them tried to hide the truth during the ritual. If their shadows would have tried to make themselves bodies, like this one had, and turned their weaknesses, their desires, into something terrible.

Viv watched her shadow drag at the creature's mossy hair. The creature tried to wrench free, but it was beset on all sides. Sasha's was too strong for the creature to escape, Micah's too quick, Viv's too vicious. But just as a spark of hope kindled in Viv—they'd done it, even without Daria's help—Micah cried out, and his shadow sank to the ground and slid back into him. Viv's broke next, creeping over the grass and into her skin like a rush of cool air, and then only Sasha's was left, furiously pummeling the creature just outside the barrier.

For a second, it looked as if Sasha's shadow might win. But then the creature rent at it with its teeth, and Sasha swayed as his shadow returned to him. They all knelt there, panting, as the creature scrabbled at the barrier.

"It wasn't enough," Micah said. "We need to ... need to do it again."

"We can't. The shadows are already spent." Viv felt desperate, panicked, the way she did when she shivered in her sweaty nightgown, wondering if this time the fever might not break.

"You need to do it," Sasha said, and Viv looked up to find him facing her mother.

Daria's face was pale. Her hair hung limp over her shoulders, and she was scratching pink lines over her arms as the thing on the other side of the door shrieked, its mouth like a bottomless hole.

"I can't," she whispered.

"You have to." Sasha's voice was harsh. Sharp. "This is what Viv sees when she's sick. What Micah sees when people treat him wrong. It's what Viv's lived with her whole fucking life. You did this to her. This is what it looks like."

Viv stared at him, shocked by his vehemence. Sasha had always been the best at knowing people—he'd seen into her heart from the beginning, breaking through all her defenses. And he loved her. If she'd ever wanted proof, it was in this: his eyes bright, his voice booming over the creature's shriek, one hand holding hers.

Daria gazed at the creature, which gibbered as it tried to dig a hole under the door.

"I don't need a doll." Her voice was small. "I already made my shadow."

She took a step forward, and Viv, despite herself, tried to get up to stop her.

"I thought a child would save my marriage," Daria said. "I always wanted one, and I thought my husband would see why once the baby was born. But he had the same sickness my aunt had, and it killed him. My boy. He wasn't even old enough to smile."

The creature hissed and flung itself against the door, and Daria took another shaky step.

"I thought I could protect the next one. So I made a spell. My aunt had told me not to use it unless I needed to, and I thought ... didn't I need it? My husband wouldn't help. He thought I was foolish to want another child so soon. So I made a shadow. I told it to protect my baby. To keep her from harm. And it ... it killed her." She was crying, still grabbing at her arms. "My third opened the door to it when he heard my voice. So

I ..." She turned to look at Viv. "I decided you were already dead. When you were sick, I prayed it would just ... I prayed the fever would take you, because the shadow was worse. I was probably the one who made you think your sickness would kill you. I treated you like you were a ghost. And when you were older, I was too afraid to admit what I'd done. All I wanted was a family, and now I've lost every one of you. But you're still alive."

Viv reached for Micah with her free hand, and he squeezed her fingers. She didn't know how to feel. Daria's truth was tragic, and terrible, and heartbreaking—but her own hurt was still there, and knowing *why* wasn't enough to heal the wounds inside her that had formed every time her mother turned her aside.

But it didn't look as if her mother was asking for forgiveness. She walked through the door and grabbed the shadow creature by the arms. It turned its gaping maw toward her and started climbing onto her, raking bloody lines into her skin.

Viv tried to stand, and Micah wrapped his arms around her to keep her at his side. "You can't. It'll kill you."

"She knows what she's doing," Sasha said, holding her by the waist. Viv watched, trapped in a rush of terror, as her mother clung to the shadow creature. It howled and shrieked, spat and babbled, tearing at Daria's hair, dragging them both to the ground. But Daria held on, even when it tried to writhe out of her grip, even when it cried the names of Viv's siblings, even when it burst into broken, wrenching sobs. She hunched over it, and the wind whirled around her like a cyclone, whipping at her hair and her gown. Sasha turned to shield Micah and Viv from the storm, and they huddled together as, one by one, the candles behind them went out.

When the wind finally died down, a single figure lay in the grass before the door. Daria's face was covered in dirt and scratch marks, and her clothes were a ruin, but when Viv approached, her eyes flickered open. "Vivian?"

Viv looked down at her through the barrier. "Is that you in there?"

"Yes." Daria groaned, sitting up. "All of me."

Viv let out a breath. "Then you should know most people call me Viv."

Daria looked up at her. Viv understood that things would never be perfect. She would never have the mother she dreamt of as a girl. But there was something to be said for sharing the darkest piece of yourself with each other, and if they couldn't be the kind of family they'd wanted, maybe they could be … something else. Something different but nonetheless good.

"Hello, Viv," Daria said.

Viv reached through the doorway, holding out her hand. "Hi, Daria. It's too dark to walk home, and my husband made a pie that's supposed to help you sleep. So you might as well come in."

Daria took Viv's hand. Viv pulled her through the door, shadow and all, and turned to introduce her to her family.

Chapter Fourteen

Snow fell over the kiln in the center of what used to be Micah's house, covering the ashes and browning leaves that carpeted the ruins. Micah brushed some leaves aside, revealing the mark of a disk he'd made before the fire swept through the house, a perfect oval in a mess of blackened stone.

"Weird to think you used to live here," Sasha said.

Micah smiled, thinking of Sasha bursting through the wall to save his great-grandmother's book. "You get used to it. Then you forget you could have anything else."

Viv, who was sitting on a fallen tree with a red shawl around her shoulders, gave Micah a knowing look.

They almost hadn't come. Micah had dismantled the door spell, and he and Viv had slept for the better part of a day. Viv said bigger workings could do that, but Micah thought it was the emotional strain as well. Having Viv's mother over, even for a night, had been exhausting.

She'd left the next morning, but she and Viv had set up a truce. They were writing each other, since they couldn't talk face-to-face without it getting too awkward. But while her mother's first two letters made Viv moody and disgruntled, she said it was what Daria could manage. It would do.

It felt like they'd barely had time to process what had happened that night. Viv couldn't sleep alone—Micah learned that when she got up from a nap, grabbed him, and dragged him back with her so she could drift off curled around him. Sasha tended to twitch at shadows, and Micah couldn't look at the place where the magical door had been without shivering. But they had each other, and the world moved on.

The last leaves were still clinging to the trees when Micah said he wanted to go to the village to declare themselves mates in front of Dragan. Sasha was setting up a fight to claim Micah as his husband in the Compound—apparently Timon, who'd decided Micah was going to marry *him* when he grew up, offered to challenge Sasha before he was informed it was against the rules. He'd written Micah an outraged letter about it, and Sasha had howled with laughter.

"We should make another kiln," Sasha said, poking around in the ashes. "Now that everyone knows there's a toymaker nearby. I got three more kids asking for dragons."

"Dragons aren't even my best," Micah protested. Viv snorted.

"Too late. Now everyone wants scales."

It seemed like they received a new request from kids in the Compound every week. Some even left presents for him, candies or carved wooden utensils or pretty stones from the beach. It was a new feeling, being able to hear from a child how much they loved their toy, and Micah was using the kiln almost daily now.

Sasha let out a triumphant cry and pulled something out of the ashes—a lump of metallic ore Micah had used to make a cat that purred when you shook it. He took the metal from

Sasha and held it to the light. It was bluish black and still polished.

"We could make our rings out of this," he said, and Viv leaned in to look.

"That'd be nice."

"Rings from the fire that brought you to us?" Sasha grinned. "All right, boss. Sounds like magic shit to me."

"Probably is." Micah wrapped the metal in a cloth and slipped it into his bag. "You all up for a walk?"

"Oh, am I ever," Viv said, rolling her eyes. Her chair was still a pile of pieces in the living room, but they were taking the journey slowly, which meant they'd probably have to sleep at Zev's place that night. Micah didn't mind.

They followed the old lines he had set up in the woods, a complex system of shells, bells, and rocks meant to alert him to visitors. They passed the box where Dragan and Zev used to leave him supplies and reached the cottage closest to the woods, where a woman was patching a chimney with her wife looking on.

"It's strange, but the village still feels familiar," Micah said, holding Viv's hand as Sasha tried to scrape together enough snow to form a ball. Sasha threw it, and it scattered, spraying snow and bits of ice. "Even that. They used to have snowball fights with the kids before the winter storms hit. I tended to sit them out."

"Oh, man, we gotta do that," Sasha said, just as Viv said, "I don't blame you."

Micah grinned at them and took a breath as Dragan's house came into view, along with the fire pit where most of the village tended to gather. Micah slowed as they approached, but the only person he saw was Zev, who was walking toward the house with his hands in his pockets. He stopped and waved when he saw them.

"Hey! You all know it's almost winter, right?"

"Is it?" Viv asked. "Tell me more."

Zev pulled a face at her, and Viv pulled one back. Then he strode over to lift her in a hug. "Good to see you, witch girl."

"You're still looking happy, wolf boy."

Zev howled softly and winked at Sasha. Then he nodded to Micah. "Good to see you, too. Uh. Any reason you're here, or ..."

"He wants to marry us," Sasha said. "*Three times.*"

Zev looked like he wasn't sure whether to laugh or not. "Three?"

"Yeah, we're that hot. Once in the fighting pits, once with rings, and then here. He says you cut your hand and shit? That's badass."

This time, Zev did laugh. "I feel like I have some catching up to do. But good for you. Really. Dragan's home—I bet we could do it now."

Micah tried not to let his nervousness show as they walked up the hill to Dragan and Zev's house. His memories of the village weren't altogether pleasant, but that was why he was here, wasn't it? To make a new memory. Something on his terms. He straightened his shoulders and picked up the pace, and when Dragan opened the door, Micah's heart only pounded a little.

"Brought some new mates for a ceremony," Zev said, and Dragan grinned.

"Fire-Keeper? You picked a handful."

Micah blushed. "I have two hands."

Dragan's eyes twinkled. "I see that. Come in, then."

Inside, there were big cushions in front of the fire, where three wolves were currently lounging. They looked like they were caught between wanting to check out the newcomers and wanting to stay warm, but the fire inevitably won out. They followed Micah with their gaze as Micah stopped in front of the dais where mating ceremonies were held.

Dragan brought out the knife, and Micah took it, pressing the edge of the blade into his palm. "I don't need fancy words. You know how I feel. What I am to you. What you are to me."

Sasha took the knife. "Keep it shallow," Viv warned, and Sasha winked at her as he cut his palm.

"I'll fight the fucking world for you if I have to," he said, and that, for Micah, was more than enough.

Viv took the knife, sighed, and pressed it to her palm. "Since I'm supposed to say something here, I'll just make it clear that these two are *mine*, and no one else can have them."

"They wouldn't dare, baby," Sasha said.

"He's right," Micah added and kissed them both.

Dragan invited them to stay the night, and after Zev, looking delighted, bandaged them up, Micah found himself seated between Sasha and Viv, unable to stop smiling. Dragan kept giving him curious looks, but it wasn't until dinner was over that he asked.

"Zev told me a little," he said as Zev wrestled with the wolves and Sasha inched closer, clearly wanting in on the sport, "but I feel like there's more to this than he's letting on."

"This?" Viv said, all innocence. Dragan gave her a stern look, which of course had no effect.

"You three," he said, gesturing. "I have a feeling this is a story I need to hear."

Micah blushed, but it was Sasha who spoke up, slinging an arm around Micah's shoulders.

"Sure thing, buddy," he said, and Micah grinned. Only Sasha would call Dragan *buddy*. "But it's pretty wild. Where should I begin? The shadow creature?"

"Shadow creature?" Dragan asked, brows raised.

"Probably not," Viv said. "Start with the witch book."

Dragan's brows rose higher still.

"No, start with Viv," Micah said.

Sasha held his hands up for silence, and remarkably, everyone listened. "I know how to start." He cleared his throat. "Once upon a time, a witch and her husband found a hot toymaker in the woods ..."

Epilogue

S *pring*

Winter fell away gradually, the dark days giving way to more light and less-cold afternoons, and it was one such afternoon that Viv gathered her lap loom and a satchel of wool and thread and fastened her cloak around her shoulders. She headed from the bedroom into the main living area, patting her new chair with the wheels on her way.

Micah had worked feverishly on the chair for the better part of two weeks, barely sleeping or eating until it was finished, despite Sasha's continual nagging that he do both. When the fever came and left her weak and gasping, the relief of being able to propel herself with her hands and not rely on someone to carry her was overwhelming. Micah's smile when she used it for the first time was bright as the sun, and Viv had nearly wept on him that night. Giving her back something that the illness took was indescribable, and Micah had held her close and whispered,

"That's what you and Sasha do for me, you know. When it gets bad in my head, you don't try to fix me. You just help me find my way back."

Thanks to the chair, Micah's "witch drinks," and Sasha's eternal optimism, while her illness had been difficult—it always was, in winter, when getting warm was even more of a challenge—it hadn't lingered as long as usual. Being able to use the chair to get around helped restore her good mood, which, she was convinced, had aided her recovery. She would never be "better"—never have the sort of good health that Sasha had—but this was something she could navigate, live with. Fight, in her own way. And having two husbands doting on her certainly didn't hurt. Even when she was cranky about needing it, deep down their love and concern always helped.

She found Micah standing by the stove, hair tied back in a ponytail and elbow-deep in an earthenware bowl he'd made that winter. They had a whole new set of dishes and bowls, since Micah had had so much time with the kiln.

"Hi," he said with a soft smile. "You need anything? Feeling all right?"

She nodded. "Yes. I thought I'd go sit in the sun for a bit. I'm feeling stronger. I thought I'd walk today."

"If you're sure," he said, kneading the dough, his powerful shoulders shifting under the simple shirt he was wearing. He'd put on some weight over the winter, and it looked good on him, though his face retained its angular lines and hadn't softened much at all. Neither had his arms, which she and Sasha appreciated.

"I am." She kissed him. "What kind of bread is that?"

"Just herbs. Your mother is still coming over, isn't she?" Micah asked, blowing a loose strand of hair out of his face.

Viv nodded. "As far as I know. I'll be back soon."

Micah smiled again and went back to his bread. He was

humming, a habit she'd never noticed until winter sent them inside to their various and sundry activities. Micah hummed, and Sasha talked. Thinking about the silence of the deep woods, of how she had felt that night in the ritual circle, Viv didn't mind the noise. Far from it.

It was sunny, and she took a deep breath, inhaling the scent of outdoor fires and *nature*. Winter was hard on everyone, but they were Lukoi, and this was what gave them the spite to keep surviving despite the dark and the cold. The snow melted, and the sun came back, and Lukos teemed with life and color. It was probably too obvious a metaphor, but Viv couldn't help it.

This time, when she fell ill during the winter, she hadn't spent her time simply imagining the sun, the flowers blooming in the meadows, the blossoms on the trees. She'd thought of them, certainly, but she'd thought about doing this: walking outside, breathing the fresh air, seeing the flowers herself.

Sasha was singing while he chopped wood, and Viv took a moment to admire him. He was standing in a patch of sunlight, shirtless, swinging the axe in time with his—very terrible—song.

"Oh, and that's the one, my favorite, she might have been the runt but god*damn* she has the sweetest cu—"

"Sasha!" Viv called. "What is that song?"

"Dunno, baby, I made it up. Why?" He rested the axe on his shoulder, looking so beautiful with his eternally messy black hair and gray eyes, his powerful chest and skin gleaming with sweat. Now that her strength was returning, she'd like to do more in bed than watch Micah wreck him into a sobbing mess. She wanted to make him sob, too. "Where you goin'?"

"Just for a walk. I thought I'd do some weaving." She held up her bag and smiled. "Don't forget my mother is coming for dinner. Micah's baking. Don't track mud into the house."

"Boots off, yeah, yeah. Boss gives me that *look* if I forget."

Viv raised her brows. "That is not a deterrent, for you."

"Well, then he won't spank me later, so, yeah. Real confusing, being me."

She shook her head fondly and went over to kiss him. He was warm, as always, skin hot to the touch as she went up on her tiptoes.

"Feeling up to it, right? Tonight, I mean. We can make it another time, if you're not."

"I'm fine," she assured him. "Really. I want to do this." She did, even if it was still a bit scary.

They'd started with Sasha's family, as it was a less stressful way for Micah to have new people in his space (even if those new people could be very loud). Sometimes he would need to excuse himself and go to the work room, but no one minded ... especially as he usually reappeared with new toys for the kids before they left.

Viv and her mother was ... a quieter affair. The first two times they'd planned to do it that spring, Viv had canceled: once because of her illness, and once because she was dreading it too much and Sasha told her, "You don't have to do this until you're ready. It's okay if you're not." It was the same thing they told Micah about family dinners with Sasha's brood, so it would be hypocritical of her to protest.

She and her mother had written letters to each other over the winter, though, and Viv had not held back in them. She was honest about her grief, the pain of loss, how it felt to cry in her bed at night because she thought her mother didn't love her. She didn't censor her anger, either, making it clear how furious she was that Sasha had to talk Daria into coming to the ritual circle that night.

Her mother's return letters were equally honest. She'd written about her own grief, losing her husband and children, her desperation to save Viv's life even if it cost her the love of her surviving child. It didn't eradicate the years of pain, but it helped, some, to know her mother's perspective. Even if it was hard to read it, sometimes, and the letters made her need to rake Sasha's back with her nails. Luckily, he never minded that.

They'd had two or three dinners by now, and it was ... awkward, with none of the exuberance of the ones with Sasha's family. But they were trying, and Viv kept all the letters from her mother, wrapped in a ribbon and tucked away in a box. She would probably read them again, at some point. She wondered if Daria kept *her* letters, too, but wasn't at a point where she could ask.

Viv found a sunny spot and spread out a blanket. The sun glinted off her wedding ring, lovingly made by Micah from the blue-black metal they'd found in his old cabin. She rubbed her thumb around it as she assembled her weaving materials: thick wool, fine thread, thicker yarn. The loom was warped and ready to go, and she picked up the tapestry needle, a long, flat piece of wood with a hole in the middle for the fibers. Another one of Micah's creations, it was easier for her to manage than the smaller needle when she was recovering from one of her fevers and wanted something to do with her hands.

She threaded the needle and got to work, occasionally glancing down to make sure the tension was even and the warp threads weren't pulling free. Micah had also improved her lap loom with notches on the top so the warping was less frustrating. Simple things like that made her life so much easier, and she wondered if he knew how much she appreciated it. How much it meant to be able to weave when she was tired, to still make something beautiful.

Then she would see him staring at her or Sasha, the way he would rub his own ring or the scar on his hand, and figured he probably did understand.

The sun was warm on her face as she let herself fall into the rhythm of weaving. She could hear the faint sound of Sasha's axe—and his horrible singing—but let that awareness drift into the background as she worked. It was a simple project. A wall hanging, one she wanted to put up in the bedroom she shared with her husbands.

She looked down, watching the colors come together, the different fabrics intertwining in the warp threads. She wove the bottom first, earthy shades to represent the ground in autumn. Black came after, thick threads to show brambles and dead trees and despair. And then came the beautiful light blue, dyed just for her by Sasha's grandmother, and pinks and oranges, and a soft yellow that made her smile and think of Micah's hair, with a soft gray on the edges for Sasha's eyes. Then there was a bright, vibrant blue, all the way to the end of the frame.

It seemed like it only took an hour or so, but by the time she drew the tapestry needle through the last row of warp threads, she was surprised to find she was shivering. The sun was setting, turning the sky brilliant colors that looked something like her weaving, but not quite. Her colors were softer, somehow.

Sasha found her a few minutes after she finished snipping the loose threads and weaving them into the back of the tapestry.

"Hey, beautiful, ready to head home? I've gotta clean off, and then maybe someone should give me a blow job, since I cut all this wood like a fucking badass ... Whatcha make this time?" Sasha held out a hand, and she took it, letting him pull her to her feet. He slid an arm around her waist, smelling like—well, sweat, mostly—and peered at the tapestry when she flipped it over.

"That's great, babe," he said, enthusiastic as always, whether about Micah's toys or a new serving dish or Viv sewing a button onto his coat. "Looks kinda like the sky right now. That what you were going for?"

She looked up and saw the brilliant sunset, heralding the coming night.

Viv shook her head, smiling, turning her face up and letting the last, lingering rays of the sun warm her as best they could. It was all right that it was going—it would be back tomorrow.

And so would they.

"Not a sunset," she said, tucking her work into her bag and turning to press her face against Sasha's chest to hear his heartbeat, steady and strong. "A sunrise."

Coming Soon

STORMFRONT, the first book in Iris Foxglove's new *Immortals Descending* series, is out this October! This series follows five immortal beings — embodying the concepts of Death, Desire, Dreams, Disaster and War — as they find their eternal mortal companions. This series is set in the same world as the previous two, and will feature several familiar faces — and places — from earlier books.

In a remote village, a man named Azaiah goes wreathed in flowers and smiling to the sacrificial altar, willing to die to keep his village safe from plague. But the Harvester has something else in store for Azaiah, and it isn't the shores of the world beyond that await him...but the cloak and scythe itself. Being Death means a long life that nevertheless requires a connection to humanity, and Azaiah learns that corruption awaits those who do not find a mortal companion to keep them tethered to the world. He finds it in Nyx, a soldier from an ancient empire and an adopted son of the Emperor, whose soul burns bright enough that Azaiah is certain immortality won't be a burden but a gift.

But then a shocking betrayal changes Nyx from a gruff soldier with a kind heart to a man bent on vengeance, swearing fealty not to Azaiah, but his sibling, Ares. With Nyx set on destroying the empire that was once his home, Azaiah is dangerously close to losing himself to the corruption that threatens those who lose their tether to the mortal world.

Nyx once loved the Empire and the family that took him in, but when the perfidy of his adopted brother results in a tragedy beyond his ability to bear, Nyx wants nothing more than to burn the world in his wake. Turning from the quiet, intriguing Azaiah toward the promise of bloody vengeance, Nyx gives his vows to Ares and watches the empire he once served fall into ruin. But as the years pass, vengeance is a cold comfort, and the man who is now called Glaive is determined to save Azaiah from being lost in the dark.

COMING OCTOBER 10, 2022

Pre-Order your copy today!

Also by Iris Foxglove

THE STARIAN CYCLE

The Traitor's Mercy

The Duke's Demon

The Prince's Vow

The Exile's Gift

The King's Mage

A STARIAN TALE

The Last Flight of Marius Chastain

SEASONS OF THE LUKOI

Winter of the Owl

Spring of the Wolf

Summer of the Wanderer

Autumn of the Witch

IMMORTALS DESCENDING

Stormfront (October 10, 2022)

About the Author

Iris Foxglove is a shared pen name between two longtime fantasy readers, Avon Gale and Fae Loxley, who are committed to writing fun, escapist queer fantasy featuring decadent, kinky stories, intricate worldbuilding and unforgettable characters.

Loved the book and want to help indie authors produce more unique content to enjoy? Leave a review on Amazon, Goodreads or wherever you like to review books. Don't forget to tell a friend!

Connect with Iris:

If you're interested in receiving information on new releases, sign up for Iris' newsletter!

If you're interested in monthly bonus content, exclusive excerpts and other perks, consider becoming a Patreon! Monthly content is available at just $1 a month!

Iris also has a Facebook group if you'd like to check it out: Iris Foxglove's Poisoned Garden

Thank You Patrons!

House of Onyx
Kim Licki
Kari Shanahan
Eva Wild
Jæ Dixon
Rosie Hallen
Gail Morse
Unpopular_Onion
justfe3hthings
JaneBuzzJane
JM
Russ
Tammy

House of Gold
Laura Taylor
Amy Schaffer
Nix Rodriguez
kenda1l
Andrea Canada
Elle Porter
Catherine Dair
Anonymous
brooklynapple
A Castilla
Breanne Jordens
Layla

www.ingramcontent.com/pod-product-compliance
Lightning Source LLC
Chambersburg PA
CBHW020908160726
47993CB00005B/1870